FORREST PUBLIC LIBRARY DISTRICT
A85900 321091
DISCARDED
D0283407

WAX

Therese Ambrosi Smith

Manufactured and printed in the United States of America.
15 14 13 12 11 1 2 3 4 5

ISBN-13: 978-0-9844000-7-2
ISBN 10: 0-9844000-7-9

PUBLISHER'S CATALOGING-IN-PUBLICATION DATA

Smith, Therese Ambrosi.
Wax / Therese Ambrosi Smith.
p. ; cm.
ISBN-13: 978-0-9844000-7-2
ISBN-10: 0-9844000-7-9
1. World War, 1939–1945—Women—United States—Fiction. 2. Women—United States—Social conditions—Fiction. 3. Female friendship—United States—Fiction. 4. Feminism—United States—Fiction. 5. Feminist fiction, American. 6. Historical fiction. I. Title.

PS3619.M5925 W29 2011
813/.6 2011926718
CIP

Edited by Virginia Shea
Cover design by Adriana Panesso Hammill
Book design by Linda Marcetti

Cover Photograph by Dorothea Lange
American, 1895–1965
End of Shift at Yard 1, September 1943

Published by Blue Star Books

Blue Star Books
903 Pacific Avenue, Suite 207A
Santa Cruz, CA 95060
www.book-hub.com

Books are available for special promotions and premiums.
For details, email news@book-hub.com

IN MEMORY OF LUCY "THE RIVETER" AMBROSI

PREFACE

ROSIE INSPIRES ME.

I can't remember when I first learned about Rosie the Riveter. She's always been there, like the national anthem and baseball. So I was surprised, two years ago, when my thirteen-year-old friend Lara explained that she thought the iconic poster from the forties was an old ad for power tools.

It was a Saturday morning in early October, and Lara came by as I was pulling a piece of spongy wood trim off the back window of my beach shack. "Just trying to stay ahead of decay," I said, and asked if she wanted to help.

She picked up my cordless drill and posed with flexed bicep; "We can do it," she said.

"You're a Rosie fan," I said.

"Who?"

"Rosie the Riveter—you know, 'We can do it!'"

Lara shrugged. "I saw it on your dishtowels," she said.

My dishtowels—she liked the graphics; the tough, albeit unpierced chick. Strong and confident, Lara can relate: she sees no limit to what she can accomplish.

The women who built the steady stream of replacement warships and aircraft deployed in World War II are elderly now. The youngest of them is more than eighty years old. While we are often reminded that we are losing our veterans at a rapid rate, less is said of the mothers, sisters and lovers, who equipped the troops and made essential contributions on the home front. They are the great and great-great grandmothers of the young women I see on the bus, texting friends. I've often wondered if today's daughters know the stories. According to Lara, "not really."

American women were Roosevelt's secret army, and Hitler gravely underestimated them. Like their soldier brothers, they too left ordinary lives to do extraordinary things. They worked in difficult and dangerous conditions, often at the limit of their physical ability. They accomplished tasks they had never imagined having the training or strength to do. They were the home half of the greatest generation. They helped save the world.

Last week, Lara, now nearly fifteen, told me about a visit she made to relatives in Canada, and how she helped lay a new hardwood floor. She spoke enthusiastically about learning to measure and cut wood, how to nail on an angle. I imagine her building her own beach shack someday, and when we all come by to warm it, I will bring her new dish towels, silk screened with the beloved image of Rosie the Riveter.

ACKNOWLEDGMENTS

MUCH LOVE AND GRATITUDE to the many people who supported me through this project:

The book was conceived when National Park Service Ranger Elizabeth Tucker, Rosie the Riveter/WWII Home Front National Historic Park, offered me a remarkable collection of oral histories.

Huge thanks to Caroline Leavitt, author, teacher and mentor, who coached me through the final pages, and to Virginia Shea who painstakingly edited them.

Many real stories informed this fiction thanks to Carol Peterson, archivist at the San Mateo County Historical Museum, and Marilyn Taylor, Alameda Navel Air Station Museum.

Lee Young, Archivist, American Truck Historical Society explained, in detail, how to drive a 1934 Ford pick-up truck, Chuck Kilian reviewed the courtroom scenes and Rube Warren assisted with "rationing research".

Librarians at the Half Moon Bay Library contacted the U.S. Fire Administration on my behalf, for loan of vintage fire science textbooks. Thanks also, to staff at the San Francisco GLBT Historical Society for their assistance.

Drew Johnson and Robin Doolin at the Oakland Museum of California helped with the licensing of the wonderful Dorothea Lange photo that Adriana Panesso used in the cover design. Thank you, Linda Marcetti for the interior book design.

Thanks also to: Diane Duffie, Bill Smith, Kim Marie Smith, Marie Miller, Lara Garay, Marion and Roy Fox, Mike Wells, Jackie Enx, Takashi Matsumora, Nidhi Mahar, Rhonda Herbert and the great Ivy Henry.

This book would not have been possible without the hard work, guidance and support from Book Hub/Blue Star Books, specifically Dan Haldeman, Melissa Munnerlyn, and Amanda Poulsen.

Hugs to Barry, for much love and encouragement on the homefront.

CHAPTER 1

May 7, 1945

AT FIRST, Tilly wasn't sure she'd heard right.

"The Germans have agreed to unconditional surrender." The announcement reverberated through the assembly gallery on loudspeakers usually reserved for emergency drills, and production slowed, and then stopped. For a moment, there was silence. Then, at once, a cheer rose from every bay and corner. Thousands of voices sang "God Bless America". Many wept. Tilly tossed her goggles and embraced the women working to her left and right. She looked across the deck to Elsie, who nodded in her direction. And then, on cue, they lowered their masks and went back to work.

No one knew what would come next; there was still fighting in the Pacific, but the war in Europe was over.

• • •

Two weeks later, Tilly tugged the old army duffel from beneath her bunk and dragged it to the door of the Airstream.

She paused to admire the lacy pattern spiders had laid across it and wondered if a fortuneteller might find her future there. With a damp towel she captured the sticky threads and beat the bag, inside and out, against the aluminum doorjamb. The dust made her sneeze. Her father had carried the bag back from the Great War.

She'd acquired few possessions while at Kaiser, so packing was light work. She'd leave most of her welder's gear behind, except for a few mementos. News clippings and the binder she'd received at orientation would go home with her. She tucked her heavy gloves into the corner. Maybe she'd use them as oven mitts—she laughed to herself and then cried. Soon she'd be home and working as a waitress; she might never do anything so important again. She had helped win a war.

Among the clutter in the small trailer she'd shared for three years was the issue of *Fore 'n' Aft* that had featured her roommate. Tilly wanted to keep it but knew that Doris would someday want to show it to her kids.

Doris had been interviewed after scoring highly on an aptitude test. It was big news, a woman with so much aptitude for so many things, and Doris was something of a phenomenon. She'd been quickly trained to install sophisticated navigation systems on Liberty Ships. But when the hulls currently on the line were launched, she'd be sent home too. It didn't matter how good she was. It was understood that returning soldiers would be hired to do their jobs.

Tilly wondered if her roommate would go back to Pittsburgh. Before the war, Doris had lived with her mother and had sold cosmetics in a downtown department store. It was hard to imagine her selling lipstick, hard to imagine her assisting women in the weighty decisions of color and application, but that's what she'd done. Everything changed after Pearl Harbor. Now it had to change back.

CHAPTER 2

October 25, 1941

IT WAS Katherine Hepburn who'd convinced Tilly she could play an important role in the drama unfolding on the world stage. *The Maltese Falcon* had come to Half Moon Bay. Tilly was so excited, she took the bus to town ahead of Mark, because she thought he'd be late and she didn't want to miss a minute. The lights were down before he slid into the seat beside her. He'd waited in line ten minutes for a fresh batch of popcorn and had bought the largest size—because she loved it—but when he passed her the bag, she barely acknowledged him. Her eyes were glued to the newsreel.

All Tilly could see at first was a person covered head to toe in canvas and gear, in overalls and a welder's mask and those big heavy gloves, holding the rod in one hand and a torch in the other. She couldn't tell it was a woman. And then Katherine Hepburn took off the mask and looked straight into the camera—straight at Tilly—and said "Democracy's in a jam." Tilly was eating popcorn by the handful, rapt, not even blinking, shoveling through the bag while Mark sat quietly beside her.

The feature film followed, but Tilly, who'd seen the future, couldn't concentrate on the exploits of Sam Spade. She was ready to take her place with women in industry. Tilly Bettencourt would leave home and work to supply the Arsenal of Democracy.

In twenty years, Tilly had never been farther north than San Francisco or farther east than San Mateo. She worked for tips and could predict, with accuracy, how much each of the regulars would give before she'd even served them. She was pretty sure everyone in town believed they knew how her life would unfold. Mark was a boyfriend who would do in a pinch, but he wasn't someone she dreamed about. She needed to get out, breathe. She needed to be part of something bigger, and what better cause was there?

"Democracy's in a jam? What's that supposed to mean?" Helen said.

Tilly had waited until her mother was pressing clothes to tell her that she'd written to the Kaiser Company. Helen reached for the starch on a shelf above the shallow cabinet that the ironing board folded into.

"They need workers," Tilly said. She grabbed a kitchen chair and sat on the opposite side of the ironing board. "They're running crews around the clock. Even women with children are working in the shipyards. They provide babysitters."

"Uh huh. And what do you think is a better deal for an industrialist like Mr. Kaiser? Hiring men, or women and baby-sitters? Tilly, use your head."

"That's the point." Tilly liked to sit when she talked with her mother because she was several inches taller, and it felt wrong to look down on her during important conversations. "I want to use my head. And my hands."

"I could use a hand. Can you pour me a glass of lemonade?"

Tilly got two cut glass tumblers out of the cabinet and pulled the pitcher from the icebox.

"There's nothing like lemonade when you're ironing," Helen said.

Tilly watched as the wrinkles disappeared from her father's shirt. She looked at the lines in her mother's face. Helen had been a great beauty, the Chamarita Queen of the Portuguese Festival in Half Moon Bay. But that was before she married, before she was Tilly's age.

Helen took a sip and resumed ironing. "I didn't raise you to build ships," she said. "I raised you to find a nice man and settle down." She unfolded her pressing cloth. "And speaking of nice men, have you talked to Mark about this?"

Tilly looked away.

"I didn't think so," Helen said. She shook her head. "What exactly do you think this little adventure is going to be like?

Do you have any idea how difficult and dangerous the work will be? Tilly, you're a waitress for heaven's sake."

"And Katherine Hepburn is an actress," Tilly said, her fist clenched beneath the table.

Helen looked up with her mouth open and stared at Tilly. "And what you saw her do was act," she said. "Do you really think that Katherine Hepburn is working as a welder? Do you think she's given up her career because of Hitler? This is Europe's war."

Tilly had no idea what Katherine Hepburn was doing. She looked into her glass as if the answer might appear in the floating lemon pulp. "But even if we're not at war we need to do our part," she said. "We need to produce. The President said so. You listened to the radio."

Helen handed Tilly Paul's best shirt and a hanger. She untangled the ties of one of her aprons and flattened it out on the ironing board. A bit of hair came loose from the knot at the nape of her neck, and she tucked it behind her ear. She rubbed the back of her hand across her forehead before she spoke. "What could be more patriotic than food production? If you're so worried about the war, feed the soldiers; feed the Europeans. Feed them vegetables. Havice is converting his flower fields. Go see him about a job." Helen didn't notice that she'd yanked the plug from the socket until it hit her in the leg and snagged her stocking. She dropped the iron and muttered words Tilly wasn't supposed to hear. Tilly seldom saw her mother so angry.

"You know," Helen said, "your aunt and uncle depend on you at the roadhouse. What kind of jam would you put them in?"

Tilly swirled the glass and took a final gulp. The lemonade wasn't very sweet. "I have to get ready for work," she said. She took her glass to the sink and rinsed it, then climbed the stairs two at a time.

In the tiny upstairs bathroom, Tilly ran warm water in the basin. The small window above the sink looked out over the marine terrace and the summer bloom on the flower fields of old Rancho Corral de Tierra. This would be the last year for flowers, according to talk at the roadhouse. Next year they'd be growing beans.

She looked toward her favorite trail. In an hour of steady hiking, Tilly could climb to North Peak. From there, using her father's old army issue field glasses, she could see all the way to the southern end of the San Francisco Bay and north to the Marin Headlands. She could see the new bridges and Mt. Diablo to the east—places farther from home than she'd ever been. If she could get a job in the shipyards, she might be able to save enough to buy a car. She wondered how hard it would be to learn to drive.

While the water warmed, Tilly twisted her long, dark hair into a knot and clipped it at the nape of her neck. She got the mix of hot and cold just right and sudsed her face, shoulders and arms. Then she dried off and rummaged in the closet for the last clean, white shirt. She gave her black pumps a shine with the damp towel and put them in a bag with the hose. The mile and a half to work was along the Great Beach, and she often walked barefoot in the sand for a good part of the way. She would clean her feet when she arrived. Her long-suffering Aunt Ida would just sigh and hand her a towel.

Looking out the kitchen window at the same view of flower fields, Helen tried to imagine her beautiful girl, her only child, behind a welder's mask. Tilly had always been a tomboy, but a very pretty tomboy. She ran her pressing cloth under the tap for only a moment.

Her sister had been with her on the night Tilly was born. Helen remembered a much younger Ida sitting with her at the kitchen table, saying she knew their husbands were running whiskey with their brother, Aldo.

"All this mystery and intrigue," Ida had said. "They think we're stupid."

Helen had made tea from the thickly growing mint she could never seem to eradicate from her garden and had poured them each a cup. She'd been grateful for Ida's company, with the baby so close. The sisters recalled how their mother and aunts had fingered rosary beads while they waited for their men: Portuguese women—Pera women—suffering high winds and late returns off the coast of Monterey, where cold up-welling currents made fishing a productive enterprise. Ida and Helen swore their lives would be different, and in a way they were.

"Our mother worried about our father drowning at sea," Ida said. "Our husbands have added getting shot or arrested."

Their brother, Aldo, had inherited the old man's fleet of three wooden trawlers and continued the family fishing tradition. During Prohibition, he discovered he could net more profitable cargo. Aldo was the captain most capable of navigating the waters between Monterey and San Francisco in darkness and through impenetrable fog, and the likeliest to out-run federal agents. He'd spent his boyhood with his immigrant grandfather in the wheelhouse.

That night the sisters tried to guess the probability of their men successfully launching dinghies undetected from an isolated cove. They were sure the feds were no match for Aldo on the water, but wondered what would happen when the extra catch arrived at Fish Alley in San Francisco.

Helen yawned and spooned honey into her mug. She felt brief and infrequent contractions. Her lower back was sore. She ran a hand over her hard belly, wondering if she'd last until the due date. She was counting on a mid-wife for the delivery.

"We have to keep the faith that they know what they're doing," Helen was saying when she suddenly felt like she'd sat in warm liquid. She looked at her cup, puzzled because it still had tea in it. She watched the expression on Ida's face as her eyes moved downward. Simultaneously, they knew. There wasn't a phone in the cottage then, so Ida ran to Moss Beach to find the midwife.

When Paul got home at daybreak to find Helen with her sister, and he held his daughter for the first time, Helen suggested that the baby should be called Paula.

"Tilly," he said. "I've always liked the name Tilly."

She was christened Matilda Ida Bettencourt at Our Lady of the Pillar, and Jose and Ida hosted a celebration at the roadhouse. Some weeks later, the men quietly changed the name of Aldo's favorite boat *Matilda C.*, to *Matilda B.*, and when Helen noticed, she couldn't help but wonder if her daughter was named after the old vessel.

Tilly was sixteen before Helen heard the full story of what the men were doing while she was giving birth. Aldo was up from Monterey and staying at the roadhouse with Ida and Jose, and they were all in the upstairs apartment eating fresh fish from his catch that Ida had prepared using her mother's recipes. They were drinking good, strong red wine and after they'd drained the third bottle, Jose brought up the old days and their career in "distribution," as he liked to call it, and the night of their first sale.

"It was just after two-thirty," he said. "Paul had been sitting at the bar with those old field glasses trying to hold them on the horizon, but he'd drunk so much coffee he couldn't steady them."

"I was worried I'd miss your signal," Paul said to Aldo, "And you'd be sitting off the point waiting—imagining that everything had come apart and that we'd been locked up somewhere."

Helen glanced over at Tilly, the only sober member of the party, who sat wide-eyed. She thought her daughter must be thinking, *Who are these people?*

Paul talked about catching sight of the first lantern the deck hand had raised up the mast, and then the second. He and Jose had paused for a moment, though they knew they were well past a change of heart.

A thousand feet south, the whiskey they'd bought with the mortgage money was loaded onto a wagon tended by two men with rifles. Ida gasped and interrupted the story to ask if they'd really intended to use them. Jose said that they weren't even loaded, and Aldo just roared with laughter.

They hauled the barrels to Lighthouse Cove and gave the food money to the light keeper. He darkened the light. Darkness was the signal to Aldo, who launched two dinghies with trustworthy men who could row in rough surf. They pulled worn oars against brass oarlocks and made good time toward shore.

Paul explained how he'd planned the operation and had been sure to schedule transport to the *Matilda C.* in an outgoing tide. He said that everything had come off so efficiently that the whiskey made its way to Jose's contacts through the canneries at Fisherman's Wharf undetected. But Helen wasn't listening. Her husband, on the night their daughter was born, had gambled both the mortgage and the food money on a bootleg venture. She said a quick prayer as she looked again at Tilly, who appeared enthralled with the story, and thanked God that He had protected her husband, brother and brother-in-law. She would need to talk to Tilly soon about this period in their family history; she was old enough now. But she could never tell her everything. There were things that even Ida didn't know.

The "distribution" business had been their life-blood through the end of Prohibition; there'd been little legitimate commerce on the coast after the railroad failed. They'd been dependent on the Ocean Shore. Without the railroad, it was simply too difficult to transport meat, milk and produce to San Francisco over Montara Mountain on an unpaved road that was impassable four months of the year, and too difficult for roadhouse patrons to come to the coast for pleasure.

Helen and Ida saw their brother more often in those days, and Aldo Pera always traveled from Monterey on the *Matilda B.* As a young girl, Tilly had used Paul's field glasses to scan the horizon for *her* fishing boat. She drew pictures of it with crayons, floating the hull on blue waves. She talked about how she'd like to fish someday in her own boat—which she once told Aldo she would christen the Aldo P.—but Aldo thought girls were bad luck on board and only took her out once, for a short spin around the harbor.

Helen sighed. Tilly was trading her girlhood dream of fishing for shipbuilding. She thought for a moment that it might be an improvement, then lightly starched her best white blouse.

It was normal that a daughter should do things differently from her mother she thought, but welding! Why did it have to be welding? She could understand that it was stifling for Tilly to work in the family business, despite Ida and Jose's generosity. She would have been happy if Tilly had applied to teacher's college or secretarial school, but no, her daughter wanted to weld in a shipyard and had sent a letter off. Helen drank more of the lemonade before laying out another shirt. She heard the front door close.

That evening Tilly had two new customers. They lingered long after the check was paid, with only coffee cups and cordial glasses remaining, and Tilly craned her neck over the server's station to watch them. The woman pulled a polished cigarette case from her purse, as her date simultaneously drew a lighter from inside his dark, double-breasted jacket. Tilly took in all the details of the woman's dress, which she suspected was silk; the drape was fluid and the skirt reached just below the knee. The color wasn't exactly silver, it was warmer; she would call it champagne. She thought she might go through her entire life and never wear anything so gorgeous. She marveled at the beautifully coiffed blond hair. How did it stay so perfectly curled? Tilly could hardly look away. She thought the pair must be from San Francisco. It was unusual to have such late diners on a Tuesday night.

One of the candles on their table was burning down, leaving white wax on white linen, but the couple ignored it and Tilly had no desire to interrupt them. They sat perfectly framed by the window and dark wood paneling, and for the moment, Tilly felt transported from the roadhouse to someplace far more elegant.

"I think they like it here," she said to Jose, "They don't appear to be in any hurry."

"Bring them each a glass of port and some Camembert, on the house," he said. The full moon was rising over the hills to the east, illuminating a fine view of softly breaking waves.

Tilly cut a small wedge of the creamy cheese for herself before arranging the gift on a silver tray. "Compliments of the owner," she said. "Please stay as long as you like." Then she faded back into her corner.

The spell was broken by the sound of heavy work boots on the plank floor; she knew who it was without looking and felt the familiar sense of annoyance. Mark took his seat in the back as he always did, but she was in no mood for a visit. She pointed toward the bar and ushered him out of the dining room, "I don't want to disturb that couple," she said, with more urgency than necessary. He would ruin everything.

She poured his coffee and went into the kitchen for a slice of his favorite apple pie, without ice cream. She couldn't tell a steady customer to go on a diet, but she thought Mark could do without the extra calories. He lived with his mother who fed him three squares a day, and Tilly figured he probably ate her pie too.

"Tips good?" he asked. He dug his fork into the crust.

"I've got things to do," she said.

From a shelf in the pantry, she counted two dozen tapers onto a tray and unobtrusively circled the floor, pulling stubs from candlesticks and replacing them. The light on the couple's table had burned completely, and they'd moved their chairs and sat shoulder to shoulder, silhouetted against the moonlight, reminding Tilly of a movie poster she'd seen. She felt as if she'd entered a different dimension when she came from the bar. And then Mark was suddenly at the gateway between the two worlds and Tilly wondered how he could have eaten so quickly. She impatiently shooed him out.

"I'll be by Saturday night," he said

She closed the heavy wooden door behind him and leaned against it for a full minute.

CHAPTER 3

December 7, 1941

HELEN WAS slicing bread for toast when she first heard the news. Through the kitchen window, she saw the truck skid into the gravel drive. Paul left the door open as he sprinted toward the house, gasping as if he'd run the entire distance from Havice Nursery. "The Japs have bombed Hawaii," he said.

She put down her knife.

"It's true." He stopped to breathe. "Pearl Harbor. Havice had the radio on in the shed."

"My God."

The phone rang. "Come down to the roadhouse," Ida said. "People will want to be together."

Jose was stocking the bar after a busy Saturday night when he heard the broadcast. He stopped, holding a bottle of Gallo in each hand. Ida put down the vase she was filling and moved beside him. He put his arms around her.

Bob and Martha Havice arrived first and took the table next to the door. They watched Jose and Paul fuss with the wooden-cased radio, moving it closer to the window to improve reception. It cracked and sputtered, but the horror in the reporters' voices sliced through. No one spoke.

Half a room away, Tilly sat alone at the last table she'd set, and Helen wondered what she was thinking. Was she frightened? They'd become accustomed to the speculation and the reports of a navel buildup in the Pacific, but now there had been an attack. And California was the logical next target for an enemy heading east. The war was no longer about European borders or the military dominance of countries half a world away. It wasn't about the Midwest or much of the rest of America. It was here, at the roadhouse: in Moss Beach and Montara.

Helen knew that Tilly's friends would enlist, as their fathers had in the Great War. This would be another Great War, or maybe a Greater War. She wondered if Tilly was thinking about Mark. She went into the kitchen and busied herself making cheese and fruit platters and tiny sandwiches for Ida to pass around the bar, because she hated to see people drink on an empty stomach, especially so early in the day.

Three hours later, the dining room emptied almost as suddenly as it had filled. The rogue wave of neighbors seeking comfort and community receded, and all was quiet, even the foghorn. Jose flipped the sign to 'closed,' something he never did on Sundays. "Under the circumstances," he said. "I think we all need a little time off." Helen went to the upstairs apartment with her husband and Ida and Jose, but with plenty of light left in the unseasonably dry December day, Tilly said she felt like walking. Helen watched from the side window as her daughter left alone. She would cross fields sown with cover crops on her way up Montara Mountain, the northernmost terminus of the Coast Range, and the barrier that had separated her world from San Francisco and points north. The slopes that Tilly could climb so easily on young legs had posed an insurmountable challenge for road and rail builders for half a century. Rising two thousand feet from the Pacific, and nearly sheer on the ocean side, Montara Mountain was a wall of granite that had kept their seaside community isolated and, until today, safe. Helen looked out over the water and considered how Hawaii suddenly seemed so close, how crossing an ocean seemed so much easier.

The fortification of the coast started immediately. Widening and realigning the highway brought laborers to town almost overnight, while communication towers sprouted every few miles. Rooms at the roadhouse were in remarkable demand, and the bar and dining room were packed most nights. Jose, ever the opportunist, was dreaming of expansion.

Helen worked more than full-time helping Ida, while Paul worked sunup to sundown with Bob Havice, converting flower and fallow fields for wartime agriculture. Soy was in greatest need and the mild coastal climate allowed two crops per year, with a third season's rotation of other vegetables.

Eventually, the war changed every aspect of their lives. On Sundays, the Boy Scout troop from Half Moon Bay collected recycling, and every able-bodied person tended a victory garden to keep food production local. Fuel and rubber were needed at the front and domestic freight could not travel at the expense of the war effort.

Tilly continued to grudgingly accept Mark's invitations but was secretly eager for his departure. She wondered what was wrong with her. All the boys were signing up to fight, and everyone was pairing up like civilization might come to an end, but she had no intention of committing to Mark.

She stopped brushing her hair and stared into the mirror at the back of her dressing table. If she couldn't look herself in the eye, how would she face him? He had joined the Navy. Soon he'd be headed to San Diego for training. She should have told him months earlier that he wasn't the man for her; she just never got around to it.

Mark was nice enough and a gentleman. He was someone to go out with when her girlfriends were with their boyfriends; it had been a convenient arrangement. She'd figured her lack of enthusiasm would eventually alienate him without her having to take more decisive action, but it hadn't.

She put the brush down and tried to think of what she would say. "San Diego is a long way away, and I don't expect you to be thinking about me," she tried. No, that wouldn't do. She couldn't make him responsible for a break-up she'd wanted all along. She'd have to come right out and say it. She took a deep breath and looked herself straight in the eye, "Mark, don't ask me to wait for you. I think it's time we went our separate ways."

She heard her mother answer the door and call her name. Nearly overcome with dread, she descended the stairs.

Helen noticed that Tilly was moving slowly, mechanically, as she slipped an arm into a jacket sleeve. She barely looked at Mark who stood in the entry hall with a bouquet. Helen hurried to the kitchen to leave the couple alone. Minutes later, she heard the door close and Tilly's footsteps on the stairs. Somehow she'd always known that Tilly would refuse the kind and sincere young man.

Tilly's routine didn't change much after Mark left. She continued working at the roadhouse, and Helen was amazed that her daughter seemed so happy after the breakup.

June 10, 1942

Tilly gave the old door a tug and entered the tiny, tidy post office lobby. Posters lining the walls reminded patrons to invest in war bonds.

"You're a little late today." Tilly had heard these words as a student. The Montara Postmistress, Lily Saximeyer, had taught her in grammar school.

"I think my aunt would rather I brought the mail in," Tilly said. "They're so busy they hardly leave the roadhouse."

Mrs. Saximeyer turned over a stack of letters, the usual business mail and a few personal items. There was an issue of *Popular Mechanics* for Jose. As she turned to leave, a man approached the door and held it open. She smiled; three months earlier it would have been unusual to see someone she hadn't known for years. Now there were so many workers in town.

"Tilly, wait a minute, I just remembered." Mrs. Saximeyer reached into the Bettencourt slot. The typewritten label had a Richmond address. Tilly's hand shook. She skipped down the front stairs and crossed the coast road.

The tide was at its lowest point, the wet sand firm underfoot. She could walk quickly just at the water's edge and recover some of her lost time, so long as the waves didn't catch the hem of her skirt.

She'd gone three-quarters of a mile, half the distance to the roadhouse, before she noticed the *Matilda B.* on the horizon. Its silhouette was not significantly different from other boats, but Tilly could pick it out in all but the thickest fog. She looked at the envelope again and could imagine Jose's voice, "It's a fool that doesn't take advantage of every opportunity."

Her Uncle Aldo was at it again. He'd retired in 1940, but he kept his favorite boat. Salmon would start running soon, and canneries in Monterey and San Francisco were staffing up to work three shifts. The local catch would feed soldiers half way around the world. "It's a fool that doesn't take advantage of every opportunity." Tilly watched a seagull wrestle with a piece of kelp. There was something it wanted tangled up in it. She looked at the envelope in her hand. The gull glanced at her then went back to its struggle, and she thought it worked with more purpose than she did.

Just south of Point Montara lighthouse, nearly all the way to the roadhouse, Tilly decided she couldn't wait. She pulled the letter from its manila sheath and read the brochure from the recruiting office. She could apprentice in a number of trades. "A welder," she said out loud. "I could learn to be a welder." Upon completion of her apprenticeship, she would earn five times what she made at the roadhouse. She stared at the surging water, considering the possibilities. The largest of the set broke against her ankles, and she did a little jig to keep her skirt above the foam. From a spot on higher ground, she re-read each word. She would be able to live away from home and save money. She took a deep breath and newly buoyant, skipped and splashed the rest of the way.

After the last patron left, Tilly hurried to finish her closing routine. She swept the floor and pulled a stool up to the bar, next to the section of rail Jose was polishing. "I got some mail today," she said, and handed him the letter. "I'm telling you first because you're my most open-minded relative."

Jose looked at the return address on the envelope. "And so Niece Tilly, I am the test case?"

She nodded.

"Well, I know what this is about from looking at the return address. So you are going to work with the Rosies?" He put the top on the can of polish and folded the cloth he was using into quarters. "Perhaps you and I should have a drink." He slipped behind the bar and poured himself two fingers of Scotch. "And what should I get you?"

"Ginger ale, please."

"One ginger ale on the rocks with two cherries, a double!" He placed the glass on a cocktail napkin in front of her and followed with a bowl of peanuts, while she sat quietly. "Now, tell me about your plans," he said.

She sipped her ginger ale. "Last fall, I sent a letter to Kaiser explaining that I wanted to come to work. And I never heard back. But now with the war on Japan and everything, they're expanding the shipyards. Uncle Jose, they really need workers, and I'm young and strong and could learn something. Something different. I could become a welder. And I'd make good money too. Oh, it's not like I don't make enough here—I mean you and Aunt Ida have been very generous..."

"You don't have to apologize," he said. "If you left to build boats, we would miss you, but we'd never hold you back. I think I can speak for my wife on this. We only want what's best for you." He took a handful of her peanuts while she pulled the stem off a maraschino cherry.

"When I applied, Mom said I was being foolish. She said the working conditions would be horrible, and I'd be working with desperate people stuck in Richmond because they'd traveled a long way to get there, with no money to get back."

Jose didn't speak right away. He rubbed his temples above his very dark eyes and sipped his Scotch. He dropped another ice cube in the glass. "Once, people came here looking for something better," he said. "That's what I did. There was nothing here then." He laughed, "I thought of myself as optimistic."

"Uncle Jose, you and Aunt Ida are like second parents to me. If you said you needed me here, I'd stay with you."

He shook his head. "Nonsense. This war will not go on forever. You will return when the job ends, and we will welcome you back. But you must not feel constrained by us. Tilly, one day Ida and I will retire and sell this business. You must not count on us forever, and we must not count on you forever. That is how life is. We must be free to find our happiness." He tossed a peanut into his open mouth. "In the meantime, I always say…"

Tilly finished the sentence, "It's a fool that doesn't take advantage of every opportunity."

"Exactly."

The next morning Ida was sliding apple pies into the hot cast iron oven when Helen arrived. She stopped and poured coffee.

"I guess you heard about Tilly's letter from Kaiser," Helen said.

"Jose told me this morning," Ida said. She poured herself a cup. "I heard Mark is being sent to the South Pacific." She added cream and sugar. "Does Tilly know?"

"I don't know," Helen said, "She hasn't mentioned it. I don't think she thinks much about him at all. It's as if she's relieved that he'll be out of her life."

"I don't think the attraction was very strong," Ida said.

"There have been so many weddings," Helen said. "I don't want my daughter to end up alone."

Helen had just turned fifteen when Paul left to fight in Europe. As a girl she'd had a crush on him, all the girls had. He was tall and lean and handsome, and the fact that he was older and a soldier made him all the more attractive. And he paid no attention to her. But when he returned three years later, and she saw him at a Farm Day dance, he made her feel as if she were the only girl in the room. She left with him that night and they were married six months later.

"Can you wash the lettuce?" Ida asked.

Helen took the box from the cooler and carried it to the sink.

August 9, 1942

Helen wondered how her husband could sleep so soundly. Tomorrow, everything would be different. Tilly would be on her own, living in a dormitory and beginning her career as a welder. She pushed against Paul, who had a tendency to sleep diagonally in the bed and sometimes made it impossible for her to stretch her legs. She wished she could turn off the conversation in her head.

She wanted to tiptoe down to Tilly's room and look in at her sleeping, but feared waking her. She rolled over and prayed silently that the war would be over soon and that all the young people would come back unharmed. Then she closed her eyes and tried to clear her mind. But sleep would not come.

Paul rose at four fifty, ten minutes before the alarm, and dressed in the dark. Helen pretended to sleep and let him believe that he could slip out without waking her, but she'd not slept one minute.

Paul yawned as he sat in the cab, waiting for his beautiful girl to emerge. The idling engine broke the stillness; even the nurserymen and fishermen slept past dawn on Sunday mornings. He thought his daughter seemed happier than she'd been for a long time. Though Paul harbored his own reservations, he knew he could simply fetch Tilly when she learned that moving to Richmond to weld wasn't the same as traveling to a foreign country for adventure.

Blackout curtains darkened the windows, but he was sure he could make out the lamp in Tilly's bedroom and the light he'd left on in the kitchen. Helen, he thought, would feign sleep to avoid a tearful farewell, and he believed Tilly would appreciate it.

He stretched out in the seat and thought about the early years of his marriage and how difficult it had been for Helen to conceive, although their relationship was passionate. With each passing month, Helen had become more distraught, and when the railroad failed, he worried seriously about the stress taking a toll on her health. It was during this time that he began to truly appreciate his in-laws. By 1921, largely due to Jose's optimism and business sense, combined with Aldo's expert seamanship, the family fortune improved significantly. When Helen announced she was pregnant, he couldn't have been happier. Every day he gave thanks for being part of the Pera clan.

He turned on the flashlight momentarily and glanced at his watch: five forty-five. The faint glow in the upstairs window disappeared. A minute later, his lanky brunette dragged an over-stuffed duffel across the threshold and kicked it onto the porch. Tilly held a handful of cookies snagged from the ceramic jar and popped one into her mouth as she closed the door quietly behind her. She hoisted the canvas bag over the rail, and it fell into the truck bed with a thud. Then she climbed into the cab and bit into a second cookie.

"Swell. Clean," she said.

She noticed, he thought. Paul had spent the previous afternoon cleaning and tuning the truck for their trip. His daughter was excited and fidgeting, and he thought that she embodied all the best of what he and Helen had to pass on.

A shower of crumbs fell from Tilly's hand to the floor. She handed a cookie to her father. "These are great," she said. "Mrs. Mueller baked them with her sugar rations—said I'd need the energy—but I left half of them for you and Mom." She quickly brushed her jeans, right leg tapping against the passenger door.

"Has she heard from her son?" Paul asked.

"He just finished basic, that's all I know," Tilly said.

Paul glanced back at the house, now entirely dark and shifted into drive. He pointed the truck west, toward the paved road. The sun wasn't above the horizon, but there was enough light for driving, and at the highway, he turned north to San Francisco. Tilly pulled a piece of red fabric from the pocket of her jacket and began playing with her long, wavy hair.

"What do you have there, Tilly?" He asked. He had to shout over the din of the Ford's engine.

She turned to face him as she tied the two ends of the scarf at the middle of the top of her head. "Aunt Ida made these scarves for me. She saw pictures of women working in factories, and they all tied their hair up."

He had to laugh. Half of him wanted his girl to have the time of her life living on her own; his other half wanted to turn around and keep her safe at home. Ida and Jose had given their gas coupons for the trip and said Tilly could come back to the roadhouse whenever she was ready. They'd hugged him and said victory would come soon.

The morning broke clear but not bright, with white foam on slate gray water, and Paul wondered how Tilly's first night in Richmond would be. Shifting winds that stirred waves usually brought a change in weather within twelve hours.

They said little as they drove north through San Pedro Point, Linda Mar, Valley Mar and the other small communities north of Montara Mountain. Each village now hosted seaward facing bunkers. Carved from the Salinian granite and sedimentary rock underlying the bluffs, the bunkers were reinforced with concrete, protecting the coast from a foreign enemy. The Pacific Ocean wasn't enough.

After an hour, they reached San Francisco, and Paul, who had no desire to deliver Tilly to the shipyard earlier than necessary, proclaimed it break time. Turning right, he stopped at a diner on Embarcadero and got the door for Tilly, who had managed to wrap her hair scarf into a turban.

A shapely, middle-aged waitress smiled at them but stayed seated, finishing her breakfast while the cook poured Paul a cup of coffee. They stared at the Bay Bridge from their seats at the counter. Five years earlier, it had existed only on blueprints and Tilly told Paul her history teacher had talked about it.

"I can't wait to drive across," she said.

"I don't know," Paul said. "I just can't get used to that thing being there." He said the same of the Golden Gate Bridge—said it ruined the view, and Tilly laughed at him.

Traffic was light, but Paul watched Tilly check her watch again and again as she waited for him to finish. She reminded him that she was expected to sign in and get her housing assignment before the afternoon's orientation. At eight, they were at the on-ramp; Tilly was clutching her seat. Bridges on the coastside were short spans over narrow creeks; now they were driving over one hundred feet above the San Francisco Bay.

"There's Treasure Island," Paul said as they approached mid-span.

Tilly craned her neck to get a good first look. She'd just graduated from high school when Ida and Jose took a few days off to go to the world's fair. They'd come back saying it was almost as good as travel.

"No need to change money or get used to different time zones," Jose had said. He'd been most impressed by the China Clipper and had dreamed of flying on it someday, but the island was conscripted by the Navy for a communications training center. Paul thought of a boy from the nursery who'd been assigned there. Treasure Island was also the point of embarkation for the Pacific Theater, and they could see the *U.S.S. Enterprise* leaving port. Red-turbaned Tilly, impressed and embarking on her own adventure, whistled as it cut through the current. She reached across the truck cab to honk the horn and waved both arms, then took Paul's field glasses for a closer look.

Paul quietly remembered his own service. He watched his daughter adjust the right lens to bring the glasses into focus. They were his only souvenir from the military. He kept them to remember the short-sightedness of war.

The old Ford shuttered to a stop at the Sinclair station on University Avenue, and Tilly tried to shield her eyes from the blinding morning sun. She squinted as a woman station attendant in a pinstriped shirt stepped out from under an awning and approached the driver's-side window.

"Yessir?" she said.

"Ten gallons, please." Paul presented the ration coupons, while Tilly looked on. She took a second look, while shading her eyes with her arm.

Paul noticed the startled expression. "You're staring," he whispered. He nudged his daughter when the woman left the window, but Tilly kept the attendant in her sights. She moved to the rear of the truck, opened the gas tank with her right hand, and simultaneously reached for the nozzle with her left; she lightly hopped over the hose and pumped gas with the grace of a dancer. Though she appeared strong, her shoulders were too narrow to fill a man's uniform shirt, and it hung loosely. The sleeves were rolled up. A black sedan pulled in; the attendant was instantly at the driver's side window taking direction and starting the flow of fuel. She returned to Paul and asked if she should check the oil.

"No thanks," he said, "I just changed it yesterday."

The windows were dusty, and the attendant grabbed a sponge and cloth to clean the windshield. Through the glass, Tilly could see that the palms of her hands were lighter than her forearms. Tilly looked down at her own hands. The woman avoided Tilly's gaze and spoke as little as possible to Paul. She tossed the sponge in the bucket, stopping seconds before the pump registered two dollars.

"So you've never seen a woman pumping gas before?" Paul turned the truck back in the direction of the main road. "Shouldn't be a big surprise," he said. "You're going to be a welder."

"Dad, I've never seen a real-life colored," Tilly said, "except in the movies."

Paul nodded and looked ahead. He didn't want Tilly to see the panic he felt. How would she do on her own? There was no traffic. He took the eastbound on-ramp to Richmond.

CHAPTER

4

June 10, 1942

"I THINK THAT powder color is a bit pink for your complexion," Doris said. She removed two more compacts from the glass case, one a tortoise shell and the other a soft green. She flipped the lids. "Maybe you'd like one of these."

The shopper lifted a sample of each pressed powder, compared the slight variations, and fixed her gaze on the rose-colored makeup. She wanted a peaches and cream complexion, but she'd been born with olive skin. Doris hated selling the wrong product. The customer wasn't always right, but Doris had to pretend that she was. Makeup was really about make believe.

The shopper moved from the too-pink powder to the too-pink rouge, and when Doris laid out some too-pink lipsticks, she knew she'd get an enthusiastic response. She made the sale.

Between customers, she wiped fingerprints off the glass display cases, stocked and arranged inventory, and generally tried to look busy. She couldn't let herself lean on the counter. The day wore on, and when six o'clock mercifully came, she punched out, took her umbrella as protection against Pittsburgh's summer showers, and caught the Liberty Avenue bus. From the stop at Twenty-Eighth, she had a short walk to the tidy two-story brick house on Dobson, where she'd lived her entire life.

She hung her hat on the coat tree in the hall, then noticed the legal size manila envelope from Kaiser next to the phone. It was addressed to her. "Mom?"

She pushed through the white saloon doors into the kitchen and lifted the lid off a large pot full of chicken stew with vegetables. Her mother was whipping potatoes. Doris couldn't resist a taste and momentarily forgot the letter. Joan stared into the bowl, muttering.

"This stuff just isn't as good as butter," she said. "Look at it. It'll never replace butter."

Doris hugged her and set two plates in the breakfast nook where they shared meals—only dinner these days. Joan had been re-assigned to the nightshift building military gliders; the Heinz plant on the north side of Pittsburgh no longer canned pickles and ketchup. And while Joan said she hated the hours, she loved the pay, so she'd cook supper for her daughter, then take a nap while Doris did the dishes. By the time she finished work at eight o'clock, Doris would be catching the bus downtown.

"I need to get a job doing something useful," Doris said opening the refrigerator. She put ice and water in two tumblers.

Joan tasted the gravy. Satisfied, she put the saltshaker on the shelf above the stove. "Did you see the letter?" She shook the last bits of whipped potatoes off the mixer.

"Yeah, it's right here," Doris said. She used a steak knife to open the envelope and read for a few minutes.

"Well?"

"They're pretty accommodating, especially for working mothers," Doris said. "Maybe you should get a job there."

"I'd have to lie about your age," Joan said. "You're a bit old for a sitter." She carried the potatoes and a loaf of bread to the table. "So what do you think?" Joan said.

"Can I leave you by yourself?" Doris asked. She spread a slice of white bread with margarine. Her mother and estranged uncle were her only family, and Doris had sensed, even as a young girl, that she would need to take care of herself. "Darling, of course I'd miss you," Joan said. "I'd miss you terribly. But it wouldn't be forever." She sat down across the table.

Doris took a spoonful of stew and let the flavors roll around in her mouth.

"Honey," Joan said, "I know how much you want to go out west. This might just be your chance."

"I'd really like to find Uncle Stanley," Doris said.

Joan put down her fork and reached across the table. She put her hand on Doris' arm. "I haven't heard from your uncle in years," she said, "so I'm inclined to believe he's still in San Francisco, since he only gets in touch when he moves."

Doris nodded. She already knew what her mother would say next.

"I don't want you to be disappointed," Joan said.

"I know, Mom," Doris said.

"Your uncle isn't anything like your father was," Joan said. "There's a physical resemblance, of course, but it ends there.

And there's something else you should know. I went a little crazy after your father's death. You were only two and I couldn't imagine how I'd get by on my own. He was our only close relative, and I think maybe I was too much of a burden. I ran him off."

"No, Mom, I don't think that's possible."

"But you don't understand. I wasn't like I am now. You can't remember of course; you were just a baby. Stanley stayed long enough to bury Frank, and then he was gone. Said he had important railroad work to get back to, and that was it. A couple of months later, he sent that photo you like, of him on the beach."

Doris crumpled the letter from Kaiser. Her mother caught her arm. "Don't worry Doris," Joan said,"I've been here for twenty-five years, and I have lots of friends. I have a good job now. I'm more worried that you'll be lonely."

Doris knew that she'd be on her own if she went to work in the shipyards. Her uncle wouldn't be far away—assuming he was still at his last known address—but she couldn't imagine that he'd help her. Still, she hoped to meet him. After her mother, he was her closest living relative. She knew he'd invested in railroads and had engineered the construction of a few small regional lines around California, but she knew little else about him. She put a big scoop of mashed potatoes on top of the stew.

"Honey," Joan said, "you're just too smart to be selling lipstick."

"I suppose I should go," Doris said.

"You're just too smart to be selling lipstick." Doris thought about her mother's words as she tried to fall asleep. She wanted to go to school, maybe study business, but she didn't have enough saved. She needed to make more money, and it would be possible now with all the boys overseas.

She had few friends—most of her co-workers seemed perfectly happy selling lipstick—and Doris preferred to spend her time alone. She wouldn't miss her job. The only person she cared about was encouraging her to go.

She gave notice the next morning. Four weeks later, in Richmond, California, she stepped off a Greyhound and into a crowd of new arrivals. She'd hardly slept on the bus and had changed clothes only once in five days. She felt sticky all over and wondered how she smelled. She ran her fingers through her shoulder-length hair from top to bottom and buttoned her jacket to the collar. The sun hadn't pierced the morning fog, and everything was damp.

Before she'd left Pittsburgh, Doris had learned as much as she could about Richmond, California. It hadn't been hard to do. Industrial output was the subject of considerable national pride, and that made it news. The reference librarian had been a big help with obscure sources that she might not have found on her own.

Kaiser had been Doris' first choice, and even though it meant traveling cross-country, she'd thought she'd be lucky to work there. She'd read that shipyards one and two covered miles of the north bay coast, using the water as a part of the assembly line, and that a third yard was nearly ready for operation. Kaiser Richmond was the largest facility of its kind in the nation, and Henry Kaiser had a reputation for treating his workers generously. Anyone who read Eleanor Roosevelt's column—and Doris read it every day—knew the First Lady thought favorably of him. One of his innovations was health insurance. Workers were entitled to "prepay" for health coverage for only fifty cents a week.

Doris had done her homework before applying, and she'd outlined her reasons for wanting the job in a carefully worded query that she'd sent to the hiring officer. She got no response at first, but then the country went to war and everything changed. They needed workers and were actively recruiting women.

She hefted her suitcase and crossed McDonald Street, heading toward the water. She'd seen the main entrance to the shipyard on her way into town. A bus marked "Shipyards" picked her up. Although it was Sunday morning, there was a perceptible buzz with people on the street moving quickly.

Doris had never traveled alone. She'd never been farther from Pittsburgh than Lake Erie, but she knew she could read a map and didn't doubt her sense of direction. She strode purposefully and handled her large suitcase well, though she had to change hands every half block. She realized too late that two smaller bags would have been more sensible. Everything about her bearing said "I'm here to land a good job."

At the entry gate, she checked in without incident, learned that her roommate, Matilda Bettencourt, hadn't arrived yet and secured the keys to her assigned housing, Airstream No. 27.

CHAPTER 5

August 9, 1942

THE FIRST TIME Sylvia saw her, Tilly was forcing a canvas duffel through the door of Airstream No. 27. The bag was as wide as the door, but fortunately, it was soft sided. Sylvia watched as Tilly manipulated the bulk of it and pushed it through. The operation reminded her of the chef stuffing sausage back at the Kansas City steakhouse that, until last month, had been her place of employment for over a decade. She was a long way from home but would finally be doing something besides slinging bourbon and steak to businessmen who didn't notice her. She'd become a relic in their eyes, a part of the history of the place. She was a woman who wore comfortable shoes, no matter how her legs looked.

Another young woman, a strawberry blond, had unpacked in Airstream No. 27 earlier in the afternoon, and Sylvia had watched her without attempting a neighborly introduction. After an hour, she left with a notebook, and Sylvia nicknamed her "Ernestine."

So Ernestine was going to have a roommate. Either that or the woman with the sausage casing luggage was in the wrong trailer. Ernestine didn't look like she would make a mistake like that, and she did have a key to the door. This new young woman appeared a whole lot less sure of herself.

Sylvia knew that the polite thing would have been to say hello, but her sister, Alice, had written of her nephew's pending deployment, and she couldn't bring herself to step outside. She had this sense of dread and knew she had to pull herself together before her shift in the morning. For now, a little gin and grapefruit juice would have to get her through the afternoon.

When Robbie's high school graduation date had drawn close, Sylvia found herself following world news with an intensity previously reserved for the Saint Louis Cardinals. If America got into the war, it could take her only nephew. She'd been a child during the Great War, lost her father to it. And life had not unfolded in a way that made a family of her own possible.

They had celebrated Robbie's milestone with a dinner after the commencement ceremony, and Sylvia had baked the cake she'd always baked for him, his childhood favorite. She'd started early in the day so the chocolate layers would have plenty of time to cool. Then she spooned marshmallow cream from the jar and blended it thoroughly with butter and vanilla, before adding the sugar and just a tablespoon of whole milk to get a good spreadable consistency. With a narrow spatula, she lifted the frosting into perfect peaks.

Her nephew was fourteen years younger than she, and she felt more like an older sister than an aunt. There was no one she cared about more. In her early twenties, she'd bought her first car and had taken him camping and fishing at Cuiver River and Big Creek. They'd made a pact to see all the state parks and historic sites in Missouri in the summers before he graduated high school, but they never made it through the list. Robbie discovered sports and dating and had less time for her.

She'd often made cupcakes for their road trips and thought he'd appreciate revisiting her famous chocolate marshmallow combination. But as she centered the top layer she froze—what if his childhood tastes had changed? She hadn't thought to ask what he might want. He was a man now.

She glanced up at the clock, relieved that the bakery would still be open. She'd stop on the way to Alice's house and buy another cake. Something more sophisticated. Something with buttercream. She'd bring both desserts, one to show she cared enough to bake his old favorite and one to show she respected the man he had become.

Her sister answered the door, and Sylvia passed her the homemade cake on top of the bakery box. Then she ran back to her car for the gift—a Black and Decker electric drill with a set of bits, a gift that said he was an adult now and needed to start his own tool collection. She'd wrapped it in dark blue paper.

At first impression, Sylvia thought Robbie's girlfriend was pleasant enough, and pretty in a modest sort of way. But she thought Robbie could do better. She left at nine to meet Dianna, who had suggested they get together for a drink.

• • •

Sylvia knocked the flag off the door as she struggled to get the key in the lock. In the dark hallway, she told herself she should have refused that last cocktail. In her private moments, of which there were many, she calculated the ratio of martinis consumed to her relative inability to do simple tasks. Difficulty unlocking the door to her small apartment was a signal that she'd imbibed enough for one evening. Sylvia took a practical view of how much alcohol was too much.

Last week, Dianna told her it was over. It had lasted seven months and might have lasted longer if the world hadn't turned itself inside out, turned her inside out. Dianna had agreed to marry her boyfriend, who'd enlisted in the Navy and was heading to San Diego for training. She was preparing to move to California. Yes, she felt passion for Sylvia, but every woman experienced "sisterly love" at some point, and it was only a fleeting thing, and it was time to go. She told Sylvia that, at thirty-two, it wasn't too late for her to find a man and settle down.

Sylvia, who had no other plans for the evening and no reason to remain functional, uncapped a cold bottle of gin and opened a jar of olives. In the morning, she would contact Kaiser and ask about job opportunities. Her nephew was gone, and she wanted to work building Liberty ships.

CHAPTER 6

TILLY LOOKED at her watch, then hesitated for only a moment at the closed doors of the auditorium. The orientation had already started. She entered with a shaft of light and quickly pulled the handle behind her. They were showing a film, and her eyes didn't adjust immediately.

"Richmond, California, which had no shipyards prior to the war, now has the capacity to produce more merchant vessels than any city in the US."

A few heads turned in her direction. She slid into the closest empty seat—in the back row between two colored women. She smiled to her left and right as she excused herself. They shifted their weight away from her. The black and white footage showed the bustle of a shift change.

"The yards comprise the most modern and efficient marine manufacturing complex in the country, and Richmond is home to more war industries than any other city of its size.

"Before 1940, the Six Companies organization, with Henry J. Kaiser at the helm, was involved in major civil engineering feats, building roads and dams, including Grand Coulee. As World War

II approached, Kaiser began to think about turning his team of veteran construction managers to shipbuilding. Kaiser got an order from the British government to build sixty ships based on an old tramp steamer design—we call them Liberty ships. Thirty of these are on order to be built right here in Richmond, California."

Tilly leaned forward in the seat to take in the aerial shot of the complex before the frame changed, then sat back and slumped, her feeling of helplessness complete. From afar, she'd imagined Richmond being a lot like home but bursting with interesting and industrious women. She had no frame of reference for working in an industrial complex. The newsreels she'd seen in the movie theater hadn't captured the energy of the place, and voiceovers had masked the din. What had seemed enormous on the big screen was dwarfed by reality, and when her father drove her to the entrance, she feared she'd be swallowed up as soon as her feet touched pavement. Paul's brow furrowed deeply as he downshifted and moved into the queue for the drop-off area.

Visitors weren't permitted beyond the gate, so good-byes had to be said in the loading zone. Tilly had wanted the job more than anything, but she felt her stomach tighten when her father unhooked the tailgate and pulled her bulging duffel from the back.

"Are you having second thoughts?" he asked as he shaded his eyes from the sun.

Tilly thought he could see right through her, and took the bag quickly. "I'm staying," she said. She didn't look at him. He put his hand on her shoulder.

"I've got to get back," he said. "Are you sure about this?"

She smiled by locking her molars and baring her front teeth. "I'm swell, Dad. You don't have to worry about me."

Paul nodded but kept his eyes on her face. Then a car honked, and he waved at the driver, hugged her, and climbed into the cab.

Tilly shouldered her gear and prepared to enter a new world, her strength and enthusiasm waning. Through the gate, she could see a purely functional environment: no greenery, nothing requiring labor better directed toward the war effort. She'd have to adjust. Every surface was hard; each one amplified and reflected noise. She wondered if she'd ever be able to sleep. She turned back toward the street in time to see the old green Ford pulling slowly toward the south, and with it went her remaining confidence. She fought back a sob and took a deep breath. She had to hold herself together. After a moment, she approached the reception station.

A woman she thought might be her mother's age sat behind one of a half dozen small, wooden desks inside an industrial gatehouse. She was the only receptionist not assisting a new employee; her nametag said "Emma." Emma smiled from behind an ample stack of paper when Tilly approached.

"I'm here to work," Tilly said. She was able to speak without crying, but her voice broke.

"I'm sorry," Emma said, "Can you say your name again?"

Tilly dropped her bag on the floor and leaned over the desk trying to read the list. The space was crowded with workers of all ages and hues. Almost everyone had luggage.

"Bettencourt?" Emma asked, "with a B?"

"Yes, Tilly."

Emma ran her pencil down the margin. "Ah, we have you down as Matilda Bettencourt." She looked up and smiled.

Tilly thought Emma might have a son in the war, and it suddenly occurred to her that she was fighting for victory, not fighting to leave home. The work she would be doing was important. "Everybody calls me Tilly," she said.

Emma handed her a map and checked "Bettencourt" off the list. "Welcome to Kaiser," she said. "This will help you get to where you need to go." She winked, "You're one of the lucky ones—you'll be housed in an Airstream."

Tilly looked down. She didn't have a lot of experience with maps. "An Airstream?" she said. Emma had placed an X at a location that seemed to be on the outer reaches of the complex.

"They're a bit like trailers." Emma paused, watching Tilly's expression. "They're travel homes...metal houses on wheels?"

Tilly nodded, but her expression betrayed her.

Emma tried again, "They're a bit behind on construction of employee apartments and dorms," she said, "so to help newcomers, they purchased the last Airstreams before the plant was converted."

Tilly read the map. The area with the X was labeled Parking Lot C. She was going to be living in a parking lot.

Emma was still talking. "They're very modern, and the girls just love them," she said.

Tilly was trying to understand how she could live in a parking lot.

"They're like little, shiny cottages, and you'll only have to share with one roommate," Emma said.

"A roommate?" Tilly hadn't considered the possibility of living with a stranger.

"As a matter of fact," Emma said, "she checked in a little earlier, from Pittsburgh, Pennsylvania."

"Pittsburgh, Pennsylvania," Tilly said. "Imagine that. All the way from Pittsburgh." Her voice was quiet. She had just taken the longest trip of her life.

"Your roommate's name is Doris Jura," Emma said. She handed Tilly a key to the Airstream and explained where to get something to eat and where the orientation would be held.

Tilly hadn't much use for maps in Montara, and she hung on Emma's every word as if a lapse in attention might leave her wandering endlessly in this strange and complicated place. She was leaving when a powerful thought came to her. She stopped abruptly, dropped the duffel and cut back in line.

"Is Doris Jura colored?" Tilly asked. Those within earshot turned and looked. Emma also stared.

"Why no, Tilly," Emma said. "We don't house whites with coloreds. You'll be working with coloreds though."

Tilly nodded and embarrassed, hoisted the bag to her shoulder.

The route to Parking Lot C was simple: out the door and turn left. Tilly headed away from the entrance along a walkway Emma had marked on the map with arrows. As directed, she went half the length of the yard along the inside the fence. She was relieved when rows of aluminum trailers came into view. She wondered if her father had reached Berkeley yet, and then forced the thought from her mind. She was here to stay.

Her Airstream looked like a silver loaf with a door and windows, and she swallowed hard when she thought about sharing it. She suspected it was only sixteen feet long, half as wide. Still, she told herself, it was hers—or half hers. She double-checked the number on the key against the one stenciled on the parking space and opened the lock.

It was magical. Had she been a child, it would have been the perfect playhouse. It was exactly as Emma had described: a modern, shiny cottage, a miniature, rounded home. She smiled as she looked around. Everything was new; the upholstery was covered with paper to keep it clean. She pulled away a corner of the wrapping and saw the beige and charcoal woven fabric. There was good wood veneer over the doors to the tiny cabinets and wall sconces were evenly spaced above the bed. It wasn't what she'd expected, but the truth was that Tilly, in her enthusiasm for getting the job, had ignored her mother's concerns and hadn't asked about accommodations.

The Airstream was new, and it was hers. She was ready to move in and grabbed her bag, but found her duffel wouldn't fit through the door. She pushed against the canvas and pulled, then removed a cookbook from her Aunt Ida that was catching on the jamb and squeezed the bag in. She was about to toss her gear on the bunk fitted opposite, when she noticed a skirt neatly laid near the pillow. She held it up to her waist, her first clue. Her roommate was tiny. She looked down at the pumps poking out from the storage space below; yes, she was a petite woman.

A giant suitcase had been stowed under the bed, where it filled the entire space. Tilly pulled it out. Tiny but mighty, she thought—it was the tallest suitcase she'd ever seen. Then she remembered that Doris had come all the way from Pittsburgh Pennsylvania, and figured she'd needed to bring a few extras along. She wondered how old Doris Jura was. Tilly slid her luggage back, suddenly feeling like a voyeur.

The table at the end nearest the door collapsed into a bed, and Tilly kicked her duffel to that side. In between were a small stove and sink, and a toilet in a tiny space that reminded her of the head on the *Matilda B.* She thought of her Uncle Aldo living with burly deck hands for days at sea and knew that she could live with one petite woman in an Airstream. She left everything but the map, afraid she'd be late for orientation.

The shipyard was built along the shore with water functioning as part of the assembly line, and work bays were evenly spaced along it. From a distance, they all looked alike. Tilly held the map with water to the west, her left, and tried to navigate through the complex. When she located a building she could identify, she discovered she was going in the wrong direction. A man noticed that she'd passed him twice, and offered to assist.

"The water is on the south side," he said.

Tilly stared in amazement. "The ocean is on the west."

"Angel, that's the bay, and you're on a peninsula," he said. "Where are you from?"

"I'm late," Tilly said. "Please point me toward the auditorium."

Doris arrived at the auditorium just as the speaker was about to begin and took a seat near the front. She thought the room might hold one hundred—it was nearly at capacity—and she noticed that nearly all were women. Roll was taken alphabetically.

"Matilda Bettencourt?"

She recognized her roommate's name and turned to look, but there was no response.

With her notebook open, Doris pulled a pencil from her jacket pocket and recorded the date. After a brief presentation about the benefits of working for Kaiser, a man explained that women could join an auxiliary union just for them, while men joined the regular union. A pretty and energetic gal dressed in red, white, and blue encouraged them to buy war bonds automatically. She said they'd pay patriotic as well as financial dividends and explained how payroll deductions worked. Doris jotted a few notes. Then it was time for the pep talk, followed by the film. The lights went down.

Half way through, as the narrator was describing the operations in Richmond, the door at the back opened and a young woman entered. Doris turned to see the afternoon light illuminate the back row of coloreds, as the late arrival looked for an empty seat. She thought it must be Matilda and smiled to herself. She'd hoped her roommate would be her age, someone who could be a friend. Matilda appeared, from her long hair and slender build, to be in her early twenties.

Doris hadn't been in Richmond more than a few hours, too short a time to meet other workers, but she'd seen the next-door neighbor and had formed an immediate, unfavorable opinion of her. From the Airstream window, Doris watched the woman smoke and drink—probably alcohol from the way she sipped it—for an hour as she stared in Doris' direction, without so much as a wave. Doris nicknamed her The Battleaxe and hoped she wouldn't be stuck living with anyone so dull or humorless. It was bad enough having The Battleaxe in a trailer, ten feet away.

Doris turned her attention back to the screen.

"Here in the yard, workers come into play with all the dynamics of materials flow and the rhythm of operations. New ships have to be produced much faster than ever before and traditional methods simply won't get the job done. Shipyards were previously thought of in terms of acres; Kaiser's yards cover miles so that the mountains of materials can be handled efficiently."

The footage shifted to women workers: welding, riveting, wiring—all were smiling.

"Fast welding techniques have nearly eliminated laborious riveting. Our yards are laid out like assembly lines, with the steel and parts flowing smoothly from flat cars to completed vessels.

"In addition to innovative time-cutting techniques already developed, modern construction of Kaiser Liberty ships utilizes seventeen banks of welding machines on each side of the hull, pre-assembly of the deck in seven sections instead of twenty-three, and complete outfitting of the deckhouses, down to bunks, fans and flooring, before assembly."

And so it continued. There was more patriotic and motivational footage, interviews with women who wanted to help the war effort, and finally a message from Henry J. Kaiser himself, thanking the new employees for their service to their country.

The lights came up, and the hostess returned to center stage. "I hope you enjoyed the film and have learned some background on our company." She paused and looked around, "Someone came in late," she said. "May I get your name for the roll?"

Tilly rose to attention and gave a half wave, "Tilly Bettencourt. You probably have me down as Matilda."

"Welcome to Kaiser."

Doris turned and smiled but couldn't get her roommate's attention.

Food, Tilly thought to herself. She was suddenly very hungry and needed groceries or the company cafeteria. She reached the back door of the auditorium first and was out before the crowd. She pulled out her map.

Doris, a minute behind, ran to catch up. "Excuse me, excuse me, Tilly?" she said, catching her breath. She smiled when Tilly turned, "I'm your roommate."

Of course, Tilly thought. She would fit into that skirt. And she was young. Tilly looked at Doris' smile and impulsively hugged her. "I'm so relieved," she said. "I've never lived away from home or had a roommate, but I think this is going to be swell."

"It's good to meet you," Doris said.

"I was going to get something to eat," Tilly said.

"You're going the wrong way," Doris told her.

Tilly looked at the map again.

"Were you late because you were lost?" Doris said.

"Completely."

"Follow me."

Tilly was surprised to find a line at three o'clock, but Doris said it was probably swing shift having an early dinner.

The food was arranged behind counters that connected in a giant U-shape, and women in uniforms and hairnets doled out reasonable portions. Signs reminded employees to take only what they could eat. "Food is a weapon—Don't waste it!"

"I'm only having coffee," Doris told a worker who seemed to recognize her.

Tilly brought her meatloaf and potatoes to the table and sat across from Doris, who was looking at the ketchup bottle.

"My mom worked for H. J. Heinz bottling ketchup and canning pickles before the war," she said. "The plant's on the north side of Pittsburgh. Now they make military gliders and my mom's a riveter."

Tilly was impressed and wondered where they were making the ketchup, but she didn't ask.

"I don't think this is really Heinz ketchup in this bottle," Doris said as if to read Tilly's mind. "They're filling it with something else." To emphasize the point she poured a little on her index finger and tasted it. "Red vinegar sludge."

Given the state of the world, Tilly thought ketchup of any kind was a luxury. She would be careful to wipe it all off her plate with the last of the meatloaf.

"I have an uncle in San Francisco," Doris said. "He's been out here more than twenty-five years, but we haven't heard from him in a long time." Tilly's mouth stayed full while Doris did most of the talking. "My father's brother—my dad died when I was still a baby, and mom never stayed in touch."

Tilly murmured some generic condolences.

"He was involved with railroad engineering," Doris said, "and some land development stuff." She was on her second cup of coffee, and Tilly wondered if the caffeine was fueling the conversation. She noticed that Doris didn't use a spoon. She would add cream and swirl the cup around. "It would be great to find him," Doris said. "Do you know much about San Francisco?"

Tilly had to admit that she didn't, though she wanted to make a good impression.

The company instructions said to bring as little as possible to Richmond, and as they took stock of their tiny space, they understood why. Tilly's duffel took up much of the floor area; she kicked it under the table.

"We can make this work," Doris said. She took a sheet of paper from her notebook and started a list while Tilly marveled at her initiative. "The place's been parked for a while so it needs a good scrubbing." She wrote "cleaning supplies." "There's no toilet paper in the bathroom," Doris continued, "and we need to locate the laundry, get some basic provisions. We'll want to get some blackout fabric and hang curtains around each of the bunks—especially if we get assigned different shifts."

Tilly sat nodding her head in agreement. Doris made a plan, and Tilly would help implement it. It was already four o'clock, and they had a lot to do before their first shift.

It was after four o'clock when Paul took the last southbound bend on Montara Mountain and the village came into view. He looked out across the beach on the west side of the Coast Highway and east to fields of vegetables. He'd seen something of the world when he fought in the Great War. He found no place more beautiful than home.

He drove the truck down the driveway to the barn. Helen was in the garden, dressed in jeans and one of his old shirts, picking beans and zucchini. A pile of weeds she'd pulled out by the roots grew at her side. He walked to where she was toiling and started to work alongside her.

"How was the drive?" she asked.

"Good till we got to the drop-off." He sat back on his haunches and looked at his wife, "I felt like I left Tilly on another planet. Do you know she's never seen a colored outside of a movie?"

Helen looked at him, eyes wide, and Paul realized his mistake. "I lit a candle for her at church this morning," she said.

Paul tossed a weed into the pile and put his arms around her. "Tilly's going to be just fine. I'm proud of her."

Helen shook her head. "She might be fine, but I won't be. I didn't sleep a wink last night and I doubt that tonight will be any better."

Paul took her hand and led her toward the house. "Perhaps we both need a nap," he said.

CHAPTER 7

August 19, 1942

SYLVIA THOUGHT that a better person would let the company know she had an extra bunk in her Airstream, but then, she had never thought of herself as exemplary. Housing was in such short supply that workers were sharing beds—day shift vacating in time for the nightshift. She had a whole company-provided trailer to herself. Maybe they forgot her because she was at the end of the line: No. 28 of row M. She enjoyed her outlaw status, mostly. Sometimes things got a little lonely, just a little, but she could hear everything that happened in Airstream No. 27, and some of it was downright entertaining.

Ernestine whose name, Sylvia discovered, was really Doris, was a constant source of amusement. She'd never come across a young woman so driven to do—well she wasn't sure what, exactly. She was just driven and absolutely thrilled that the war had presented her with an opportunity to excel. Rumor had it that Doris had scored high on a technical aptitude test—higher than any of the men, and they were going to do a feature on her in *Fore 'n' Aft*. Sylvia smirked inwardly. She could just imagine Doris-Ernestine saving copies of the newsletter for her grandchildren.

The other young woman seemed rather pleasant, very friendly and innocent. She'd be quite a beauty, Sylvia thought, if she ever figured out how to make the most of her physical attributes.

The morning was warm, and Sylvia sat on the aluminum stairs connected to her twenty-eight inch aluminum entry, taking her morning coffee and cigarettes in the sun. The spread of her hips was ample, and she had to sit one step below the doorjamb or risk getting stuck in the narrow opening. She chuckled when she heard her neighbor's alarm clock ring and then heard Tilly's head make contact with the rounded metal ceiling above her bunk. This was a daily occurrence, and Sylvia had once heard Doris suggest that Tilly alternate head and foot position each night, to flatten the sides of her head evenly. "You don't want an asymmetrical head," Doris had said.

Sylvia could appreciate a woman with a good sense of humor. Maybe Doris-Ernestine had some redeeming qualities.

The door and all the windows of their Airstream were open, and Sylvia saw Doris hold a dish above a pan of boiling water—concocting heaven knew what. It sure didn't smell like coffee. It smelled like candles. Was she melting wax?

She heard Tilly ask Doris what she was doing, and then heard Doris shout, "Don't throw water on it." There were flames in Airstream No. 27; Sylvia managed to shed her indifference. She grabbed her small fire extinguisher—she was never without one since she'd witnessed a bad kitchen fire in one of her Kansas City steak joints—and rushed through the door to Tilly and Doris' astonishment. The Airstream was suddenly full of smoke and surfactant, and the three women tumbled outside. Doris recovered her composure first and thanked Sylvia for the attempted rescue, even though it was obvious that Doris had already smothered the fire with a damp towel. Sylvia realized that her neighbors now knew she'd been watching them, and about the time she thought she'd just crawl away in embarrassment, Tilly put her right hand out and said, "Pleased to finally meet you."

The only reasonable thing to do then, while the smoke cleared, was to invite Tilly and Doris into her camp for coffee, though it meant sharing her rations. She poured them each half a cup from what was left of her morning brew and made a new pot, while Doris explained that she was making candles from the packing material the navigational equipment was shipped in.

"As far as I can tell," Doris said, "no one is using it for anything, so I thought I might as well play around with it."

"Doris is already working O.T., can you believe it?" Tilly said. "In the electrical division."

"Sure beats selling lipstick," Doris said.

"Selling lipstick?" Sylvia had a belly laugh over that one, and Tilly had to admit that it would have been something to see.

They talked about how their first payday would be on Friday and how they'd all signed up to buy war bonds.

"There's not much I want that isn't rationed," Sylvia said, "I might as well save up for silk pajamas after victory." She would bank the remarkable sum of thirteen hundred dollars per year, more if she got overtime. She said that contemplating her accumulating wealth helped her forget her muscle aches. Something about that, and saving for silk pajamas, struck Doris as funny, and as she laughed out loud, Sylvia decided that she could learn to like her. And she had to admit, the candle-making business was a pretty creative idea.

Their new home, the shipyard, was to Sylvia a colossal industrialized hive, highly organized, with all energy flowing to a single purpose for three shifts, everyday. Her regular schedule was Saturday through Thursday, with potential overtime. Tilly's schedule was identical. Doris worked swing, but often stayed on into the night shift. Their collective mission: To restore the fleet—replace vessels destroyed by German U-Boats. As Sylvia labored coating decks with a non-skid surface, she tried to forget why so many ships were needed. "Each of these boats can carry the population of a small town outside of Kansas City," she wrote home to her sister. Always in her mind were Robbie and the boys he served with.

• • •

With the bracing around the completed hull removed, the air horn sounded, and workers left their tools to watch. Towing commenced. As the vessel slid from the marine way, Sylvia and Tilly saw it come alive. It was a real Liberty ship. They cheered and hugged as it was moved to the outfitting dock where a technical crew, including Doris, would install operating equipment in final preparation for the sea trial. Tilly was giddy.

"It's always exciting," a woman next to Sylvia said. "It just doesn't get old."

At the end of shift, Tilly picked up her first real paycheck; she'd need to open a bank account. Payday at the roadhouse had been an informal affair—Jose would simply open the register and count out the bills. She explained this to Sylvia as they walked downtown. As she scrutinized the pay stub, she stopped abruptly. "There must be some mistake," Tilly said.

Sylvia looked over her shoulder, "What seems to be the problem?"

Tilly explained that they had deducted the correct amount for war bonds, but there were other deductions she didn't understand.

Sylvia laughed at her and explained how income taxes worked. "About four percent," she said. "They need money to build all these boats."

When hull #1553 was christened the *Mary Cassatt*, Tilly, Doris and Sylvia toasted with mugs of rationed coffee and vowed to have a proper celebration when they had a night off together. They had all worked on the vessel, and it was completed, from keel to christening, in forty-four days. Sylvia, holding a brush and posing in her splattered overalls, pointed out that their first common vessel was named for a woman painter.

"Next thing we know," Tilly said, "you'll want one christened the Sylvia Manning."

Tilly began as a tacker, a spot welder, though she had other options. When asked to state a preference, welding was all that came to mind: Katherine Hepburn welding. As an apprentice, her task was to make simple connections between steel plates, usually on the tops of decks. Her goals were promotion, membership in the women's version of the boilermakers union, and significantly increased earnings.

Jim Benson, her mentor and coach, had been conscripted from retirement to train the truly inexperienced. A forty-year veteran of the trade, Benson answered the patriotic call after war was declared and mastered the new techniques for submerged arc welding. He somehow summoned the patience to teach tender recruits the skills of a manufacturing force, monitoring the effort from his office two stories up the south wall of the main assembly gallery. His office resembled a steel crate with windows; occasionally Benson used it just to let off steam. He was a thorough and demanding teacher.

"You need to keep your face shield down no matter how much you're sweating," he'd say again and again, "and remember that looking at the arc will burn your eyes."

With a rod in her left hand and the torch in her right, Tilly imitated the techniques Benson demonstrated, without the same results. Her gloves and helmet, the most critical pieces of protective wear, were also the most cumbersome; she often felt like she was fighting herself. The goggles cut beneath her eyes. Benson assured her the rhythm for the work would come—like fluidity for knitting or crocheting—but she'd never learned to do either.

"Hold it this way." He demonstrated the proper angle for applying just the right amount of molten metal and Tilly fumbled in her oversized gear to try and produce equivalent results. She remembered the ease with which she performed her job as a waitress, lowered her mask, and turned on the torch. She would learn. With each shift, she gained greater confidence.

After six weeks, Benson approached her when the line took a water break. "Tilly the Tacker," he called. She stopped guzzling and wiped her mouth on her sleeve. Her hair was soaked through, and perspiration ran down the side of her nose when she looked up at him.

"Let's try you out on an interior seam," he said. "Stick around after shift change." He told Tilly to find him after the swing shift started and pointed toward a woman working the job she'd be learning. To date, all her welds had been on decks—decks she could kneel on. Working on the inside meant welding at odd angles, and sometimes overhead. The work required greater skill, strength, and stamina. Benson said that Tilly would be shadowing a woman named Lydia, and that Lydia would show her the ropes.

It was hard to concentrate as she waited for the shift to end, but eventually Tilly was led to her new workstation. She stood at the top of a ladder on the starboard side of the cavernous hull, then climbed the rungs between the deck levels. With her mask up and her gloves in her right hand, she held on with her left, took a deep breath and lowered herself one step. The heat from the burning torches swallowed her, and she was glad she hadn't eaten for several hours. She'd stay enveloped by that heat—how different from working on the top deck, where the wind off the bay could be chilling.

Lydia put a torch in Tilly's hand, then shouted a few commands, her voice nearly inaudible against the ambient noise. Most of the instruction came in the form of demonstration and imitation; Tilly struggled to lay her beads of molten metal in a cohesive strand. She'd never worked on a vertical surface before and was astonished at how much more difficult it was. Try as she might, every weld she performed required a "do over" by Lydia. They went on for an hour, and Tilly, already tired from a full days work, became increasingly frustrated.

"You're up to it," Benson said. "You just need to relax."

Tilly was dismissed for the day and climbed out of the hull feeling lightheaded, not sure if she should attribute it to excitement, exhaustion or dehydration.

She removed her helmet and gloves, consumed another quart of water, and punched out. Suddenly, it was twenty degrees cooler and her soaked overalls chilled her. She tossed her small duffel over her shoulder and hurried to the women's locker room.

Doris was working swing, and there was no response when Tilly knocked on Sylvia's door. She continued to dinner alone and lonely, eager to share the promotion news. She passed an empty phone booth and dug a nickel from her jeans.

"What number please?"

Tilly quickly changed her mind. Her mother was too worried about the welding to be happy, and if she called Ida and

Jose instead, well, that would be a slight. She sighed and put the receiver back on the cradle. The night called for something a little out of the ordinary.

She walked along Canal Street and out the main gate of the complex, continued east to Cutting Boulevard, then hopped a bus to MacDonald Avenue. Sidewalks in downtown Richmond were crowded, shops open late to accommodate the day shift, and business was brisk. Tilly didn't immediately think of food.

She scanned the windows for dresses on display, but she was unable to focus on what she saw and too disinterested to really shop. Trying on clothes would waste effort—six days a week she wore denim or canvas. In one window she caught her reflection and noticed her hair. She turned for a look at how it draped across her back and held up a tress to check the ends. It was long, all one length as it had always been. She looked around at women on the street. They were coiffed. Tilly had never had a real haircut, and she wondered what she would look like. She smiled. She could afford to find out.

The sign said "Gloria's" and the shop didn't look busy. For a moment Tilly thought it might be a bad sign, but decided that if Gloria had time for a walk-up, then it was meant to be. She turned the knob.

Bells tinkled overhead, and she entered a rose-colored world. The salon was small, with two chairs, floral wallpaper, pink-painted baseboard; everything smelled unnaturally, unpleasantly sweet. She was reconsidering when a woman with a very blond head popped out from behind a hooded dryer she was adjusting over a client. She simultaneously greeted and guided Tilly, by the shoulder, to an empty station before a giant oval mirror. She ran her dramatically manicured fingers through Tilly's locks, evaluating the gorgeous crop of untouched brunette waves.

"I was thinking about getting a haircut, you know, a style." Tilly said, "That is if you have time—I can come back later." She started to rise.

"My name is Gloria," the beautician said gently pushing her back into the chair. "As soon as I brush out Julia, we can talk."

Tilly slid back in the chair, shoulders up around her ears.

"Have a look through these," Gloria said, handing her some magazines, "and see if you spot something you like." She returned to the beauty in progress as Tilly turned the pages, alternately checking her own image.

This is ridiculous, Tilly thought. Try as she might, she couldn't imagine the hair in the pictures on her head. Through the mirror, she watched Gloria's reflection dote on Julia's silky auburn curls. A very satisfied customer, Julia booked her next appointment and tipped generously.

"All the women in the pictures look beautiful," Tilly said, "but they're not me."

"My dear, you are very beautiful," Gloria said, and then she began to work quickly as if she knew all along what she wanted to do and was simply asking for Tilly's opinion to be polite. "Let's take a bit of this length off and call more attention to that lovely face of yours."

Telling herself not to worry, Tilly held her head steady and closed her eyes. She tried to imagine Montara beach at high tide. The damage wouldn't be permanent.

The scissors sliced through a fistful of hair that Gloria let drop to the floor; Tilly stiffened and pressed her eyelids together tightly. She could see her mother holding up her hair and trimming the ends. Gloria's jaw was set as she worked.

Occasionally, Tilly stole a look—what was left of her dark mane hung limp at the shoulders and she had long bangs. Gloria had wheeled a basket on a stand next to the chair and was fussing with rollers and clips. Tilly got her turn under the dryer, where she tried to imagine how she would ever manage setting her own hair. She wondered how she would store the necessary paraphernalia in the Airstream.

When Gloria finished brushing, fluffing and spraying, she handed Tilly a mirror for a look at her handiwork. She was beaming; Tilly was incredulous. Her hair was parted on her right, waved off her forehead and rolled under just at her shoulders. Everything was smoothed into place and so shiny it reflected light. She resembled a brunette Bacall, Gloria told her. Tilly didn't follow Vogue models and wasn't used to this level of glamour. She felt very self-conscious—as if she were trying to pass as a different person. She paid and thanked Gloria who was effusive about how gorgeous she looked.

Tilly's hair bounced in the breeze, and she felt lighter as she walked back toward the shipyard. She liked the feeling, and it caused her to walk with a bit more lift. Her stomach started to rumble, the cooler, evening air rousing her appetite. It was getting dark.

She found a diner and took a seat alone at the long chrome counter, enjoying the aroma of frying onions and grilling beef. The short-order cook cut thick slices of cheddar for the burgers on the grill, and she watched the cheese melt and coat the beef patties, transforming them into something sublime. She swallowed. She felt uncomfortable with her appearance and sat, hunched over the menu, even though she knew exactly what she wanted.

The waitress took her order, and Tilly alternately swirled her ice and sipped her water as she waited for her food. Someone dropped coins into the jukebox. The Andrews Sisters sang through small speakers mounted on the counter.

A young man in uniform entered and sat next to her. He cleared his throat, but she didn't acknowledge him.

"Hello Sugar, have you been rationed?" he said.

Tilly looked over her shoulder.

"Come on Angel, you know I'm talking to you."

She almost choked on the ice cube she had in her mouth. "Thank you," she said. She stared straight ahead. She was uncomfortable when men she didn't know approached her.

The waitress brought her lemonade and turned to the young man. "What'll it be, Sailor?"

"How about a cheeseburger and a chocolate malt."

She pulled a pencil out of her bun and scratched a few notes on a pad.

"Hey, I'm sorry if I came on a little strong there," the young man said.

Tilly had seen other women become playful when approached by men, but she never felt playful. Her meal was delivered to her relief, and she gave her full attention to the cheeseburger: the golden bun covered with sesame seeds, the melted cheese, ketchup, mustard and pickles. The condiment-slick between the bun and the lettuce did not intimidate her. She ate without dignity, positioning her body at a slight angle away from the sailor.

"Name's Joe."

"Pleased to meet you." She nodded at him but didn't offer her name, and they finished their meals in silence. Tilly walked back to Parking Lot C alone.

"Wow. That haircut looks great on you." Silvia was sitting on the stoop of her Airstream, coffee and cigarette in hand. She could see the transformation in the dim light spilling from her trailer door. Her ash glowed as she flicked it to the asphalt. "Got a hot date this weekend?"

"No," Tilly said.

"Well, you will before long."

Tilly sat on the asphalt in front of her, happy to have someone to share her promotion with. She told Sylvia how she got her hair cut because she'd wanted to celebrate. "I never realized how different I looked from everyone else until this afternoon. My hair still looked like it did when I was a girl."

Silvia nodded and smiled. "Congratulations honey, on both promotions." She blew a blue smoke ring.

Tilly was glad it was dark because she felt the blood rise in her cheeks and didn't want Sylvia to see her blushing. She looked at her feet. It felt good to be admired by Sylvia.

CHAPTER 8

DORIS DID A double take when Tilly opened the door to the Airstream. She was sitting on the bunk, cross-legged and in tears. Tilly poured her a glass of water and sat on the settee, opposite.

Doris passed the letter from home and Tilly read aloud.

"Darling, I hate to give you this awful news, but your Uncle Stanley died suddenly in San Francisco…"

Tilly paused and looked up, "I'm so sorry."

"He lived alone in a small flat on Eddy Street. The apartment manager found him; they believe he had a heart attack. I was contacted by a police officer as Stanley's next of kin—ours was the only address for a 'Jura' in his personal effects. He was cremated—it was the only practical solution given the war and the difficulty in shipping a body across state lines. The ashes will be sent here.

"I've been asked to assist with Stanley's personal possessions. There is, as I'm sure you realize, an extreme need for housing in San Francisco. At this point, I see no purpose in

trying to salvage what's there if it means paying rent on the apartment and delaying the time when it can be made available to a new tenant. I let them know that you are in Richmond, and how to contact you through Kaiser, should anything come up requiring immediate response. I know how hard you're working darling, but you and I are the only relatives left. If you can get to San Francisco, please visit the address below and check in at the front office.

"With respect to your uncle's state near the end of his life, it appears that he led a frugal and far more cautious existence in his middle years than in his early ones. Whatever fortunes he made and lost were mostly lost, and he kept to himself and lived simply. It's a tragedy that he never met you, as you would have been the light of his life..."

"I can't really grieve," Doris said, "I never knew him." She dried her eyes with her sleeve. "I'm more upset because I've come this far, but never made it across the bay." She drank the water. "Now my mother really is my only family. And this scares me, because it can end so quickly."

Tilly said she understood and that she realized how lucky she was to have grown up around her uncles, Jose and Aldo.

"What I remember of Stanley," Doris said, "is from a photo in the hallway. He was on a sunny beach, young and barefoot. His life seemed so much more exciting than ours."

Tilly leaned back and pulled her knees to her chest. "It's hard to believe we've already been here for two months."

"Continuous overtime is going to wear me down," Doris said. "I don't have the energy to do my laundry anymore, but I need to do this."

"I'll go with you," Tilly said.

They boarded the bus at six o'clock in the morning and found the entrance to the Ben Hur Apartments by nine. Doris had worked until midnight and had slept little. "It's a good thing you came with me," she told Tilly, who woke her from a dead sleep when they reached the stop on Van Ness Avenue. "And I've been meaning to tell you," Doris smiled, "your hair looks great."

The building superintendent responded slowly to the bell; they waited on the mat. A peeling blue door opened to reveal an unshaven man unlatching the chain. He was wearing a white, cotton undershirt with deep-cut armholes and dark hair curling at the neck.

"My late uncle rented one of your apartments," Doris said. "I believe you've talked with my mother."

It was cooler in San Francisco than Richmond, the fog more persistent, and the light jacket Doris wore proved inadequate protection from the chill. She realized she was hugging herself and dropped her hands to her sides.

"I just heard about my uncle yesterday," she said. "Is there anything we can do?"

"Stanley took the apartment furnished," he said. "His clothes are there, and some personal stuff, not a lot. I have a girl coming tomorrow to clean." He was checking a board with keys hanging from it as he spoke. "I talked to your mother about giving the clothes to a relief agency, but so far nothing's been removed."

Doris nodded.

"It would be good if you could go through his files and take what you think is important. No one here knew much about him."

Doris took the key; it had the number three thirteen on it.

"It's on the third floor." He pointed to the stairs. "The elevator probably won't get fixed until after the war—just can't get parts."

She nodded again. "Thank you."

"I'm sorry for your loss," he said.

Doris had to fuss with the lock, but when it clicked, the door opened effortlessly. The drapes were drawn, the air stale. She lifted blinds and cracked a couple of windows to illuminate a cheerless space filled with dark mahogany, aged upholstery and worn carpet. A small kitchen was unused, lacking pots, utensils or food.

"I guess he ate out a lot," Tilly said, finding only colas and tomato juice in the refrigerator.

Doris found an opener mounted under the counter and offered Tilly a Coke. "This feels like a hotel room," she said. "I wonder if he lived somewhere else."

One towel hung on the rack in the bathroom below a shelf with a few toiletries. A pearl-handled razor and shaving brush had been left on the sink.

"He made his bed in the morning," Tilly said.

There wasn't a lot of clothing, but what he had appeared to be of high quality and average size. Doris held up a jacket. "Looks like he favored suits and silk ties," she said and shook her head. "Not the romantic beach bum." She pretended to find her reflection in a spit-shined boot. "I prefer to remember him as a barefooted free spirit."

Between the living room and the bedroom was a small office, and Doris took a seat at the desk after declaring that nothing about his wardrobe or possessions was remarkable or worth the effort to ship to Pennsylvania. "We've got to get through his papers before the five o'clock bus."

A total of four drawers: two in a desk that matched the rest of the furniture and two in a freestanding cabinet, housed business and personal records. All were unlocked.

Doris wondered if Stanley had died working. The office was the only area of the apartment that appeared used. She shuddered to think that his heart might have failed while he sat in the very chair she now occupied. He died alone, without comfort, without family. And when her mother passed, she would also be alone. She felt the tears coming as she looked across the desk at Tilly. "Thank you so much for coming with me," she said and forced herself to focus. She had hours of reading ahead of her.

Sliding the first desk drawer open, Doris started with "Banking." There were records from several institutions, but most were old. "I'd say these accounts are closed," she said, "they've been inactive for years." She pulled out the first set of current documents to mail to her mother. "She'll find it amusing that her European brother-in-law banked in Chinatown."

They pored over the ledgers but found nothing unusual. He didn't seem to have paid for another residence—at least not from his Bank of Canton account. Statements showed intermittent, sizable deposits, reasonable for a man paid per project, and fairly regular withdrawals. The apartment and the club where he took his meals were his biggest expenses. There was no evidence that he owned a car, though expired registration receipts showed he'd owned luxury vehicles in the past. He occasionally paid for tailoring or dry cleaning.

Tilly sat on the floor in front of the freestanding cabinet, flipping through project files that appeared to be work-related—various engineering projects and studies he'd authored. "These are copies," she said.

"Let's assume his clients have the originals," Doris said.

Tilly moved on. She opened the second drawer and near the back, found documents from the Ocean Shore Company. "Doris, look at these." She removed several folders and spread them around her on the floor. "The Ocean Shore Railroad ran through my home town. It went bankrupt before I was born."

"I wonder if that's the railroad I heard about growing up," Doris said. "My mother told me Stanley was away on railroad business."

"In the early days, my family depended on it," Tilly said. "My aunt and uncle opened their roadhouse in 1910 to serve travelers and when the railroad failed, they nearly went bankrupt too."

Doris abandoned her examination of bank records and continued to read alongside Tilly. As they probed deeper, she spied "Title to Real Estate in Montara" typed across the top of another file. Tilly let out a yelp and Doris felt her pulse speed for a moment, only to find more records referencing the bankruptcy and correspondence with the Ocean Shore Holding Company. There was no parcel map, deed or tax record.

"I wish I knew more," Doris said. "I wish there was a diary in all this." They searched page by page, without finding a description of property.

"If Stanley owned land," Doris said, "it's probably been sold. It would have been fun to look for it."

"Come and visit after the war," Tilly said. "There's evidence of his work everywhere. In some places you can still see where they ran the tracks."

"I would love to see that," Doris said.

"Around Montara Mountain—on a stretch they call Devil's Slide—they couldn't keep it from falling into the surf," Tilly said. "They just couldn't keep the trains running."

"That's probably when Uncle Stanley cashed out—after the railroad went out of business," Doris said.

"Yes," Tilly said, "a lot of people left then. There wasn't a paved road to the coast for a long time, and it was really hard to make a living. My dad and uncles resorted to bootlegging to keep food on the table."

Doris held up some sketches—elevations and a perspective, of what looked like a resort hotel called Bluegate. "Lovely," she said. "I wonder if this ever got built."

The wood-frame building was detailed in the Victorian style, with tall bay windows and a graceful porch wrapped around the west wing, and Tilly said it would have been a perfect spot for watching the sunset.

"Probably another one of my uncle's failed development schemes," Doris said.

They worked through reams of paper: copies of tax returns, certificates for various licenses, and a current passport. There were war bonds purchased at regular intervals.

As the afternoon wore on, Doris tried to prioritize what to pack. She discarded the railroad files saying, "I doubt that anyone cares anymore," and set aside what was current to mail to her mother. Tilly followed her lead, adding to the mailing box.

After several hours spent reading and sneezing in the dusty environment, Doris worked her way to the back of the final drawer. She found a slim folder with "life insurance" handwritten on the tab. This she would also send home. It contained a sealed manila envelope labeled "Last Will and Testament."

CHAPTER 9

TILLY'S EYES were watering, and she thought she felt something under her left lid—debris from the gritty assembly gallery. She blew her nose in a bandana, ran a rough canvas sleeve across her brow and retreated behind her mask. Her goggles fogged. Tears streamed down her face and mixed with sweat, another layer of discomfort. She was more annoyed than alarmed.

The line stopped for a water break. She struggled for precious minutes, prying her eyes open with filthy fingertips in an attempt to force moisture onto her corneas, to flush out the foreign particles.

"Everything okay?" Lydia said, looking up from her water jug.

"Got something in my eye, don't worry," Tilly said. "I'll get it out." She didn't want the attention. She dried the inside of the goggles.

She hustled back to her station, her head beginning to throb. No one ever said this work would be easy. She took a deep breath. Women fired arc welders on her left and right, their flash noticeable if she turned her head the right way.

With one hand on the rod and the other on the torch, she created a puddle, then joined sheets of steel one drop of molten metal at a time, aware that a faulty weld could sink a ship. Poorly made seams had been known to literally unzip. She lifted her face mask frequently to closely inspect the beads she created for uniformity, and to adjust those damn goggles. Any void would require the work be redone, and Tilly found it difficult to see imperfections through two layers of eye protection.

A particularly bright flash—a strong pulsing light—from her left side caused her to drop her mask. She had two more hours to go, and fought to stay focused.

Her eyes now felt as if hot sand had been poured into them. Her headache gained intensity, and her self-diagnosis was dehydration. She filled a quart jar with tepid water and drank it. She'd stop by the clinic to see about salt tablets.

The afternoon wore on and she began to see halos. Something was seriously wrong—she feared she might not last the day—but she shied from her supervisor. She told herself she was strong enough to get through. She didn't want Benson to reconsider her promotion.

She heard the air horn signal the end of shift and slumped forward, dropping the rod. She rested her head on the hull for a moment, while her co-workers stepped around her. It was finally over. After a moment, relief revived her like pure oxygen, and she told herself it would get easier going forward. She stripped off the gloves and used the handrail as she descended, not yet steady on her feet.

The afternoon sun was warm and at just the right angle to be blinding if she walked toward it. Tilly squinted; her tears burned. She crossed the street for shade and it happened: she blinked and lost her vision. It was as if her eyelids closed and a semi-opaque film spread over the lenses. She tried to blink the film away, but as she did, the light grew dimmer.

She cried out and stumbled. She felt a firm grip on her forearm.

"What's the problem, honey?" The voice was maternal. Tilly reached for the steady hand with both of hers.

"I can't see. Help me." Her voice cracked, and she started to cry. The woman looked at her eyes and their blind movement. What should have been white was pink crossed with lacy red lines.

"Let's get you to the clinic, honey. Keep your eyes closed now." She guided Tilly by working her left arm like a rudder. She was shorter and heavier, and she felt solid as Tilly leaned into her. Tilly waved her right arm as they walked, uselessly searching the air. She tripped on a raised piece of sidewalk. "You be careful now," her guide said. "A sprain takes longer to heal than arc eye."

Tilly instinctively turned toward the voice.

"I've seen you around welding," the voice said. "I'm a welder too."

Tilly learned that her rescuer's name was Elsie and that she was working the same shift—caddy corner from her station. Tilly didn't remember seeing a woman there. Was she so worried about herself that she didn't notice her co-workers? Elsie said something that Tilly didn't hear.

"I asked," Elsie said, "you wearing your goggles all the time? All the time you're working?"

"Well, I have to check my seams," Tilly said.

"Uh huh," Elsie said, "you have to check your work while you wear your goggles."

"But I'm welding with a torch," Tilly said. "I never looked at an arc."

"Which is a good thing," Elsie said. "It means you'll recover in a couple days. Now step up here so you don't trip on the curb."

They slowly crossed the yard, and when they reached the clinic, Elsie guided Tilly through the door and pointed her toward the reception desk.

"I'll wait outside and walk you home when you're done," she said. "You just ask someone to walk you back out." Tilly hesitated and started to ask why Elsie didn't want to wait inside.

"Honey, in case you haven't noticed," Elsie said, "whites and coloreds don't spend time together. Let's make this easy, I haven't got all day."

Tilly started. She'd never considered that Elsie could be anything but a white woman. In fact, she'd imagined that she looked a little like her Aunt Ida.

"Go on," Elsie said. "Go on in there and get your medicine. I have young ones at home waiting for me."

Tilly did as she was told. She tripped over the first step, caught herself and managed to get through the door just before a man pushed his way out. A receptionist came to her aid. As she sat in an armless chair waiting for treatment, she thought about Elsie standing outside. She remembered something she'd read, something the president had said. He said it was a Nazi technique to pit race against race.

She'd spent the last month avoiding coloreds; she wasn't sure why. She had no reason to. There weren't any coloreds in Montara or Moss Beach; she had no history with them. But here you stayed away from them. It was just what you did, the way the system was set up.

Tilly was wearing a black patch over each eye when a nurse led her out of the clinic. Elsie stepped forward and offered her arm.

"They told me I have arc eye," she said.

"Uh huh," Elsie said. "Honey, a blind man could see that."

Tilly was confused by her discomfort in the company of such a kind woman and spoke little on the way to Parking Lot C, though she had many questions. Foremost in her thoughts was: Why did you want to help me?

Elsie got her into the Airstream and wished her well. "I've got to get home to my little ones," she said.

"How I can ever thank you for your kindness?" Tilly said. She offered her hand. She told Elsie she'd be looking for her at work, and that she wanted to recognize her on the street.

"It was nothing, honey, just one person helping another," Elsie said. "You'd have done the same."

Tilly had thirty-two hours blind and confined to think about Elsie's parting words, but she couldn't imagine herself helping a stumbling black woman get treatment. Would she have stood outside the clinic waiting to walk her home? She was forced to admit that she wouldn't have.

"I don't know why," she told Doris, "but this whole thing has rattled me. I mean being helped by a colored."

Since she'd been at Kaiser, Tilly'd seen many black men and women hard at work. As far as she could tell, none of them tap danced or played upright pianos. She thought about Katherine Hepburn's red hair tumbling out from under that welder's mask. Her mother had been right. Katherine Hepburn was an actress. Real women had their hair shellacked with sweat. The work was dangerous and difficult, and everyone who did it, regardless of color or background, was helping win the war. They were all in it together.

"I feel like we see the world up close here," Doris said. "It looks different."

Tilly knew it was morning when she heard Doris get up. She removed the eye patches; she could see. Her eyes needed some time to adjust to the daylight, but her vision was fine—a glorious day. She bounced out of her bunk without banging her head on the ceiling, dressed and knocked on Sylvia's door for the walk to the mess. What she saw was heartbreaking.

Sylvia hugged her and cried into her shoulder. Tilly knew she had to say something.

"How bad is it?" She asked.

"He's dead." Sylvia managed to get out between sobs.

Tilly felt a weight at her core, and felt it drop. She'd been so stupid that she'd been injured and forced to spend a day and a half prone in the Airstream. Soldiers were dying.

"You need to go," Sylvia said. "We both do. We have to keep working."

Tilly nodded and helped her friend through the shipyard. She worked her shift with a new intensity, then went to the field hospital to donate blood. As she watched the ruby-colored liquid flow from her forearm to the bag, she thought about Sylvia. She ached for her friend—felt a heaviness she'd never experienced before. The nurse told her to unclench her fist.

Sylvia's worst fear had been realized in a telegram that her supervisor delivered at shift's end. Sylvia would later wonder if the Western Union carrier arrived at the break, or if it was customary for workers to receive news from home on their own time, so that work could continue uninterrupted. But it really didn't matter. Robbie was dead. He'd been killed in the South Pacific, and his remains would be in transit for days. She'd had nightmares about her nephew dying in combat; when it was confirmed, she initially felt an odd quiet relief. It carried her through the locker room in a kind of trance, but outside in the sunlight she broke down, sobbing, leaning against the corner of the building until she could summon the composure to head in the direction of her Airstream. Not surprisingly, no one stopped and asked what was wrong or if they could help. They knew there wasn't anything anyone could do, save work for victory and hope it would all end soon.

Sylvia eventually got through to her sister's place on the phone. Her brother-in-law said Alice had finally fallen asleep, and he didn't want to wake her. The doctor had prescribed medication for her nerves, and Sylvia wished she had something to take the edge off.

She slipped into a bar on Canal Street and ordered a double martini. When a soldier asked if she wanted some company, she burst into tears. He held her hand then, and put an arm around her. He ordered another round. She thought he must be ten years younger—not much older than Robbie. As the second double martini began to relax her, she cried less and talked more, told the young soldier that her nephew had been her motivation for working at Kaiser.

"We all need you gals supporting us," he said. "When you work for one of us, you work for all of us."

The evening wore on; they sat on adjacent bar stools, eventually needing to prop each other up. She knew a route to Parking Lot C that didn't require passing "the checkpoint," as she liked to call it, and brought her new friend back to her empty Airstream. She didn't want to be alone, and the young man reminded her so much of Robbie. She hoped that her nephew had had sex before he died.

She let him have her, not because she wanted him, but because she felt like she owed him something for his time. The soldier was gone in the morning, and try as she might, Sylvia couldn't remember his name.

Tilly had found her crying in bed, and had tried to console her. As Sylvia walked through the shipyard, arm-in-arm with Tilly, she was mortified by the thought that Tilly might have seen the soldier leave.

• • •

Joan Jura received the documents Doris had posted and contacted an attorney about a proper reading of the sealed will before she wrote her daughter:

"I shared your concern, but after checking, learned that the dramatic 'reading of the will' scenes we're so familiar with from novels and movies aren't the norm or legally necessary. There is no requirement for a public reading, so long as the will was recorded in the county it was authored in—in this case, San Mateo County. After I learned it was proper to do so, I opened Stanley's Last Will and Testament and found to my delight, that you are an heiress."

Doris read the letter again. Her uncle had left her a fifty percent share in something called the Bluegate Partnership. By the terms of his estate, she was now the managing partner.

"Managing Partner, imagine that," Tilly said. "What's the Bluegate Partnership?"

"I don't know," Doris said. "Remember those old sketches we found in my uncle's files? They were over twenty years old."

"You own half a hotel?" Tilly said. "Can I work for you after the war?"

"That would sure be nice," Doris said. "My mother says that nothing in the will explains the partnership agreement. We don't know what I've inherited or who owns the other half." She slid the letter back into the envelope. "There's probably nothing to it. Mysterious end to my mysterious uncle." She looked out the window, secretly hoping there was more. Eventually, they'd lose their jobs, and she'd be a sales clerk again.

"'Managing Partner' sounds impressive," Tilly said.

"The will was made out in Redwood City, and my mother thinks most of Stanley's business was conducted in San Mateo County," Doris said.

"That's my home county," Tilly said. "I wonder if my folks have ever heard of Bluegate."

Doris passed Tilly the letter.

"Redwood City is a long way from here," Tilly said, "more than twice the distance to San Francisco."

"It'll have to wait till the job ends," Doris said. "I don't suppose there's any rush." She took the letter from Tilly and slipped it into a book on her bunk. Their routine continued without variation for another five months.

December 25, 1942

They were together on Christmas. Though they had time off, it was only a day, and no one had the means to travel. It was raining hard, drumming on the Airstream. It had been a little more than a year since Pearl Harbor, and it appeared the war would go on for some time.

In November, the U.S.S. *San Francisco* had engaged in the battle of Guadalcanal in the South Pacific, and ninety-eight men lost their lives. The namesake vessel managed to limp home to a hero's welcome and the city put its best face forward, but no one was under any illusion that the war would end quickly.

Sylvia mixed gin and tonics for Tilly and Doris. They sat in her Airstream, because it was somewhat less cluttered, and Sylvia pulled out a deck of cards to fill the conversation void. No one said much, though they knew they had it easy. They were, if not home, on the home front.

Doris had talked to her mother earlier in the day and missed her terribly, but at the table, she felt a kinship with Tilly and Sylvia that she'd never experienced with other girlfriends. Perhaps it was their shared mission, or maybe it was because Tilly and Sylvia seemed different from other women: stronger, more practical. Whatever the reason, it was a gift to have met them.

Sylvia passed the deck and told Doris it was her turn to deal.

CHAPTER 10

March 3, 1945

DORIS SAID it looked like they were winning the war. She read aloud from the front page of the *San Francisco Chronicle* while Tilly made coffee. She read the papers religiously, following the allies' progress. Troops were crossing Belgium and Luxembourg to enter German territory. She stretched back in the settee.

The smell of brewing mud reminded Tilly of home, and lately she was thinking more about where she would go after the war. Her family expected her to return. "Production's slowing," she said during a lull in the late spring rains that had made casual conversation, in the aluminum Airstream, impossible. She looked out the window at an asphalt parking lot littered with trailers. Some had potted tomato plants in front: miniature victory gardens. They too, reminded her of home.

"It says here that the country is nearly bankrupt," Doris said. "The war will have to end soon."

Tilly poured the first cup and passed it to Doris. Then she passed the cream. "The first week, I didn't think I'd ever get used to this life," she said, "but here I'm useful in some important way."

"I can't go back to selling lipstick at Gimbels." Doris said. She turned back to her newspaper and Tilly made herself a peanut butter sandwich.

Tilly heard Sylvia whistling outside, and Doris reached across the upholstered bench seat, worn by years of continuous use, to unlatch the door. Sylvia always seemed to know when their coffee was ready. She had her favorite mug in hand.

"Can you believe it?" Sylvia said. "We all have a night off. We're never off at the same time."

Tilly couldn't understand why she was so excited. She didn't want anything to change. "Production's slowing," she said.

Doris looked up, "We know."

Tilly suspected that when the layoffs came, Doris would have the most difficult time adjusting, even though she was closest to total exhaustion. She'd made the most of the opportunity, but it didn't matter how good she was. They understood that returning soldiers would be hired to do their work.

Sylvia slid in beside her on the settee. Years as a painter had done little to reduce the spread of her hips, and the Airstream was suddenly crowded, but Tilly didn't move away. They sat elbow to elbow.

"We've never properly celebrated the *Mary Cassatt*," Sylvia said.

"Wasn't she sunk?" Doris said. She filled Sylvia's mug.

"She was lent to the Russians," Sylvia said. "But it doesn't matter. We built her, and she was launched in forty-four days."

Tilly and Doris looked at her. Tilly took another bite of her sandwich and said, "I don't know how you keep track of all our hulls."

Sylvia snorted and put her cup down abruptly, "What do you think I keep in that little metal box? Recipes?"

"You're serious?" Doris said. "You have a card for each hull?"

"Of course," Sylvia said. "I'm keeping track, and we're winning. We've out-produced them. It's time to celebrate."

Tilly climbed under the back berth to find her duffel bag, squeezed it through the door to knock some of the dust and cobwebs off, and retrieved the only good dress she owned. She'd worn it to her senior formal five years earlier. It had never been a great dress, but now it hung loosely on her frame. She thought she looked like a violet crayon and tried, without success, to shake wrinkles from the pencil skirt. They guessed she'd lost ten pounds. Doris suggested that they needed to start a full transition back to civilian life.

"Eating?" Tilly said, trying to tie the belt tighter.

"No, shopping," Doris said. "We've been too busy making money."

Sylvia selected The Blue Diamond for dinner and dancing, largely because she'd heard the owner had black market connections. "They've slipped the yoke of rationing," she said. "It has to be more fun." When Doris protested, Sylvia said they could put patriotism aside for one night.

They left Parking Lot C in a cab after many minutes of mutual admiration. Sylvia tried to lure the driver into joining them when she said she didn't get out nearly enough.

"Maybe I'll see you gals later," she said as Sylvia paid the fare.

Tilly started her evening-long struggle with a new pair of heels, the highest she'd ever owned, relieved to make it inside the club without incident. She stood at the hostess podium and stared, while Doris and Sylvia read the menu. She hadn't thought places like the Blue Diamond existed outside of the movies. The roadhouse served fine food in a friendly atmosphere, and Tilly'd been proud, if not satisfied, to be a part of it. The Blue Diamond was about escape, excess, and extravagance. There were no windows to the outside world and the lighting was low. If sound could be described as a color, what she heard would be smoky blue. Fabrics were heavy, velvety, lush, and they deadened the ambient noise so that intimate conversation was possible; couples sat close together. The carpet felt like down underfoot. The people looked different too, more fashionable, sophisticated. Tilly felt awkward.

"All this place needs is men," Doris said.

But Tilly couldn't take her eyes off Sylvia, who was wearing a new emerald green dress that clung to her ample curves. She'd touched up the roots of her bottle-red hair and wore perfume that was more spicy than sweet. Tilly decided that Sylvia might be the sexiest woman she'd ever met. Not sexy like a pinup, but sexy like a real woman.

She slid into the plush horseshoe shaped corner booth, with Doris on one side and Sylvia on the other. Doris immediately ordered a bottle of champagne to go with their appetizers.

Sylvia said they had to try escargot.

"You want me to eat snails?" Tilly said, and then looked around to see if anyone had heard her say it. She wanted to belong.

"I've had them before," Sylvia said.

Doris filled their champagne flutes and put the bottle back on ice. "I'm game," she said.

Tilly drank the first glass quickly, not experienced with the consequences. She'd had sips of champagne to go with wedding cake, but she had never drunk much. For her first course, she chose the safer sausage-stuffed mushrooms, while Doris opted for raw oysters. By the time the order came, Tilly was feeling warm and adventurous.

Sylvia offered a buttery snail, and Doris said she liked it.

"Okay, I'll try one," Tilly said.

Sylvia slid closer to her and their thighs touched, sending a thrill through Tilly like she'd never experienced. She backed away, then took Sylvia's offering from the small cocktail fork. It was warm and chewy with just enough garlic.

"I'll suggest my aunt and uncle start serving these at the roadhouse," she stammered, "gardeners' special."

Sylvia offered another, holding it inches from Tilly's lips, and Tilly leaned into her. They were bare legged, having drawn stocking seams on their calves with eyebrow pencil, and the feeling of Sylvia's skin brought a flush to Tilly's cheeks. She drank the second glass of champagne as if it were water, "I think I understand why champagne is so special," she said.

A tray of shucked oysters arrived, and they alternated cucumber mignonette with cocktail sauce. "An aphrodisiac," Sylvia said looking directly into Tilly's eyes.

Doris poured Tilly's third glass of champagne and asked for another bottle, indifferent to the cost. "We've earned this," she said as she sat back in the plush upholstery. "It's been three years of very hard work."

The vocalist was glamorous in a yellow gown and sparkling earrings. She had a remarkable range. A young officer came to their table and asked Doris if she wanted to dance. Tilly and Sylvia watched for only a moment before Sylvia was feeding Tilly oysters with a little silver pick. She held the shells to catch all the liquid, and after Tilly ate the meat, she drank the juice. Tilly didn't know what was happening in this strange communion, but she felt like electrical currents were running through the booth and her thighs.

Sylvia excused herself for the ladies lounge, and Tilly tried to concentrate on the band. The vocalist's voice was clear, from the heart or soul, she wasn't sure which. For the first time in years, she wondered where Mark might be. She'd last seen him at the roadhouse on his way out of town. It was the day after she'd refused his marriage proposal. How ridiculous, she thought, being married to Mark. She sighed, seated alone at the table, staring straight ahead. The truth was that she felt no attraction at all for him. She watched as Sylvia took the dance floor, cutting in on Doris and the Marine. Then she saw the two women dance to "String of Pearls"—rather well she thought, once they decided who would lead. Sylvia looked over her shoulder and winked.

CHAPTER 11

May 18, 1945

THIS LOOKS thicker than normal, Tilly thought as she took her paycheck from the friendly clerk, who knew her by name. There was some sort of correspondence enclosed. She stared.

It was ten days after VE Day; it had been a momentous month. The president had died in April, less than three weeks before Hitler committed suicide. Then came the surrender.

Tilly took a deep breath and started to peel back the flap. For a moment, her mind drifted to the day she received her first correspondence from Kaiser, from her grammar school teacher turned postmistress. She snapped back to the present when she heard a co-worker.

"Damn, it's over."

Tilly shoved the envelope into the pocket of her overalls without looking at the contents, and walked out into the overcast May morning.

She was no longer needed, at least not here. It was a good thing, she told herself, the boys were coming home. But she didn't feel happy. She walked down Cutting Boulevard, following the route she'd taken the night of her promotion to welder. The hulls she'd worked on would be finished and launched, but there'd be no new construction. She stopped at the first phone booth and dialed a familiar number.

"Niece Tilly, this is a most excellent surprise! Are you well?"

"Oh yes," Tilly said. "We've won at least half the war."

"It is a great victory, and you have done your part," Jose said.

"Yes, it seems I've completed my part. Kaiser is laying off workers." As she said it she realized she might cry, and she couldn't let her uncle hear that.

"I see. Well, this is quite a coincidence. Your Aunt Ida and I were speaking about this just yesterday. With the war ending, people will have more time for leisure, except for us, because we will have to serve them all. We were hoping you'd come back to work for us."

Tilly caught herself before her voice cracked. She didn't want to be a waitress for the rest of her life, but she didn't have any plans. She hadn't had time to think about what she'd do next. Whatever she felt about its confines, the coast was home. It was what she'd been working to protect. At that moment, she missed her uncle terribly. "I can't wait to see you and Aunt Ida. I miss you, Uncle Jose."

"And we have missed you," he said. "It will be a homecoming."

"I have some things to take care of before I leave," she paused, "Uncle Jose, I haven't talked to my parents yet. I'd appreciate it if you and Aunt Ida could keep this under your hats."

"I understand completely. Take your time. We'll be here when you come home."

Tilly knew he didn't understand. She didn't understand herself.

She thought she wanted coffee and a pastry, but the mood in the diner was subdued after the euphoria of the previous week. They had done their jobs well and it was time to go. She went back to the Airstream to tell Doris she'd be moving on; then she cried at the thought of telling Sylvia.

She didn't understand her crazy feelings for Sylvia, except that they were terribly wrong. Women didn't desire other women. The champagne had affected her.

She'd drunk too much the night they all went out, and Sylvia and Doris had helped her into bed. The next morning, when she realized that they had undressed her, she went crazy thinking about Sylvia's touch. She tried to remember what happened that night, but she'd blacked out when she got to the Airstream and her bunk. She was terrified at how much she wanted Sylvia.

It was a full week before she called her father, and although she thought about Sylvia constantly, she worked to avoid her. Sylvia named her "Loiterer in the Land of C." No one seemed to care that she stayed; no one was in line for her bunk. She wasn't ready to give up her independence, but she hadn't found any other options. When she finally called home, she told Paul she'd take the bus to San Francisco and save him the drive across the bay.

So now she was packing, and with her few mementos were a thousand memories of what she and the others had accomplished. In less than twenty-four hours, she'd be home with her parents. She'd be a waitress again.

A green salad sat undressed on the settee table. Doris uncorked a jug of red wine and passed around jelly jar glasses while Sylvia stirred her self-proclaimed famous spaghetti sauce on the small propane burner.

"Which bus are you taking tomorrow?" Sylvia asked.

"The six-twenty gets me into San Francisco early. It's the best schedule for my dad," Tilly said.

Sylvia poured her wine. "You might not want much of this then."

I want all of it, Tilly thought. I don't want to leave. "I've never had a sister," she said. "You two are my sisters now." She took a drink of the Chianti and sat back in the seat looking tired, despite a full week of unemployment.

Doris gave her a hug.

"I apologize," Tilly said. "I shouldn't be feeling sorry for myself. I have a home to return to, and I'll be back to work at my old job the day after tomorrow." She drank more. "Remember Elsie who took me to the clinic when I had arc eye? She got laid off too, but she doesn't have anything lined up. She's taking the bus back to New Orleans."

"The time went by so quickly; we never had a chance to make plans," Doris said. "When the ships on the line are launched we'll be sent home too."

"Now come on girls," Sylvia said. "This is our last night together in The Land of C. Let's have a little more optimism. We'll be at peace soon." She adjusted the seasonings and gave the sauce a final stir. Her red hair color was starting to fade. "All those love-starved men will be returning to wine and dine you marriage-age treasures. Life will be good," Sylvia said. She looked at Tilly.

Tilly winced.

Sylvia drained the spaghetti into a bowl and loaded three plates. Then she ladled the rich meat sauce on top.

Tilly took the first bite. She twirled her fork and wrapped the length of the spaghetti around the tines. "Thank you so much, Sylvia. I'll never forget this meal."

"It's perfect except for one thing." Doris pulled two white tapered candles out from under the table. Two small Coke bottles served as candleholders.

"If you set fire to my Airstream…" Sylvia pulled her fire extinguisher out of a little cabinet near the toilet, "I never got this thing recharged after your last mishap." She laughed and took a match from her cigarette case.

Doris raised a jelly jar. "To the future."

• • •

Paul had barely carried Tilly's duffel into the house before Helen set a bowl of vegetable soup and two ham sandwiches in front of her.

She'd been preoccupied on the drive home with feelings she couldn't share with her dad. She remembered the panic she'd felt when she first arrived at the shipyard and watched the old green Ford turn toward home. That had been a different girl.

"I'm fine Mom, really," Tilly said. "I've just been working hard for three years."

"You seem so worn down, and so thin," Helen said.

"Just give me a day to adjust," Tilly said. "I'll be back at the roadhouse tomorrow." To prove she had energy, Tilly grabbed her hiking boots and set off across fields of soybeans, to see if her favorite trail over Montara Mountain was open or still under the control of the War Department. When a guard turned her back, she walked to Gray Whale Cove, where she knew she'd be alone, and sat on the sand watching cold pillows of fog blow in from the Pacific. They were still fighting battles out there, beyond her horizon.

When she'd left for Kaiser, she hadn't considered how hard it would be to return home. There was the initial joy of seeing her family, but then, nothing.

She thought about Sylvia, who would be leaving Kaiser soon, and decided that it was best that she never see her again. She'd burned her address over the stub of one of Doris' candles. Whatever she'd felt wasn't normal, she knew that, and she knew it was probably related to her periods. She'd stopped cycling about a year into her time at Richmond; a company nurse said it was because her body weight was too low. She looked at her arm and flexed a muscle. She was thin. Her mother was right, she needed to eat more. She needed to get her hormones up and running, and everything would be okay.

Within three weeks of Tilly's departure, Sylvia was laid off. She spent her remaining nights in the clubs she'd been too busy to frequent when production was in full swing. A woman named Eve sat on the barstool next to Sylvia and said she was going to Reno because slinging drinks in a casino might be her best employment option. Then, while Sylvia was thinking she might go to Reno too, Eve slid her hand along Sylvia's thigh and quietly encouraged her to come along.

"I can see myself driving around with one of these trailers someday," Sylvia told Doris as she packed her things. "Maybe visit some of those National Parks."

They hugged and waited at the gate while the driver loaded three over-stuffed bags. As Sylvia began her journey over the Sierras to Nevada, Doris waved standing on tiptoe, and when the bus rolled into the distance she squinted in the sunlight until it disappeared, feeling very much alone. She was now the sole inhabitant of the Land of C.

Preoccupied by uncertainty, she wandered through the once bustling shipyard on autopilot. She was on her own, as she'd been for most of her life. She'd thought much about starting her own business, but she couldn't decide where. Though she missed her mother, Pittsburgh didn't feel right. She would need to find a way to make a reasonable living, and after three years without winter, she'd developed an affinity for California. She wondered what Los Angeles was like.

The Airstream was no longer the charming "shiny cottage" she had been given on day one. It was simply substandard housing, or no housing. They'd been camping for three years.

She began packing to leave; it wouldn't be long. In her estimation, the ships still in production would be completed in the next few weeks. As she fitted books into a cardboard box, a letter from her mother fell from inside a dust cover. She read it again. She was Managing Partner of Bluegate. She looked out the window at the perfect day and told herself her next move would be to Redwood City.

• • •

The "Help Wanted" sign in the window of the Broadway Bakery caught Doris' attention as she walked toward the County Recorder's Office. Settling her uncle's affairs might take some time, and she would need all of her savings for the business. She asked to see the manager. Cookies, muffins and cakes were the same all over America, she thought. She'd seen nearly identical displays in Richmond and Pittsburgh.

Doris didn't notice the manager, Nancy Adams, watching her and was startled when she spoke.

"Young lady," she said. "Where are you from?" She slid her glasses up her nose.

"I've just been laid off from Kaiser in Richmond." Doris extended her hand, hoping the manager would ask what she'd done for the war effort.

"Do you have any similar work experience? Do any work in retail?"

Doris swallowed hard, "Before the war, I sold cosmetics at a big department store in downtown Pittsburgh. I was good at it." She was concentrating on her smile, telling herself how important it was.

Nancy shook her head and laughed. "Cosmetics? This job will be easy."

Doris was taking a giant step backward, but did so with a grin plastered across her face. She was hired; she hid her disappointment at the hourly wage and was inked onto the schedule from four in the morning until noon. Nancy sized her up for a uniform and said she would personally train her.

"Thank you for the opportunity, Mrs. Adams," Doris said.

Bakers pushed racks loaded with cooling bread and pastry to the sales counter at five, when Doris ritually flipped the sign from "closed" to "open." She had to hustle to keep up, but was already immune to the once seductive smells. By midmorning, she'd feel sticky and sweaty. She brewed coffee to fill the last of the urns.

Longshoremen were the earliest of the regulars. They started work at dawn loading freight in the busy bayside harbor that had once been the port of sale for redwoods logged from the Coast Range and shipped north to San Francisco. Now the cargo was equipment produced on the peninsula for delivery to the Pacific theater. Redwood City was important enough to San Mateo County to be designated the seat of government.

"Good morning, George." Doris handed him a warm glazed before he said a word. She made her customers feel special.

"It's Frank's turn to buy," he said. It was their daily routine, testing her memory.

"Are you going to let him get away with that?" Doris asked.

They left, and she released the smile she always managed, wiped the glass on the pastry cases and shined the chrome below. Three weeks earlier, at five times the hourly rate, she'd been considered the best at wiring navigational systems on Liberty ships.

Doris noted the time—six twenty-five—then looked for the tall, lean man. He was outside the front window, right on schedule. He came at the same time every day, always alone, dressed for work-—in construction, she guessed. He never looked her in the eye; this heightened her curiosity. She wondered if he'd been in the war. When he approached, she pulled the devil's food cake from the case and started to cut a generous wedge. He glanced down just at the moment she was lifting it into a small pink box.

"Don't tell me you're switching to angel food," she said, holding the cake in the air.

"I'll have my usual," he said.

"My name's Doris," she said. She transferred the frosting covered knife to her left hand and extended her right.

"John," he said. "Pleased to meet you."

He took the package, and as he was leaving, held the door for a woman, all without uttering a sound. It struck Doris as she watched that something about him was familiar.

Having a shift that ended at noon was the best part of the job. It left afternoons free for research—which she'd divided into two categories: Bluegate inheritance and Bluegate Candles. If her uncle had left nothing of value, she would still adopt his business name, but answering the inheritance questions was her first priority. It was impossible to concentrate on the business plan with the mystery unsolved. At any rate, she promised herself she would leave the bakery by Thanksgiving.

Doris practically jogged back to the county building when her shift was over, relieved to be away from the heat of the ovens on a scorcher of a summer day. Her curiosity had kept her going for weeks, but as the avenues she traveled led to dead ends, she wondered how much energy she should continue to invest in her uncle's past. Repeated trips to the courthouse and recorder's office on different afternoons had been unproductive. It was entirely possible that he'd had nothing left to bequeath.

"My inheritance is half ownership in something called the Bluegate Partnership," she explained to the matronly assessor's assistant. "I think it once owned land on the San Mateo Coast, and I want to find the other partner or owners."

Anna Nelson gave Doris her full attention and was still asking questions fifteen minutes later, trying to ferret every bit of information. Did she have an address? Did she know when the property was sold? Doris felt foolish.

"I couldn't find business license records or a partnership agreement," Doris said. "I couldn't trace my uncle in the San Mateo County archives, though he'd recorded his will within the past two years." She told Anna she was increasingly frustrated and berated herself daily, because she believed she'd once had everything she needed. She'd thought often of the afternoon spent in her uncle's apartment and her decision to send old files to the dump.

"So I'm your bureaucrat of last resort?" Anna smiled at her. "Give me a little time," she said.

Two and a half days later, Anna Nelson delivered. Doris resisted the urge to hug her, thanked her profusely and ran from the government building to a payphone, almost too excited to dial the number. She hung up and started over. Her mother's voice came on the line and she gushed. "My inheritance is half ownership of a five-acre cove near Tilly's hometown." It was a windy afternoon, and the phone booth rattled. She shouted to be heard, leaning against the door to try to muffle the noise.

"Did you find the name of the co-owner?" Joan said.

"No, the whole thing's pretty convoluted," Doris said. "A woman who's been helping me says she hasn't seen anything like it in twenty-five years."

"But you found the recorded deed?"

"Mrs. Nelson did. It says—now let me read this, I wrote it all down: It's a deed in favor of the Bluegate Partnership with management rights passing to Stanley Jura's heir. It acknowledges that there's a silent partner." Doris noticed a man outside the booth, waiting.

"Maybe the silent partner is a married woman Stanley had a liaison with," her mother said. "Or, maybe the owner of the land owed him money."

"Mom, do you know anything about Uncle Stanley's scheme to build a hotel? Because it's starting to make some sense. I saw a sketch of a hotel in his files in San Francisco. It was called Bluegate. And now I've discovered that the Bluegate Partnership owns a five-acre cove on the coast, twenty miles south of San Francisco. I think Uncle Stanley planned to build a waterfront place."

"He spent a lot of time over there working on the railroad," Joan said, "but he was more interested in real estate than anything. Have you seen the property?"

"No. It's taken until today to find out that he had any assets at all," Doris said. "As far as I can tell, this is it: the sum of Uncle Stanley's holdings. This and those bonds and savings you have."

"If he chose the cove for a resort and managed to hang onto it through the lean years, it must be one remarkable spot," Joan said. "Honey, I know you're saving your money, but get an attorney over there that knows the county. Find out what to do about this unnamed partner."

When her three minutes were up, Doris promised to write as soon as she got to Montara and saw the land. She dropped more coins in the phone and asked the operator to connect her to the Marine View Roadhouse.

The man waiting outside the booth paced back and forth along the curb, his hair spiking in the unusual summer wind. He tried to make eye contact with Doris as the call was answered.

"Tilly is not here now, but I expect her shortly. May I take your number for her to call you back?" The voice was smooth and lightly accented. Tilly'd spoke fondly of her Uncle Jose on many occasions.

"It's probably best that I call back. I'm Doris."

"Ah, the famous Doris," Jose said. "I have heard so much about you. I hope you will be able to visit someday."

"I'm hoping Tilly can help me find a ride," she said.

Doris wondered how far from the roadhouse her inherited land was. She hoped it was close by. She left the booth to the anxious man and stood watching while he placed his call. Then she turned away.

With half an hour to burn, she leafed through magazines at the closest newsstand, checking her watch every two minutes. She bought a coke and drank it quickly, then picked up a copy of National Geographic. She stared at the cover, a picture of a black sand beach. "Stanley on the beach," she said aloud. She thought of the old photo she'd looked at a thousand times. The trees that framed the view weren't palms, they were pines or cypress or something. "He was in California!" She tried to remember every detail—did he own the beach in the photo? And then another thought, more intriguing: who was behind the camera?

• • •

"So, Niece Tilly," Jose said, "the famous Doris is coming for a visit?" Tilly had just replaced the receiver on the kitchen wall phone.

"How did you know?" she said. She carved a giant turkey leg and scooped a double serving of dressing on an oversized dinner plate that she doused with rich gravy. She happily thought the meal might add twelve hundred calories to her daily total. She'd have one or two slices of pie for dessert.

"You forget that I am your answering service," he said. He wagged a finger at her, and she smiled. "I did not want to spoil the surprise by telling you. You must tell us what her favorite food is so that we can have a Famous Doris Special in her honor."

Tilly laughed to think of how her friend would react to a "Famous Doris Special," but her aunt and uncle loved to honor their favorite customers. "Specials for Special People" Jose always said. They went into the bar and Tilly pulled up a chair facing him.

"Uncle Jose, Doris' last name is Jura, and her Uncle Stanley once worked for the railroad. I think he was a construction engineer or manager. Did you ever cross paths in the early days?"

Jose leaned against the bar and blew a smoke ring. "Jura, Stanley Jura. I have not thought about him for decades but yes, he was a regular customer." He stubbed out the cigarette in a glass ashtray and emptied it below the bar.

The next day, Doris couldn't keep her eyes off the clock. Her investigation had finally yielded some useful information, and she was anxious to get back to the courthouse. She raced through her routine in half the usual time, as if she could will the morning to pass quickly. She grazed the cookie assortment, something she'd never done before, barely tasting what she popped into her mouth.

At six twenty-five, Punctual John, Consumer of Devil's Food Cake, entered and grunted hello, which she considered an enormous improvement in their daily communication. She got a good look at his eyes for the first time and understood why he'd seemed so familiar.

The morning wore on. She calculated the minutes until her shift ended, then the seconds. Her relief finally arrived and tied on an apron.

"I'm so happy to see you," Doris said breathlessly as she charged the exit.

By ten past noon, armed with the property information she'd received the day before and a new list of questions about silent partnerships, Doris returned to the recorder's office asking if it might be possible to research an old development proposal. A middle-aged man who couldn't keep from rubbing his temples took his time before responding.

"Miss Jura, I hate to burst your bubble because you seem to be a pretty good sleuth, but there's a big difference between finding a link to a plot of land and finding a link to a twenty-five year old idea."

"I understand," Doris said. She remained calm, a portrait of patience. "But I need to know who owns the other half of my inheritance."

The clerk, who had seen a lot of her, flipped pages in an old index, alternately adjusting his glasses while he looked for something useful. Finally he said, "Do you really want to know, or is your goal to use the property? Because it seems to me"—he paused for effect—"that you might be better off if the silent partner was never found."

Doris took a half step back from the counter and looked at him. "Can I get clear title?" she said. "I mean legally?" She hadn't considered the possibility that she might become the sole owner.

"Probably not." The clerk turned the document so she could read it, and pointed to the critical clause. "Your uncle is listed as managing partner on the deed and has bequeathed his position to you. It's expected that you will manage the asset, pay the taxes and do whatever needs to be done. If you have a plan to increase the value of the property, I'd say it's your responsibility to implement it."

Doris liked what she was hearing, but she feared the clerk was simply trying to get rid of her. "But what about the silent partner?"

"You will take steps to locate him."

"How will I know when I've done enough?"

"Well there's only so much you can do." He pulled out a pad of paper and started a list. "Go over to the coast and talk to folks that have been there for a while and see if you get any leads. Post notices and run ads in the local papers. If no one offers any information on the whereabouts, I think it's safe to start making plans." He handed her the notes.

She stood stoically on her side of the counter. "What if an imposter comes forward?" she said.

He scratched his head, "You must be specific. Accept nothing less than a recorded partnership agreement that bears your uncle's signature. There has to be one. If there's a partnership, there's a partnership agreement somewhere."

Doris shook her head. "It's hard for me to believe that someone would just walk away from five acres of waterfront property."

"You have to remember Miss Jura, that land on the coast wasn't worth much back then. You couldn't get to it. The railroad failed and the Depression came; it was probably more of a liability than an asset. Do what you can to locate the partner, but consider the possibility that he may be dead or Bluegate long forgotten."

Doris had a restless night processing what she'd learned and was going through her morning routine in a fog when she heard the bells on the door; she hadn't turned the closed sign over. It was only four forty-five.

"They're open," a woman in a sapphire evening gown called to her date. Her red hair fell across the shoulders of a tuxedo jacket she'd wrapped around herself. The woman didn't acknowledge Doris, but after her date said good morning, she laughed and said, "Morning, yes I guess it is morning."

Doris felt like an extra on a movie set, in a scene with great stars; she had no power to tell them the bakery was closed. She pushed the cooling rack she was unloading aside and washed her sticky hands.

"The Danish are still warm," she said.

"A warm Dane," the woman said, and laughed again. "Imagine a warm Dane."

Doris tried to imagine what was so funny.

"I want to eat cake," the man said. He pointed at a four-layer chocolate with chocolate ganache.

"One slice or two?" Doris asked.

"The whole cake."

It took every ten and twenty she had in the register to change the bill he gave her, and she wondered how she'd make it through the morning.

She hurried to finish her opening routine, suddenly feeling her life was small and insignificant, no matter how hard she worked or how great her ambition.

Saturday was her day off. Doris left the rooming house early and was at the bus stop before seven. The number seventy-three went by, and she coughed exhaust. She wanted the fifty-six. The fifty-six bus would take her nine miles north to San Mateo to meet a ride Tilly had arranged, west to the coast, to her uncle's cove. She hadn't yet seen the Pacific.

She'd prepared, gathering all the available property information, doubting there'd be surveyor's markers or fencing to help her define the boundaries in a larger landscape. She considered how she might locate exactly what she'd inherited, and traced a parcel plan and other maps she thought might be useful. The acreage was beachfront and not far from the lighthouse. Tilly suggested they meet at the Marine View at nine to begin their search.

The day was cool, and as she waited at the rendezvous point, Doris tried to will her ride to appear. She'd been told to meet a man named Hank who'd be passing through after unloading vegetables for the Saturday morning market, but no one came.

A bus back to Redwood City passed, and then another. She checked the time again, and by eight-thirty, she gave up. She started walking. Worst case she thought, she could cover the distance "over the hill" by early afternoon.

The sun broke through the clouds and felt warm on her back; she faced a breeze that blew her hair over her shoulders. She smiled, happy to be out and hiking west. A car slowed momentarily but continued on. She shrugged and kept going, mindful of sharp curves and a nearly nonexistent shoulder. She listened carefully for oncoming vehicles and stepped off the pavement into the leaf litter as they approached.

Shortly after nine, an International pickup with toolboxes passed on her left, and she saw the driver check his rear view mirror. When the brake lights came on, she jogged forward, bag slung over her shoulder, delighted at the prospect of a ride. She thought she recognized the man in the cab through the back window. He didn't get the door for her; she tugged on the handle and climbed in. The truck was tidy. He was neat or had cleaned it recently.

"Good morning," he said.

Doris did a double take.

"You're not walking to Half Moon Bay are you?"

"As a matter of fact," she said, "I am—well, I'm going past Half Moon Bay. To Moss Beach."

"Moss Beach?" His eyebrows were raised.

She explained that she'd planned to meet a friend, "actually a friend of a friend, but after an hour, I gave up."

Punctual John, Consumer of Chocolate Cake shook his head. "It's about fourteen miles, seven of them uphill, just to get to the Coast Road." He told her he was visiting folks he'd known for a long time in Half Moon Bay, but wasn't on any particular schedule. He offered to make the detour to the Marine View—said everyone knew where the Marine View was. Doris was grateful.

They rounded the first hairpin turn as they climbed, and Doris held her hand over her stomach to try to muffle the sound. She'd been too excited to eat breakfast. Outside, the canopy was changing, with sunlight filtering through second-growth redwoods sprouted from stumps.

He took the curves in gentle succession, after warning her about motion sickness. "The road can be brutal," he said. "This section takes about an hour to drive."

Doris looked at her watch.

They went across an earthen dam between two lakes, and to break the awkward silence, she asked about them. John explained that they were part of the water supply for San Francisco.

"There are good springs in this area, and one's been tapped just over the summit—good thing to know about when you're walking." He glanced sideways at her, "Fourteen miles can work up quite a thirst."

She slid slightly in her seat. A few more minutes passed before she felt compelled to speak over the noise of the engine. She watched the dense vegetation and felt the road become so narrow, she could reach out through the window and touch a tree trunk.

"Can I ask you a question?" she said.

"Go ahead, ask," he said.

"How long have you been eating chocolate cake for breakfast? It's not what you'd call a healthy habit."

"Healthy?" He steered around a tight bend. "I'm a hell of a lot healthier than the guys that didn't make it back from Normandy. I broke an arm. It was embarrassing."

"Utah Beach?" Doris asked. She wasn't sure why she asked.

John looked at her, "Good guess." He looked back toward the road after hitting a soft spot near the edge of the pavement. "Yeah, Utah."

Doris nodded. She wanted to say how lucky he was, but she thought he might not see it that way. "I worked for Kaiser," she said. "My supervisor lost a son at Omaha."

"I wish I could meet someone not touched by Omaha," he said.

The truck ceased its labor and Doris knew they were on the downhill stretch. She felt herself relax and breathe a bit easier. Just outside of Half Moon Bay, at the bottom of the hill, the horizon opened again and they passed an old cemetery. She wanted to make a joke about the trip not being that bad, but thought better of it. They were now approaching the Coast Road and the final leg of their journey.

Expansive fields of peas, beans, artichokes, cabbages, Brussels sprouts and other cool-weather crops Doris couldn't identify were thriving on the fertile soils of the marine terrace, and beyond she could see white water—real white water. The closest Doris had been to a beach was on Lake Erie. She craned her neck to see out the west side, the driver's side of the truck.

"Just a few more miles," John said.

It appeared to Doris that the coastline actually got more spectacular as they traveled north.

The sign announcing the Marine View Roadhouse was on the paved road, though the Roadhouse itself was down a curving drive. There was a drop-off just beyond the cobblestone apron behind the restaurant, and from the approach it looked as if the building was perched on the edge of the world. The bar and dining room were sited for unobstructed views; crashing waves were audible from everywhere on the property. The exterior clapboard siding was well maintained, despite a weathered appearance. Coastal landscaping around the entrance was immaculately kept. Doris sat in the cab with the door open for several minutes, taking it all in from her slightly elevated perch.

"You're late, we were worried," Tilly said. The front door slammed in her wake. Before Doris could explain what had happened, Tilly got her in a bear hug and lifted her, as John and Jose shook hands.

"And now," Jose said, "I hope my favorite niece Tilly will introduce me to the famous Doris."

Doris smiled as Jose bowed slightly.

"You're really here." Tilly said.

Doris put her arm around Tilly's waist and was about to ask if she'd heard from Sylvia, when she looked up and saw John staring at Tilly. Their eyes locked. They had the same dark blue, nearly violet eyes.

"I'm Tilly, thank you for driving Doris here," she said.

John nodded without shifting his gaze, and then turned to leave.

Tilly held the door to the dining room.

Doris began to describe her trip and stopped mid-sentence. She gazed at the view that had captured the imagination of so many. The railroad, the land speculation, the development schemes, she understood it all. The view was explanation enough.

The room was all dark wood paneling and plank floor, the windows a giant frame for a perfect composition of wind blown cypress and rocky surf. A small beach at the base of the bluffs would be nearly nonexistent at high tide, and the cliff was deeply carved by storms. The bar ran perpendicular to the shore and the view was partially captured by the mirrored back bar. Old brass oil lamps were mounted along the walls.

"We only use them during power failures now," Tilly said, "Aunt Ida doesn't like cleaning them or the smell of burning oil."

There were candles on each of the linen-covered tables.

Doris' first impression of Ida was of a very happy woman. She was wiping her hands on her apron as Tilly led the way to the kitchen, where fresh baked pies sat on the counter. Ida was shorter than Tilly, with dark eyes. She wore her long, black hair pulled back and pinned up, since she spent much of her day cooking, but Doris thought she was beautiful. She wondered if she would ever feel as content as Ida looked.

"These pies are beautiful, Mrs. Torres, but you shouldn't have gone to the trouble," she said.

"No, you must call me Ida," she said. "And thank you for the compliment. I enjoy this. It's my work. There is also a strawberry-rhubarb in the oven, which is Tilly's favorite." She motioned toward the dining room and arranged the service while Jose pointed out old railroad photos hung on the walls.

"I have a surprise for you." Tilly was cutting a wedge of warm apple pie, having already devoured a slice of banana cream. She looked to Jose. Doris put down her fork and smiled.

"Well," he dabbed his mouth with his napkin, "your last name was familiar to me, and when I heard that your uncle worked for the railroad, I remembered."

"You knew him?" Doris asked.

"He was a regular customer when he was in town working, but I cannot say that I knew much about him," Jose said. "The railroad put him up at the Montara Hotel, but he took many of his meals here because he loved Ida's cooking." Jose took a sip of his coffee. "Stanley was the engineer brought in at the end, when it appeared their many problems wouldn't be solved. In fact, they weren't, which was most unfortunate for all of us, but Stanley's position made him an outsider with the Ocean Shore boys."

Doris glanced toward one of the old railroad photos on the wall. "Did you know about any land he owned?" she said.

"No," Jose said. "I don't remember anything about him buying land."

She unfolded one of the maps she'd traced and smoothed it on the table.

Jose shook his head. "I didn't know he owned the cove between Fourteenth and Sixteenth Streets. I suppose most of the folks around here thought that property belonged to the state. You see, the State of California acquired a fair amount of the old railroad right-of-way for a future highway during the foreclosure sale."

"Do you remember any friends, colleagues?" Doris asked.

"Tilly tells me he had a silent partner," Jose said, "but I knew nothing about that. Had I known your uncle was so mysterious, I would have pried." He winked. "All I know is that he was refined and reserved, and he always seemed to have enough money. I'm sorry that I do not know more."

Doris leaned back in her chair. "My inheritance makes me the managing partner of Bluegate," she said, "but I have no idea what I'm managing or who my silent partner is."

Jose paused and took another bite of pie. "You have found that you are a landowner," he said, using an index finger for emphasis, "the other information will come in time. If you are the managing partner, you must manage the assets. Do what you can to locate the other person or persons, but if you don't find him, or I suppose her," he smiled, "then you must move forward to the best of your ability. That is what your uncle would want you to do."

Doris stared. She'd now been advised, twice, that not finding the silent partner might be a better outcome than finding him—or her. She ran her fingers through her hair. She needed a plan for the candle factory. Everything else was a distraction. If the silent partner didn't come forward, she'd start what she believed would be a profitable business. She now had a location for it, on land she already owned, in a place that would be attractive to tourists.

Tilly led Doris to the cove after they'd eaten as much pie as they could. It was just north of the roadhouse and immediately south of Point Montara. It was small with a sandy beach and protected by a row of cypress trees that framed the view. Just beyond the tide line, rocks caused the surf to break and spray. Tilly explained that, during prohibition, her Uncle Aldo would navigate the *Matilda B.* around the reef to pick up shipments of whiskey destined for San Francisco speakeasies.

Off shore and on the horizon, the Farallon Islands were a sharp silhouette against clear skies. Doris consulted the first of two maps she'd traced in the County Assessor's office and oriented herself to the water. It fit. It did fit. It had to be the place. She found a spot on the sand central to her holding and sat on her heels. She thought about the old photo of her uncle on the beach and tried to remember the details that had surely been changed by time and weather.

"I think my uncle was photographed at this very spot," she said.

Tilly knelt next to her. "I can't believe this is yours," she said.

"It might be the most beautiful place I've been," Doris said. "No wonder my uncle held it for so many years. When he had little else, he had this." It was the sort of place travelers might like to stop and take in the view, and maybe buy candles. Doris was imagining a busy workshop and a thriving business.

"Tilly, Doris, come quick!" Ida sprinted toward the cove.

"I don't believe I've ever seen my aunt run," Tilly said. She was on her feet. "Oh God, I hope nothing's happened to Uncle Jose." The women rushed to the trail and met Ida at the top. Whatever it was, Ida was beaming.

"The war is over!" she said. "Japan has just surrendered."

The three women embraced on the side of the road. A driver heading south honked and waved. The country was again at peace.

CHAPTER 12

September 10, 1945

JUDGE ROBERT CALLEN scanned the legal notices daily in the morning edition of the San Mateo Times, a habit he'd had for thirty years. Occasionally something would catch his eye: a foreclosure, a divorce. This morning it was a small announcement that started with the sentence, "Heir and managing partner of Bluegate seeks silent partner to a 1925 land transaction in San Mateo County…" He put the paper down on his desk and used a tissue to clean his glasses, then swiveled his leather chair around to look out the bay window. "So Stanley's dead," he said quietly to the tuxedo cat curled up on a cushion on the window seat. The cat lay purring in the morning sunshine.

CHAPTER 13

Reno, NV
September 5, 1945

Dear Tilly,

Hallelujah, we have won the war! I hope you're doing well. I haven't heard from any Land of C alumnae, and I'm assuming no news is good news. I sure do miss the little community we had out there.

I couldn't face life back in Kansas City, working at the Hotel Savoy, so I've relocated to Reno, NV. The dry weather suits me and Reno sure is a lively town. Perhaps I can lure you and Doris out for a visit. Every day's a celebration.

I miss painting. Seems no one wants to hire an ex-Kaiser painter for much besides slinging drinks and serving food. Maybe I can work in a casino on the classy end of the spectrum.

I found an apartment above the five and dime on Second. It's small, but after the Airstream I feel like I can get lost in it.

There's already so much construction going on—amazing given the shortages. The big developers are looking at the land outside of the little downtown and everyone's pairing up and talking about how great it would be to have a couple of acres. I'd love to start a little company to paint all the new houses that are sure to be built.

Remember our big night out at the Blue Diamond? I'm going out on a limb here, but I think I should tell you that I know what it's like to fall in love with a woman and that there are plenty of women in the world that have had that experience. No one talks about it, but honey, it's okay to let your hair down.

I'm not sure how long I'll stay in Reno. I'll send a forwarding address when I go and hope you will also stay in touch.

I sure do miss our morning coffees.

All the best Till,

Sylvia

• • •

The "Seeking Silent Partner…" notice was posted on a cypress tree; Doris had consulted a lawyer in Redwood City and carefully followed his instructions. She was doing everything possible to find the other heir. Tilly watched a flock of brown pelicans skim over the waves. She asked herself how she could have taken Bluegate Cove for granted. Now she stopped daily on her walk to the roadhouse.

"Favorite Niece Tilly," Jose said. He opened the door for her.

"I've just been by Doris' magical cove." She hung up her jacket.

"Her uncle knew real estate. It is most unfortunate that he never realized his dream. I believe he was a man of vision, and as is the case with men of vision, a bit ahead of his time."

Tilly was preoccupied with worries she couldn't share and was only half listening to Jose. The unopened letter from Sylvia was in her jacket pocket.

"Now would be a good time to open a shop on the coast," Jose said. He looked for a reaction.

Tilly remembered that Jose was talking to her and looked up.

"I believe that Doris is wise to be thinking about investing in her own place, don't you?" he said. He reached behind the bar, barely turning away from Tilly, and poured them each a cup of coffee.

Tilly nodded. "She needs a partner. Or she needs to borrow more money. She wants me to buy in."

"And you are thinking this might be a good thing?" Jose asked.

"I don't know," Tilly said. "I don't know anything about business. My mother thinks I'll waste my savings." Tilly looked down at her hands. "She thinks I should save what I earned because I'll want to buy a house after I'm married."

Jose poured some cream in his coffee and leaned against the back bar while he enjoyed the first sips. "Paul sat on the same stool you are now on, drinking coffee and waiting for Aldo in the hours before you were born." He laughed. "We were starting a new business then too."

Tilly nodded and looked away.

"I will not argue the wisdom in saving money for a home," Jose said. "But you must ask yourself if you are invested wisely. Perhaps investing in a new company is a good thing, no?" He tapped on the bar for emphasis, "A company that makes things tourists may want to buy."

"What would you do, Uncle Jose?" She knew the answer, but wanted to hear him say it. She took a sip of her coffee.

"These will be good years," he said. "From what I've seen of Doris, she's a smart one, that girl."

"You wouldn't believe how smart she is," Tilly said. "She excelled at every aptitude test they could come up with at Kaiser."

"And you work well together?" Jose said.

"We lived in a trailer together for three years so, yes, we get along swell."

"What is your hesitancy, then?"

"I'm afraid we won't make it," Tilly said. "My mother's concerned that candles are too frivolous to invest in, and well, women don't go into business."

Jose waved an arm toward the dining room full of candle-topped tables and said, "Women don't go into business? My dear niece, don't let your Aunt Ida hear that." He shook his head and rolled up a sleeve. "There are things worse than failure, Tilly. There are always risks, but there are also rewards."

"I'm so confused," she said. "I should be thinking about marriage and a family, but I'm not. I think that's why my mother's so concerned. She thinks I'll become a lonely, old woman."

Jose laughed. "You are young, strong and beautiful. I'm guessing that your heart tells you to take this chance. Am I right?"

She nodded.

He winked. "It's a fool that doesn't take advantage of every opportunity." He drained his coffee, and she took both cups to the bus tub, then tied her black apron around her black skirt. She took the unopened letter from Sylvia from her jacket pocket, tore it into pieces and buried it in the trash.

• • •

"Good morning, Tilly," Helen said. She was setting up the coffee pot and looked over her shoulder as Tilly came down the stairs. She paused as if trying to decide whether or not she needed to brew more—Tilly was up earlier than usual. "Coffee?"

"Maybe later," Tilly said.

Helen put the percolator on the stove. She had filled a small saucepan with cold water and was taking eggs from the refrigerator. "Can I boil you one?"

"Sure. I'll have two." Tilly rubbed her temples. She'd slept fitfully. "Mom, I've decided I want to buy into the candle business."

Helen turned away from the stove with an egg in hand. Tilly thought for a moment that she'd drop it.

"Doris needs my decision and I can't make myself say no," Tilly said. "All of your warnings and arguments make perfect sense, but deep down, what I really want is to be challenged, and I may never get a better opportunity." She exhaled. She'd said it. As she watched subtle expressions cross her mother's face, Tilly understood that Helen was seeing a different future than the one she'd imagined for her child.

"I've made my decision," Tilly said. "Please wish me luck." Helen nodded and gently put the egg in the water.

• • •

As a boy, John Callen would sometimes visit his grandfather, he called him "Judge," at his courthouse office, and they'd walk to the bakery for cookies. He liked to blame the judge for his sweet tooth.

"Fortunately," his grandfather said, "you've adopted one of my lesser vices."

• • •

Doris glanced up at the clock. "You're late."

"I hope you haven't sold out," John said.

She pulled the devil's food from the case and grabbed a knife.

"I'm taking a couple of days off," he said. "I finished the Fredrick house."

"You're a builder?" She paused with the knife in the air, more interested than he'd thought she'd be.

"A carpenter mostly, but I like working alone so I do a little of everything."

Doris carefully marked the slices on the top of the fresh chocolate cake, then looked up at John before cutting. "Would you give me an estimate for construction of a building on the coast?" She pushed down on the knife and lifted the wedge of cake into the small pink box.

"Building a house over there? Tired of the walk?" He winked. She was cute and spunky, he thought.

She turned her back to him and filled a paper cup with black coffee. "Not a house, more of a barn. A big utility building, with a small storefront."

He raised his eyebrows, "May I ask what for?"

"Making and selling candles," She said. She punched numbers into the register. "That'll be twenty-five cents."

He reached into his pocket for two dimes and a nickel, and watched Doris serve a mother and young son. They bought cookies too. An important part of childhood. He sipped his coffee and enjoyed listening to them.

When they were alone again Doris said, "The navigational equipment I was installing at Kaiser came packed in wax that was easy to work with. I thought that wax would be cheap and plentiful after the war."

"And you've got a supplier?" he said.

"Yeah, I can get it at a good price." She told him about Bluegate Cove, and how she thought tourists would stop and shop, and then looked at his cup. "Can I top that off for you?" She re-filled his coffee. "My friend, Tilly, the woman you met, and I both saved most of our earnings, and Tilly's decided that she'd like to come on as my partner."

John recalled the beautiful, tall, blue-eyed brunette and suddenly took a heightened interest in the proposition. It would be nice to spend some time on the coast. "Do you know how large a building you'll need?" he said.

"We need one we can afford," she said. "I don't know what it costs to build things so it's hard for me to make decisions."

"I'm interested," he said. "Sketch your ideas for me." Then, with no particular plans for the afternoon, John drove west and headed to the Marine View for a nice lunch.

He was disappointed that Tilly didn't recognize him. Jose had given him a seat with a view, and Tilly delivered the menu and pitcher of water to his table. She turned when he said her name and paused for a moment.

"You're Doris' friend from the bakery," she said.

"I'm a steady customer, yes."

"She told me," Tilly said. She went back to his table and filled his glass. "It was good you saw her walking. My friend Hank was supposed to give her a ride but never got out of bed. He had a little too much to drink the night before."

John took the menu as she recited the lunch special.

"Garlic chicken with braised artichoke hearts. It comes with French onion soup and salad."

He gave back the menu without looking. "Pretty fancy lunch special for a Tuesday," he said.

"My aunt and uncle wouldn't have it any other way."

He ordered it with French dressing and a cup of coffee, then closely watched every step she took on her way to the kitchen. With a pen and note pad, he listed materials he'd need to price in Half Moon Bay: concrete, wood in various dimensions, plumbing, heating and electrical equipment, industrial style windows. They'd need a loading dock and a rollup-door.

Tilly interrupted him with the coffee and a basket of warm bread with butter.

"So you gals are going to start a candle-making business?" he said.

"I'm buying in as a partner," Tilly said. "Doris is the mastermind."

"She asked me for a construction estimate," John said.

"We need to find someone who will give us a fair price," Tilly said.

"I'll do what I can," John said, "but I'm a businessman too." He squared his shoulders.

"Yes, of course," Tilly said.

John partially deflated.

She entered the kitchen just as Ida took the soup from under the broiler. When she returned with the ceramic bowl covered with bubbling cheese, John put down his pen and concentrated on the meal.

• • •

It was disorienting to see her father in the passenger seat. Tilly was used to him sitting to her left. She sat up straight at the wheel, left hand firmly at the ten o'clock position, right on the gear shift connected beneath the floor boards. Her eyes were fixed ahead of the stationary vehicle, as if she were already driving in traffic.

"You have a hand for the wheel and a hand for the shifter, but only two feet for three pedals and a starter button," Paul said. "That's the hard part."

Tilly nodded. "But I do have big feet. That should help."

"The shifting pattern," Paul continued, "is like an H."

"Okay." She moved the lever, pausing in the neutral space between the forward gears. She rubbed her hands on her thighs to dry her sweaty palms. He'd ask her to start the engine any time now.

"Make sure you're in neutral when you start, then pull this knob. It chokes off air to the carburetor and lets more fuel in. Push down on the gas pedal once, maybe twice, but no more. Then turn the key on the dash to the right. Don't forget the start button on the floor by the gas pedal. Once the engine turns over, give it a few minutes to start running smoothly, then push the choke knob in and let the air come back. You'll know when she's running smoothly."

Tilly repeated the starting sequence and ran through the shifting pattern two more times before pulling the choke lever and pumping the gas. She turned the key. The old truck made a straining sound that begged patience from her, but her natural reaction was to give the pedal another strong push. The engine coughed and stalled.

"You flooded her," her father said.

Tilly sat back in the seat. She looked at the torn canvas above her head. She'd had no idea driving was so difficult.

"Give it a couple of minutes," Paul said.

She counted aloud to one hundred and eighty.

"Don't give it more fuel, start it in neutral."

Tilly tried to comply.

"You forgot the start button."

Her right foot swiveled from pedal to button and back to the accelerator.

The engine turned over and Paul reached across the cab to adjust the choke. He yelled over the noise, "Ready to put it in gear?"

"I'm ready," she said.

"Okay, give her a little gas as you let out the clutch."

Tilly looked at her father for a second, closed her mouth without asking the question on her lips, and shifted into gear. The truck lurched forward and stopped dead.

"You have to give it gas before you let the clutch out."

"What if I need to use the brake?" She yelled and then realized it wasn't necessary over a stalled engine.

"Use the hand brake on your left, under the dash."

Tilly exhaled and repositioned herself in the seat. "I can do this," she said under her breath.

"Now start from the top; choke out." Tilly started in neutral, engaged the clutch, shifted into first and gave the engine gas. Paul reached over and pushed the choke lever in as the truck made an erratic leap forward.

"Ah, Tilly," Ida said as she watched the lesson start and stop. "It surprises me that she hasn't learned to drive until now." She moved from where she stood to the porch swing, and sat next to her sister. The engine went silent again. "You're quiet, Helen. Are you worried Tilly will get into an accident?"

"I'm worried about the candle project," Helen said.

"Doris seems like a fine, young woman," Ida said.

"She's a long way from home," Helen said, "and neither she nor Tilly knows a thing about business."

"They will learn quickly," Ida said.

"Or lose everything," Helen said.

Ida sat back against the cushions and took her younger sister's hand. "The two of them are so excited about working for themselves. Don't you feel excited for them?"

"If Doris thought milking cows was a good idea, Tilly would want to milk cows," Helen said. "Doris is the sister she never had. Tilly hasn't thought anything through."

"They've been talking to Jose almost every day about their plan," Ida said. "Doris has been reading an accounting book."

"My point exactly." Helen looked away and waved her left hand in her sister's direction. "A little knowledge is a dangerous thing. My big concern is what will happen when the other owner shows up."

"That property's been sitting there since the railroad failed," Ida said. "The co-owner's probably dead."

"Mark my words," Helen said, "someone will come after that cove."

They watched as Paul coached Tilly in a reverse maneuver and couldn't help but laugh as the truck lurched forward and backward.

"I hope Paul doesn't get whiplash," Helen said. She turned toward her sister. "Both of those girls will be married in a couple of years. They should be buying houses. Prices are going up so fast now."

Ida sighed. "It's time to let go, Helen. Even if she fails, she'll be no worse off than if she'd never gone to Richmond. And she'll be so much wiser."

Helen winced at the mention of Richmond. She'd been so negative when Tilly decided to work for Kaiser, and she'd regretted it.

The truck jerked twice and then, by some miracle, settled into a smooth forward drive.

"She's young and ambitious, and waitressing isn't enough for her," Ida said.

Helen looked hard into Ida's eyes. "You could train her to take on more responsibility. She can do more than wait tables. Then you and Jose would be free to take time off."

Ida pushed against the back of the porch swing and rocked it. "Of course we could do that, and if we asked Tilly to take more on, she would do it because she loves us, not because she loves running an inn. This candle business will be hers."

Helen looked at her hands for several minutes. When she spoke her voice was soft. "At least she'll be here on the coast."

Ida gave her a hug. "I believe these will be very good years; Tilly will thrive." Helen nodded and Ida continued, "I'll never forget meeting Doris, she had just attempted to walk over the hill from San Mateo." She shook her head. "She's an exceptional, young woman. And now she'll build a business on her uncle's land."

Helen forced a smile. "The world is surely different," she said.

The truck went down the hill and came back around. Tilly was beaming. Her window was open, and she was punching the horn and waving at her aunt and mother.

• • •

Jose filled three tall glasses with cracked ice, tonic water and lime and settled into his occasional role as small business advisor. Tilly and Doris, who reverently attended his sessions, sipped their drinks and sat attentively in the otherwise empty bar. Aware of his responsibility, Jose did his best to prove worthy of their admiration. He carefully read every sentence of the outline Doris had typed on Ida's old Underwood.

"Of course I am not a lawyer, but it appears that you have been very thorough." He smiled broadly in Doris' direction. Tilly was also smiling at her. "You have carefully outlined the work you want to have done and what you are willing to pay. It is clear that you will reimburse John for all materials and expenses upon presentation of invoices, and that you will pay him weekly for labor, on Fridays. This is all very good." He took a drink of the tonic water. "I would advise that you clearly state a deadline for completion. You may want to consult with Bob Havice on how long it will take to build. He has similar warehouse buildings."

Doris made a note to talk to Havice on her to-do list.

"But in the end," Jose said, "after you have done all the research, you must go to the law office in San Mateo and get a lawyer to prepare a proper contract. I can give you a name."

Both women nodded at Jose and then at each other.

"Thank you for your help," Doris said. "I value your advice more than you imagine."

"I do too, Uncle Jose. We're so lucky to have you."

"Of course all this flattery, it will make me blush." He put a hand to his cheek and batted his eyelashes while Tilly and Doris snorted and rolled their eyes. "And now I have a question for you. I noticed that John's last name is Callen. Is he perhaps related to the famous Judge Callen?"

Tilly and Doris looked at one another.

"He's never said anything about it," Doris said. "I could ask."

"Judge Callen is an old friend whom Ida and I have not seen in several years. If you think of it, inquire about him."

• • •

Doris served the morning regulars while her boss watched though the bakery window. Nancy Adams considered her good fortune. She had a very bright young woman working the early shift; she'd never been late or missed a day. Several customers had mentioned how much they liked Doris.

Business was brisk. Orders for wedding cakes and the dessert catering package had quadrupled, and Nancy was beginning to think she should train an assistant manager. The more she got to know Doris, the more she liked her.

She got change after the bank opened, and as Doris filled the drawer, she laid out the terms of a promotion. "You can continue to work day shift; I'll begin your training with ordering and inventory. When you assume your new responsibilities, you'll be paid five cents an hour more. I'll adjust your pay as you learn."

Doris looked up, "I'm interested, but I've been looking at other opportunities. Can I give you my answer tomorrow?"

Nancy was surprised, but recovered quickly. "By all means. I'll stop by tomorrow." As she was leaving the bakery she looked over her shoulder, "Well, maybe thirty cents an hour isn't enough. Let's make it thirty-five."

"That's very generous," Doris said.

Nancy Adams left the bakery wondering who was trying to steal her best employee.

The minute she could get to a pay phone, Doris called Tilly and told her about the job offer. "I wanted to be around for construction," she said, "but it would be so good to practice running a business on one that's already successful. I'll learn about keeping inventory, doing invoices and ordering, that sort of thing." Tilly didn't respond right away and Doris continued, "I might not get a job on the coast that will teach me this much, and I have a room here..."

Tilly cut her off, "It's okay, Doris. You've done all the work on the business so far, and I've been a cheerleader. I need to pull my weight. You're not asking much; you're asking me to baby-sit the project and make sure John finishes—is that right?" The voice Doris heard over the line did not betray Tilly. In fact, Tilly was clutching the backrest of the chair nearest the phone, almost doubled over in panic.

"Well yes," Doris said. "I've checked John's references and as far as I can tell he's honest and capable. I don't think he's going to try to take advantage of us, but you'll need to monitor the work and the payment schedule."

For the life of Tilly, she could never figure out how Doris knew these things. Where did her knowledge of everything come from?

"You'll get a lot of phone calls from me, D., but I'll do my best."

"Tilly, thank you so much. I really think this will be best for our business."

Tilly hung up the phone and flopped down in the chair she'd been using for support. She stared straight ahead. Doris had just put her in charge of building the factory.

Doris worked out the final details with John and the lawyer Jose had recommended, and mailed the contract to Tilly. Her hands shook as she read it. She shared it with Jose, who acted like a proud papa.

"You are going into business and building a candle factory," he told her. "I couldn't be more excited for you."

It took a few weeks, but the burden of responsibility weighed in. On the first day of construction, Tilly woke before dawn, turned on the light to get a look at the clock, and wound the mechanism as if it would make time pass quickly. She buried her head in her pillow. Sleep would not come. When she couldn't take another minute of staring at the ceiling, she dressed quietly and padded downstairs to the kitchen.

Moonlight spilled between the cypress trees planted parallel to the house, and she watched a raccoon cross the yard as she scrambled two eggs. She cooked them in a generous pool of melted butter, ate them with toast and scrambled two more. She rocked on the porch swing with the plate in her lap as light rose over fields her father had recently tilled; finally, it was time for her familiar walk south along the beach toward the roadhouse.

At Bluegate Cove, she sat on her heels and pulled the sleeves of her worn woolen sweater over her hands as she listened to rhythmic surf playing against the steady downbeat of the foghorn. She became nearly hypnotized.

Just before seven, John parked his red International Harvester on the shoulder near the center of the property, jarring Tilly from her daydream. A Ford pick-up carrying survey equipment followed, and John introduced his wizened partner, Vern. The old surveyor unrolled the plan set on the hood and the men became engrossed in their work, occasionally looking up and pointing.

Tilly stood a respectful distance from the conference, curious, but not enough to interrupt their conversation. She watched her shadow become more defined as the sun rose higher above the horizon. She would need to call Doris and give a full report, but what would she say? They came, they pored over the plans, and they drove some stakes into the ground? She maintained her position on the sidelines.

John looked over his shoulder and addressed her as if he suddenly remembered she was there.

"Ah, nothing's wrong." She shrugged. "I was just, well I was just curious about how you get started." She wouldn't tell him that Doris had put her in charge.

"Well, the first step," John said, "is to find the property corners and lay out the footprint of the building, stake the foundation and provide offset stakes. We'll lay out the driveway and loading dock, utility lines, anything that needs to be included in the initial grading. Later, after you're satisfied with how it all fits, we'll bring in the equipment."

"I see, yes." She wrung her hands. She wondered what an "offset stake" was. "Well it certainly sounds like you've thought all this through very well," she said. The two men looked at each other. Vern raised an eyebrow. She shifted her weight on her feet and turned to leave; she didn't want them to see the blush of blood rising in her neck and cheeks. "I'll see you later," she said.

"Sure. We'll be here," John said.

The stairs to the back door of her aunt and uncle's apartment were at the edge of the cliff, and Tilly paused on the landing to look out over the rocks protecting the cove. Waves lapped gently; the wind wouldn't come up until afternoon. There was no better view, she thought. It was as if the roadhouse apartment floated above the beach—from the inside this seemed especially true. All the windows were oversized and uncovered.

Her favorite room, the kitchen, was painted bright yellow with white trim and wainscot.

When asked why they chose to live in the apartment when they could afford a nice home, Jose said "We have plenty of room to entertain guests—we just take them downstairs to the bar."

"Well this is a pleasant surprise," Ida said as she held the door to the screened porch where they took breakfast in good weather. "Have you come by for coffee?" She was wearing a flowered dressing gown, and her hair hung loose. Tilly thought she looked like a young woman.

Jose was using the white towel around his neck to collect the water dripping from his hair. "If I remember what I read in the contract correctly," he said, "this is the morning construction starts, yes? Perhaps we must have a groundbreaking ceremony."

Ida poured a cup of coffee for Tilly. There were eggs and toast on a blue platter in the center of the table. "Help yourself," she said.

Tilly shook her head.

"Is something wrong?" Ida said. She passed the cream.

"No," Tilly said. "I mean nothing bad has happened."

Her aunt and uncle sat looking at her.

"Doris put me in charge of construction," Tilly said, "and I don't have a clue what I'm doing." She sighed, "I went out there and made a fool of myself. Doris would know what to do; somehow she always knows what to do. I have to be told." She sat back in her chair and pushed the coffee away. "I don't know how to do this, but I have to do it. Doris can't be responsible for everything."

Jose looked at Ida and cleared his throat. "I know exactly how you feel." He leaned forward on his left arm.

"You do?" Tilly said.

He nodded, "You forget, my dear niece, that the Marine View Roadhouse was once a sketch on the back of an envelope. Ida and I were your age then and had to heavily mortgage the land to build. We were, as you say, babies in the woods."

"I guess I'd forgotten that," Tilly said. "You've been here for my whole life." She pulled her coffee cup toward her and took a sip. "How did you learn? How did you get through?"

Ida smiled. She put a poached egg on a slice of toast. "We made mistakes," she said. "Lots of them."

Tilly swallowed and looked up at her.

Jose continued, "No one comes out of the mother's womb knowing these things. You must learn. And when you do new things, it is inevitable that you make mistakes."

"But I don't know what to do, period," Tilly said. "Right or wrong."

Ida nodded. "You're bringing back memories," she said. "A mistake we made was thinking we needed to know how to construct the building. That wasn't important. We hired a good and honest builder. What we had to do was make sure the building would be adequate for our business."

"For an example," Jose gestured to make a point, "the shelves behind the bar had to be a comfortable height for me. I am not the tallest of bartenders, but I am the one working every night."

Ida was braiding her hair and twisting it into a knot. "There were details about the kitchen and pantry that I had to go over carefully," she said, and Jose nodded.

"Make sure the materials that are on site are the ones you've specified," Jose said. "If not, you must reject them."

Tilly asked for a pen and paper and wrote down everything they told her, until they had to excuse themselves to dress for work.

She felt lighter as she cleared the dishes and hugged her aunt and uncle.

"I know you will do a good job," Jose said.

Buoyed by her aunt and uncle's confidence in her, Tilly walked back to the cove, and when John saw her, he called her over. He led her to a line of numbered wooden stakes that were hammered into the ground. "That's your driveway," he said.

The driveway! Tilly stood back and looked at the row. She remembered the curve on the drawing with a sense of awe. Here was the turnaround marked on the land.

"I'm not sure you want your customers looking past that cypress tree when they're pulling out," John said. In the northeast corner of the property was the oldest, loveliest tree of the lot. She saw the problem, although her driving experience was very limited.

"No, this won't do," she said. "And I don't want to take the tree out."

They debated options that included redesigning the entry or moving the building. "It's your call," John told her.

Tilly started and blinked. She'd never been in charge of anything. "Let's just tighten the curve of the drive a bit," she said. "I don't want to make any major changes."

Vern nodded and looked at John. "That's what I'd do," he said.

Tilly felt suddenly relieved, excited, empowered. Her shoulders reflexively squared. She had made a decision and they would take her direction. She couldn't wait to see the new alignment staked. She raced home to get ready to work the lunch shift. She would call Doris in the afternoon and tell her about day one.

"Noon," John said.

Vern, who was checking the bearing for the south wall of the building, paused.

"We can grab a bite and check in," John said.

Vern pulled up his transom and tripod with a single motion and hoisted it onto his shoulder while John moved some notebooks off the passenger seat.

They drove the mile north to the Montara Hotel, the affordable alternative to the Marine View. What it lacked in scenery it made up for with cheap food and generous drinks. Mid-day the locals, mostly nurserymen and truck farmers, broke for food, beer and gossip.

They took a small table near the back of the room. The crowd was noisy, but it was impossible to ignore the conversation at the bar.

"You think you can make money in candles?"

"Yeah, candlelight dinners. You just have to get the right rich husband." They all laughed.

"Problem is," another man said, "the dames have more money now than we do. Uncle Sam did not pay as well as Henry Kaiser," he pointed at the air with his index finger for emphasis, "and dames today are thinking they should be making more money than we are."

"They want to be captains of industry!" Everyone laughed.

"Captainettes."

"No, you have it all wrong-o," the man to the left said, "They are thinking we should be making more money so we can spend it on them!" There was more laughter.

"That Tilly Bettencourt's a looker. I wouldn't mind spending some money on her."

"She can find herself a rich daddy." The bartender chimed in, "Doris ain't bad either. She's a cutie."

Vern raised his eyebrows, "Apparently your little project is the big news in town." He drank his Coke from the bottle.

"I picked up Doris one morning walking west from San Mateo," John said. "She didn't have a ride and wanted to see her land. If I hadn't stopped, I have no doubt she would've walked the entire distance." He glanced back toward the bar. "Those guys will be begging for jobs making candles," he said. "My money's on the girls."

CHAPTER 14

San Mateo County Sheriff Dennis Wick got his marching orders from the President of the Board of Supervisors in a letter that opened with:

> *"As you are aware, the Board has decided to take a proactive approach to law enforcement in our coastal communities. More and more travelers are taking the new road over the Coast Range on weekends, and there has been a rise in the number of subdivision applications that will, in short order, result in an increased resident population. Coastsiders have done an adequate job of policing themselves, but it is now time to provide a higher level of service."*

"They've decided we need a substation over there," he said to his second in command and handed off the letter. He leaned back in his leather chair and scratched the top of his head.

"Sounds like a promotional opportunity," the lieutenant said. "That should make the boys happy."

"I'm not sure we should call it a promotion," Wick said. "Not much goes on over there now that the bootleggers are gone. Let's call it a special assignment."

"Know who you want to send, boss?"

• • •

Deputy Michael Carry, son of the late Sheriff George Carry, slammed the driver's side door of his patrol car, after a gentler attempt failed to engage the catch on the lock. He'd argued unsuccessfully that a newer vehicle was in order. "I'll be traveling back and forth to headquarters," he said. "I need reliable transportation."

Sheriff Dennis Wick said he'd get his turn in the rotation.

A short, stocky, rather bovine man, Mike Carry's physical appearance belied his nervous energy and motivation. If the family reputation weren't enough to drive him, there was this: being the first, setting the standard for coastside law enforcement. He regarded his appointment as an historic event.

Straightening his shoulders, he wiped the dust off the Sheriff's Department insignia on the door. Despite his dissatisfaction with the vehicle, he was thrilled with the assignment he perceived as an opportunity to "call the shots." Though the overwhelming response from the ranks was that the job was banishment to a dull, damp, and foggy part of the county, Carry assumed his new role with great vigor.

He arrived alone, unsure what to expect. Since the post had been ordained by the Board of Supervisors, he thought it not unreasonable to assume that some form of ceremony would be arranged. He drove to the post office as instructed, to be shown to his quarters.

"It's the Moss Beach Post Office, not the one in Montara," the Sheriff's matronly secretary had reminded him.

He smiled. She was prudent to be specific, he thought. His realm would include all of Half Moon Bay to the south, El Granada, Princeton-by-the-Sea, and Moss Beach, with Montara to the north. He was already imagining a squad of deputies under his command, patrolling his nine-mile stretch of coastline. "One thing at a time, Mike my boy," he said to himself.

When no one greeted him, Carry entered the squat, masonry building and waited by the counter, ignored, while customers bought stamps and shared gossip. A small terrier yipped outside, and Carry resisted the urge to go out and give it a scratch behind the ears. Eventually, the line cleared and the Postmaster showed him to a very small room, more suitable as a storage closet. The narrow space was more than twice as long as it was wide and Carry thought there'd be just enough room for him to squeeze by a normal size desk.

"I'm sorry that it doesn't have a window," the Postmaster said. He waved his hands around. "We can probably put one in—this here's an outside wall." He explained that they had held packages there when the road was impassable. "The sheriff didn't want to spend much money, and we said we could give you this for free. I thought it'd be a good thing to have a deputy sheriff located in the post office." He shook Carry's hand. "Welcome to Moss Beach."

A customer rang the bell on the counter. "We can get a phone hooked up for you," the Postmaster said over his shoulder.

"I guess you'll be wanting your own number, though we'd be happy to take messages."

Carry pushed back his hat. He'd expected the space would be ready for him but quickly realized that setting up an office was part of "calling the shots." He smiled broadly and dug a tape measure from the gear in his trunk.

With little reported crime, the young deputy struggled to define his role in the community. Many residents doubted that post-war prosperity was reason enough to suddenly send a sworn officer of the law out to patrol. In fact, the lack of law enforcement was precisely why some chose to live so far from the government center. That Mike Carry was the son of a former county sheriff who had declared war on bootleggers during prohibition did not add to his popularity. Coastsiders had long memories.

Michael Carry never visited the Marine View Roadhouse at night, and he wasn't part of the social circle that frequented the Montara Hotel bar, but he did forage for meals at the local eateries.

Ida told her sister that she felt sorry for "The Lone Ranger," as she peeled hard-boiled eggs for the house salad. "It must be tough," she said, "to be so young and still responsible for keeping the peace."

Helen smirked. "Even when we were at war, we were at peace," she said. "Nothing ever happens here." She looked out the window for a moment and said, "Tilly hasn't gone out since she's been back from Kaiser. All these guys are back from war and my beautiful daughter can't seem to get a date." She thought about the call she'd taken the night before, from a Kaiser friend of Tilly's named Sylvia. Sylvia was working in Reno. From what Helen knew of Reno, nice, single girls didn't go there to live. She'd given Tilly the number, but Tilly showed no interest in returning the call. In many ways, her daughter was unfathomable.

"So Mrs. Bettencourt, are you related to Tilly Bettencourt building the project just up the road?" Deputy Carry stirred cream into the cup until the coffee was a light beige.

"Tilly's my daughter," she said.

"I get notice of the building permits issued out here. I stop by, make sure things are okay, no materials have been stolen or anything." He puffed his chest out a bit. "It helps to keep order."

"We appreciate what you do," Ida said as she placed the plate in front of him. "I got these sour cherries fresh yesterday. This pie might be a bit tart, but it's a nice change."

Carry's fork slid through the flakey pastry that Ida had dusted with sugar before baking. The sugar had melted with the butter in the dough at just the right temperature to create a kind of golden brown caramel rind on the top of the pie. Its sweetness exactly balanced the tartness of the fruit. He paused with the first bite in his mouth before he swallowed. "It's divine," he said.

Helen Bettencourt said it was good to have a sheriff's deputy as a steady customer. "We hope you'll stop by often,

Deputy Carry. Perhaps, soon, we'll be able to lure you to Sunday supper at our home."

• • •

Sylvia wondered if Helen had forgotten to tell Tilly she'd called, or if Helen was appalled that Sylvia had called from Reno and neglected to pass on the message. She never thought Tilly would deliberately avoid her. Hadn't she called her "sister"?

There was opportunity in Reno; Eve had been right about that. Sure, she was slinging hash in a diner now, but workers were finishing the Mapes Hotel and Casino. She'd already set her sights on a job in the Sky Room—which she'd heard would seat four hundred and be open twenty-four hours a day. There'd be lots of good jobs; high rollers, she thought, would be good tippers. And even though Eve had been more or less a one-night stand, she had become a friend.

Doris had written something of starting the candle business and taking Tilly on as partner, but Sylvia couldn't imagine Tilly settling on the coast straight away. A little time away from the confines of family and community would do her good if only she'd get in touch. She heard the cook pound the bell and went to grab the order from under the heat lamp. She needed to focus on her work.

• • •

John Callen looked up from his work. The day was clear and bright enough for the Farallon Islands to be visible, twenty-five miles offshore. He couldn't complain about his new project. His clients were delightful, his accommodations at the

Montara Hotel were comfortable enough, and he enjoyed the quiet of the coast.

Callen avoided alcohol, believing that it would rob him of hours; he'd lost enough time as a Marine. He knew few of the local guys but didn't regret it. For him, the coastsider of greatest interest, he had to admit with consternation, was his leggy client.

He avoided taking meals at the Marine View, though he found the quality of the food superb, because he wanted to maintain an air of professionalism around Tilly. She was paying his bills; he had to keep reminding himself of that. Each week, he daydreamed about asking her out to Nick's in Pacifica for dinner and dancing, or to Half Moon Bay for a show, but then he'd convince himself to wait until the factory was built.

Concrete arrived for the foundation, and John couldn't leave the site until the lot was poured. He worked full steam until three o'clock, when he checked his watch and acknowledged the rumbling in his stomach. Too late now for lunch, he thought.

Jose looked up from polishing glassware when the door opened. John removed his cap and smoothed his hair.

"It is good to see you," Jose said. "I understand from my niece that the work is going very well." He put a cocktail napkin on the bar, and John wrapped his legs around a stool.

"I aim to keep my customers happy," John said.

"That is what we must do in business," Jose said. "What can I do to serve you?"

"I'm a little late for lunch, what's on the dessert menu?" John said.

"My wife made a chocolate cream pie this morning that is extraordinary."

"Gotta try it. And a cup of coffee, please."

Jose disappeared into the kitchen and returned with the coffee and a napkin and fork. He leaned against the counter as John added milk and sugar. "There's something I've been meaning to ask, that I believe my niece forgot about."

John stopped stirring and looked up.

"Are you related to Judge Robert Callen?" Jose asked.

One of the kitchen staff brought the order, topped with freshly whipped cream.

"He's my grandfather," John said. "Do you know him?"

"I consider Judge Callen a good friend to the coast," Jose said. "He settled many a score after the railroad failed. How is his health?"

"No problems to speak of," John said. "My grandmother's also well." He took a bite of the pie and closed his eyes. "This is delicious. I used to buy devil's food cake from Doris each morning. I do miss it."

"I will let my wife know," Jose said. "Do not be surprised if you find a special chocolate cake dessert on the menu."

John smiled and took another bite. "I may need to eat two of these."

"In this case," Jose said, "they are on the house. And please, John, give my regards to your grandfather. It has been too long since we have seen him."

• • •

"You invited Mike Carry to dinner?" Tilly leaned back in the chair and stared at the kitchen ceiling.

"He's a nice, young man from a good family, and he doesn't know many people here," Helen said.

"He's a flat tire, Mom. People avoid him."

Helen did her best to convince Tilly that it would be good to befriend him. "You're starting a new business, and he's opened the first sheriff's substation on the coast. Surely, you recognize that you're future community leaders."

Tilly told herself to remain calm—that her mother's intentions were good. "I'm busy Sunday," she said in what she hoped was a neutral voice. "I'm meeting Doris to go over some stuff for the business. It's the only time we both have off." She put the milk bottle back in the refrigerator, deaf to her mother's protests, and walked to the beach. Having her own business wouldn't be enough. She needed her own place.

Her periods had finally started. It had taken nearly a year of eating to the point of discomfort to get close to her pre-war weight. Things would be normal if only she could find a man she was attracted to.

Tilly could understand that her mother felt sorry for Carry—she'd heard the gossip. Among the most outrageous stories was that Carry was discharged from the army when he accidentally shot himself in the leg. He'd never be accepted, she thought. His father had been respected, if not liked.

She crossed a field of young artichoke plants that wouldn't fruit until next season, happy to see the pre-war vegetable rotation coming back. She made a beeline to a small abandoned house at the very edge of the village that was disappearing under leaf litter and aggressive cape ivy. "Bell Cottage" was routed into a wooden sign above the door.

She tried to remember when Lydia Bell died. Maybe it was ten years ago. Lydia had shared the cottage with Peg for decades, and when Lydia died the younger Peg stayed on. Tilly had heard about Peg's passing while she was at Kaiser. Little maintenance had been done on the place while the old spinsters were alive, and now it was in a serious state of disrepair. Ivy had a stranglehold on the small front porch; the wooden steps sagged. The paint was so worn and weathered it was impossible to know its original color.

Tilly had never been inside. She pulled some vegetation away from a side window and rubbed the grime off the glass with her sleeve. There was furniture in the small front parlor. Giant cobwebs draped from the overhead light fixtures and the water-stained curtains seemed to be rotting in place. From the kitchen window, she could see jars of preserves left on the shelves. She'd fantasized about having a place of her own, and this would do nicely if it were fixed up.

• • •

John was making good progress, Tilly thought, as she stood inside the foundation and looked at the outline of the factory. The forms were being stripped from the stem walls and John was preparing to pour the concrete slab for the factory floor. He noticed the puzzled look on her face. "Is something wrong, Tilly?" he asked.

"Of course I know the building's the right size," she said, "but I expected it to look bigger." She walked around the inside perimeter, remembering the hulls at Kaiser. They were cavernous and many stories high.

"It will look bigger when the walls go up," John said, and smiled. "Trust me."

She looked at him. Doris mentioned that she found him handsome. He was a good-looking man, Tilly had to agree. Maybe he'd ask Doris for a date. Doris would like that.

"You're seeing the space relative to everything in the neighborhood right now, since it's all open," he said. "When the walls go up, it'll look different."

The sheriff's patrol car pulled into the drive and Deputy Carry slid out from under the wheel, about fifty feet away. He shouted across the distance. "Tilly, I've been looking for you."

She stepped over the foundation forms and started to walk in his direction.

"*The Postman Always Rings Twice* is opening in Half Moon Bay tonight," Carry said. "I'll pick you up and we can have a bite on the way to the movie."

Why, she thought, did he set himself up for public humiliation? Desperate for a graceful escape, she looked at her feet. "I've already made other plans for the evening." It was the best she could come up with.

"Oh. Some other time then." He pivoted and slid back into the patrol car, barely clearing the steering wheel with his girth. Gravel sprayed on the shoulder of the road as he lurched out onto the pavement. She heard John break into laughter.

"Liar," he said.

"My mother's encouraging him," Tilly said. "She talks to him all the time."

"Not many people do," John said.

"I don't like lying to him," Tilly said. She brushed the loose dirt off her jeans and turned to leave.

"I think I can help you out," John said. "With Mike Carry, I mean."

"How's that?" she asked.

"If you went out with me tonight," John said, "well, you wouldn't be lying."

This was unexpected. Tilly could think of a number of reasons why it was a bad idea: She liked John but not as a potential date, and besides, he was in her employ. She didn't want to hurt Doris, but she thought it had taken a lot for John to ask. Maybe if she went her mother would stop trying to get her together with Mike Carry. That would be a relief. After a couple of dates, she could simply tell John that the relationship couldn't go anywhere as long as she had to supervise him. It would work for a while anyway, and then maybe she could figure out some way to get him together with Doris.

"We could drive into Half Moon Bay and see *The Postman Always Rings Twice*," he said.

"Their love was a flame that destroyed!" Tilly posed with the back of her hand held dramatically against her forehead as she read the words that floated above the photo of Lana Turner and John Garfield. "Isn't there supposed to be a postman?" she said. She was uncomfortable and knew she was acting like an idiot, but she couldn't help it. She kept telling herself she shouldn't have come. Doris had put her in charge of managing the project. What would Doris say if she knew? This could only be a one-time thing.

Tilly was leaning under the overhang as they stood in line for tickets. The fog was particularly thick, as it sometimes got in the evenings when the weather was warming up over the hill, and a persistent mist was dampening everything, including her enthusiasm. Maybe she could just tell him she'd changed her mind or wasn't feeling well. Once inside the lobby, there'd be no turning back.

"Unfortunately, they don't serve popcorn at the road-house" Tilly said. "Uncle Jose is partial to peanuts."

John took the hint and bought the biggest bag. He asked for salt and melted butter, but only after checking with her. They took their seats midway down the auditorium.

"A newsreel I saw in this very theater convinced me that I should work for the war effort," Tilly said. "Maybe you saw it. Katherine Hepburn was in this welder's outfit and took off the mask, and that gorgeous red hair of hers spilled out and she said, straight into the camera 'Democracy's in a jam'. That did it for me."

"She didn't inspire you to become Woman of the Year?" John said.

Tilly rolled her eyes. "Don't be ridiculous John, that's just Hollywood."

The lights went down, and the first reel ran. A drifter found himself coerced into staying on at a lunch counter and gas station to help the proprietor and his much younger blond wife, played by Lana Turner, who seemed to own only white clothing.

“See any similarity to the roadhouse?” John elbowed Tilly when the first reel had played out and the crowd was heading to the lobby for intermission.

“Absolutely none. Aunt Ida and Uncle Jose would never hang a hamburger sign out front.”

John looked in the popcorn bag, then turned it upside down, “Hungry?”

“Not as much as I was,” she said.

“I can see you’re not going to be a cheap date,” he said. “Do you need some more Coke to wash all the popcorn down with?”

“No, I haven’t tapped my hump yet,” she said. Then she laughed at her own joke, and the woman sitting in the next row, overhearing their exchange, started to giggle. John grinned and shook his head.

Tilly leaned to her right side when the house lights went down, sitting as far from John as possible while occupying the adjacent seat. Her legs were crossed and angled away from him.

“You know,” she said later, as John started the truck’s engine, “The Lana Turner character had ice water in her veins, but I think today a lot of women might sympathize with her desire to make something of the business rather than follow her husband to Northern Canada to nurse his ailing sister. And I do believe she would have been successful.”

John rubbed the back of his neck.

“I hope Doris sees it,” Tilly said.

They were quiet during the drive back to Montara and then Tilly told him they probably shouldn't date while the factory was being built.

• • •

Paul gave Tilly the keys to the pickup, reminding her to drive safely. She drove over the hill slowly, challenged by tight curves and steep grades, and breathed easier when she cleared the redwoods. She carefully followed Doris' directions to the diner. She was famished, but Doris put so much paper, so many brochures in front of her, that there wasn't room for a plate. She ordered a chocolate shake.

"We'll only purchase a few pieces of equipment to get started," Doris said, "but we'll need to grow with the ones we choose. We want to fully depreciate our tools."

Tilly stared, impressed. Doris had probably read and reread every business textbook she could get her hands on, and no doubt, pestered the owner of the bakery to explain what she didn't understand. Tilly hoped to absorb some of Doris' brilliance, which she was sure she could see reflected in the diner's stainless steel.

"We need the best quality melter we can afford," Doris said. "Dipped and molded candles take a higher temperature wax. So to keep all options open, we want a melting machine that's efficient and can run hot."

Tilly nodded. It all made perfect sense. She slurped some milkshake wishing she'd done some research of her own, but it had never occurred to her that candle making could have so many variables.

"There's enough room to add a second melting machine when we need it," Doris said. She produced sketches on graph paper; she'd considered how her preferred machines would fit on the factory floor and explained how she'd accommodate expansion as the business grew.

Tilly had called the meeting because John was ready to wire the factory, and he needed to know where to install the electrical outlets. He'd also recommended adding future capacity.

"You gals will be sorry later if you have to come back and upsize everything," he'd said.

Tilly couldn't answer his questions. She looked at Doris' sketches of the factory floor and had an overwhelming feeling that she wasn't smart enough to be in business, and that it would only be a matter of time before Doris realized it.

"Have you heard from Sylvia?" Doris asked while she was waiting for the check. "I got a letter from her last week asking if you were okay. She was concerned that she had the wrong address."

Tilly looked toward the window. "I'm a horrible correspondent," she said.

• • •

Helen shelled peas near the sink in the rear of the Marine View kitchen. Her sister had been too busy to visit all weekend, and now it was Monday and they were back at work. The weather had turned sunny, and throngs of tourists had driven the paved road and stopped for food and drink. Jose was elated. "We must think about expansion." He was talking to his wife and anyone else who would listen. "Tourism is finally coming to the coast." He had spent most of the evening sketching a plan to enlarge the dining room with more white water view tables. "The tourists, they all want a table with a view, and of course, we have the very best here at the Marine View."

"It's hard to believe the war in Europe has been over for a year," Ida said. She was adding herbs to the house salad dressing. "It's so good to see people enjoying life." She turned to her sister, who was shelling peas. "I understand Tilly had a nice time on Friday evening with John."

Helen smiled and nodded. "They make such a handsome couple," she said.

"But ladies, I have not told you the best part." Jose said. "I was talking with John last week and learned that his grandfather is none other than our dear Judge Callen."

The peas fell through Helen's fingers. "Judge Robert Callen?" She said.

"Yes, our old friend," Jose said. "I am hoping he will be drawn to the coast for a visit."

"It's been much too long," Ida said. Neither Jose nor Ida noticed that Helen was staring straight ahead. She rose and gathered the peas from the floor and went to the sink to rinse them. Through the window, she could see Tilly, black skirt and white shirt, barefoot, coming up the beach to work, as she'd always done before the war. John was beside her, tool belt around his waist, carrying a hammer. He turned back toward the candle factory as they approached the roadhouse. He'd taken a break to walk with her for a few minutes. Helen thought about Judge Callen at the bar drinking bootleg whiskey and angling for a share of her husband's bankruptcy payout from the railroad, twenty-five years earlier.

• • •

They left early the next morning for Redwood City; Tilly reading from her list of questions for Doris while John drove.

"Have I forgotten anything?" she asked.

"Ventilation," he said. "Doris probably knows how much heat the equipment gives off. I know you're going to need fans by the paraffin melters."

Tilly tried to make a note as John hit a pothole. "Slow down," she said.

"It won't improve the road," he said.

There was plenty of parking on the street. John took the first space and led Tilly down Broadway.

"Where did you say we're going?" she asked.

"It's a surprise," John said. "You gals are business women now, and you need to go where the deal makers go." He stopped in front of the copper sheathed doors of the City Hotel.

"Here?" Tilly said. "Can we afford this?"

"As long as you don't eat anything." He opened the door and entered behind her.

Doris hadn't arrived; the waitress brought them coffee, and Tilly asked John what the old Carry-Callen feuds were about.

"My grandfather was Sheriff Carry's nemesis," John said.

"Any relation to Deputy Carry?" Tilly stirred a bit more cream into her cup.

"Yeah, his father—his late father. When Sheriff Carry died the judge was truly broken up about it."

"They were friends?" Tilly asked.

"Oh no, my grandfather and Mike's dad were at odds over everything," John said. "For my grandfather, the world is many shades of gray. For Carry, there was only black and white."

"But your grandfather mourned his passing?"

"He lost his favorite adversary."

The waitress filled a third cup as Doris opened her notebook and asked John to go over the construction schedule; then she talked about equipment. They double-checked the power and installation requirements for each piece, went over the budget and finally ordered lunch.

"Now a personal matter," she said, clearing the table and making room for food. "I'm going to need a place to live."

Tilly knew Doris would sleep on a cot in the storeroom if she had to, but figured that after three years in an Airstream and another in a rooming house, she was hoping for a little more comfort.

"It looks like we'll be in business full time by early October, and we might get some Christmas orders," Doris said.

"That's a good thing," John remarked as he buttered bread.

"Yes, but I'm going to have to give up my job here and move out to the coast within the next couple of months."

"I'm looking forward to the day." Tilly leaned back in her chair and spread her arms wide.

"I guess you won't want to live at the Montara Hotel and take your meals with the guys, will you?" John said, "There's not much available housing on the coast."

Doris turned to Tilly. "Do you think you can help me find a room or a cottage of some sort to stay in?"

"Want a roommate?" Tilly asked. "There's an old cottage on the north side of Montara that's been vacant for the last couple of years. The old woman who lived there died and they never moved her things. I've been thinking about trying to rent it, though it's a wreck."

Doris shrugged, unconcerned about having to do some work. "If it's a wreck, no one else will want it."

CHAPTER

15

March 10, 1925

"JUDGE, you gonna sit in this office all day?" Cora, the Callen's housekeeper, brushed crumbs from the desktop onto a plate and cleared the coffee service. Her navy and white dotted dress covered an ample form, and she peered down at the judge as she pondered the empty creamer. "Either you're drinkin' your coffee on the milky side or you're feedin' that damn cat again."

Judge Callen checked the gold pocket watch that had been his grandfather's. "I'll be out of your way in a few minutes," he said. "Has Katherine left yet?"

"She's gone down to Broadway to some temperance meeting," Cora said. "Told me she'd be back before lunch. Judge, you are letting that cat shed all over your office."

"Well, I'll be going then."

"You comin' home for lunch, Judge?"

"Is my cat safe alone in the house with you?"

Cora grinned and walked toward the door.

"I'll be at the courthouse most of the day," he said. He ran his fingers through his thinning salt and pepper hair. When he stood, he was a head taller than she. "Tell Mrs. Callen that I'll see her for dinner."

An added benefit of adjudicating the Ocean Shore bankruptcy, was that it gave the judge a reason to visit the coast for business. It was a part of the county he found more accepting of folks enjoying a little fun; it was also out of the bounds of his wife's social network. The judge straightened his tie, buttoned his jacket and closed the door to his office. Jezebeau immediately slid to his chair and stretched out in the combined warmth of residual body heat and morning sun, spreading gray and black cat hair on the worn upholstery.

From his home on Maple Street the judge could chose between two routes to the courthouse, via Whipple Avenue or Birch Street. He usually chose the Whipple option although it was a slightly longer walk, because it took him past the sheriff's headquarters and afforded the best opportunity to encounter George Carry. Sheriff George Carry possessed a literal view of the law and was given to the dogged pursuit of justice, to the amusement of Judge Callen. Carry was continually frustrated to find some of his best investigative work unraveled in Callen's courtroom. Over the years, he had developed an epic grudge against the judge, which he tried unsuccessfully to hide. He was perceptive enough to know how much Callen enjoyed getting the better of him. Five years into prohibition, Carry was happy that he was required to turn bootleggers over to federal agents, because it meant they could never be prosecuted by San

Mateo County. Callen and his cronies were among those with a serious taste for Irish whiskey.

"Good morning, Sheriff." Judge Callen caught George Carry coming down the stairs. He extended his hand.

Carry hesitated, wiped his right palm on the thigh of his wool trousers as if he had to dry it, and accepted the judge's offer. "Good morning," he said.

When Carry released his grip the judge continued, "Why, it's a beautiful day, isn't it?"

Carry looked at Callen, then stepped around him and walked up the street in the opposite direction. The judge grinned and turned toward the courthouse, where he had a full morning's work ahead of him.

CHAPTER 16

September 4, 1946

"DO YOU HAVE any idea how much you'll have to spend to make that cottage habitable?" Helen was leaning against the kitchen counter, eating a peach.

"John's going over there this morning to have a look," Tilly said. "What we spend will be deducted from the rent."

Helen stiffened. Anyone but John Callen. She didn't believe Tilly when she said he was just a friend. They spent too much time together. Helen feared her daughter might marry into the Callen clan, her worst nightmare. "The Callens—you don't know them like I do," she said. "That famous judge Jose calls a 'friend' was the worst kind of parasite, the most corrupt official in San Mateo County."

"You can't judge John by his grandfather," Tilly said.

Helen threw the peach pit into the trash. "I wish you'd give some of the other young men around here the time of day," she said. "You can do better." She felt a throbbing just below the hairline.

John finished his ham and egg breakfast and signed his room number on the check. He left a nice tip for the flirtatious, newly blond waitress. He'd give a lot to have Tilly flirt with him like that, even just a little. He'd never seen her flirt. Maybe dames that gorgeous didn't have to, and that made them all the more interesting.

He had to take Tilly at her word when she said she couldn't date him while she was monitoring his contract. He was rather impressed by the way she handled herself, but he was starting to think the job was an excuse. What if he asked the waitress out? That would send a message, but he thought better of it. As far as he could tell, Tilly wasn't interested in anyone else. He grabbed a flashlight, screwdriver and wrench from the toolbox on his truck and walked the short distance to meet her at the cottage.

The vegetation around the north side was thick and especially lush after a wet, warm spring. John beat a path through the thornier plants for Tilly. A couple of porch planks were loose. Vines grew up to the front door.

"We won't have time to throw a garden party this year," she said, putting her father's leather work gloves on and pulling blackberry brambles away from the wood siding. "In the meantime, we'll have berries in our pancakes."

John bounced on the front steps; they felt spongy beneath his weight. "We should at least tighten up the entry," he said. "I don't want you to fall through." The screen door was attached to the frame by a single hinge with only half of its screws in the decaying jamb. "Did you bring paper? I think we'd better start a list."

Tilly sighed. "I don't know if I brought enough paper." She fished for the key in her jeans pocket, and it easily turned the lock after she jiggled it. Nothing happened when she flipped the light switch closest to the door.

"Looks like you have lots of roommates," John said as he raised the blinds. There were signs of nesting rodents.

Tilly sneezed twice, looked around and leaned against the wall. "I wanted to pull this off for Doris, I really did." She knocked down a web that looked like a fishing net and blocked the entry to the kitchen. Though the place was filthy, it appeared dry and free of mildew.

John was scanning the ceiling in the front room with a flashlight, looking for water damage. "Wanted to do this? Are you saying you're not interested anymore?" His light paused in one corner, but he dismissed the dark spot as collected grime. The paint appeared to be peeling from sheer age.

"I'm not sure we have enough time and money to take it on," she said.

John checked the walls and ceiling then moved to the kitchen while Tilly took her own survey. The cottage had once been charming, with wooden plank floors, painted wainscot and simple trim around the windows and doors. An old wood-burning cook stove and a large enameled cast-iron sink graced the kitchen. With the drain boards on each side, the sink was six feet long, with a rag of a skirt gathered beneath. There were shelves in the pantry that still had rusting cans on them. "It's an archeological site," she said. Indoor plumbing had been added and a claw-foot slipper tub was installed in the bathroom. About eight hundred square feet total, it was everything they needed.

"You should take it," John said after his preliminary check. "If you don't, I will."

"You think we should take it?"

"This place is old, built of redwood, with large timbers for its size. Look at the ceiling: It's in good condition except for a little water damage in one place—the corner of the back bedroom." They walked down the short hallway so he could point out the trouble spot, and Tilly's skin felt clammy when she realized she was alone with John in the bedroom of the empty cottage. What was wrong with her? She thought about the gals who said they envied her.

"The roof's in reasonable shape," he said. "I'll patch that leak and clean the gutters."

She nodded and turned quickly for the front room.

"I'll check the attic," John said, following her, "but the electrical's new and it's probably okay. We need to check the well and pump."

She was beginning to tune him out. He was acting too husbandly—trying to impress her—trying to make himself indispensable.

"It's a couple of days work for me," he said, "no more."

Tilly nodded in agreement. She just wanted him to leave. She suddenly felt as if the space was too small to contain both of them, but he kept talking.

"I'm sure you can handle the cleaning and painting. And then there's the matter of the yard and maybe a coat of paint on the outside," he said. "It will take time, Tilly, but I think you're more than capable of doing this."

Of course I'm *capable*, she thought.

She looked at each room again. She smiled and thanked John for his advice. She didn't want to ask him for help and had no idea how long it would take to do everything on the list. She could only afford to pay him for a couple of days' work. "I know if Doris were here she'd be up for the challenge," she said. "She'd already have a list of things to do and materials to get." She opened the firebox on the stove and imagined feeding kindling into it before breakfast. She'd have to learn to split wood. "I guess I have nothing to lose by taking it. If it gets to be too much for Doris and me, we can let you have it."

She pulled the paper and pen from her back pocket and started a list.

• • •

Paul rose at five. He tiptoed to the kitchen to allow Helen an extra hour of sleep. With the coffee on, he started the toast and got the cast-iron pan hot for his eggs. He retrieved the paper from the porch and read while he cooked. He almost dropped the pitcher of orange juice when Tilly came up behind him.

"I'm sorry I startled you," she yawned.

"Didn't you work last night?" he said.

She stretched her right arm up over her head. "I did, but I have two jobs now. I'm going to start on the Bell cottage this morning."

Paul lifted his right eyebrow and pulled out a chair. He motioned for her to sit and put his plate in front of her. "Then you better eat a good breakfast," he said. He poured her a cup of coffee and broke two more eggs into the frying pan.

"Can I drop you off at the nursery and take the truck to El Granada Hardware?" Tilly asked.

Paul held her equipment list in one hand and the egg turner in the other. "I can lend you some of these things," he said.

She shook her head, "No, if we're going to set up house we need to invest. And Dad, you're going to have to teach me to split wood, the cottage has a wood-burning stove in the kitchen."

Now both eyebrows were raised. He flipped his eggs onto a dish and sat across the table. She placed the to-do and materials lists in front of him, and he put the newspaper aside. She had it all planned out. He was fairly sure Tilly had never sanded a floor or caulked a window, but if she could learn to weld she could do this. "Of course you can use the truck," he said, and smiled at her a long time.

Tilly went straight to the hardware store after she drove him to work and was waiting at the door when Floyd flipped the sign to open. He barely recognized her in overalls with her hair tied up. She'd waited fifteen minutes for him, fidgeting as if someone had wound her tightly.

"Don't tell me you gals have decided to fire Callen and build that factory yourselves," he said.

Tilly laughed. "Just doing some home improvement."

Floyd shook his head. "Tell me why a treasure like you is running around loose. If I wasn't already married..." Tilly handed him the full-page shopping list to cut him off.

"A nice start to the day," he said, and she gave a sigh of relief. She hated fielding questions about her marital status. Floyd motioned for her to follow him around the store as he loaded her cart, then helped her out of the store with her purchases.

She was at the cottage before eight o'clock, and the first item she unloaded from the back of the truck was the broom; she wanted to rid her future home of cobwebs and rodent feces before she spent another day inside. Water from the tap was a rusty brown, and she let it run before filling her new pail. She used a soap that Floyd recommended and sang while she worked.

The curtains would need to be replaced; she pulled them all down. They practically fell apart in her hands. Outside she lopped off the most aggressive vegetation so she could get to the windows. She cleaned the screens and hosed the exterior; spider webs hung from gutters and shutters and the balustrade around the porch.

At three-forty she checked her watch. She was starving but didn't have time to eat before work. She hustled to the roadhouse and set up the dining room, worked through the dinner rush, then collapsed into bed at the end of her shift. When she returned to the cottage the next morning, she could appreciate what she'd accomplished; simply washing the windows had brightened the interior significantly. She smiled to herself as she looked around. She could start thinking about colors. And at that moment, when she thought of painting the room, she could see Sylvia in her splattered painter's pants, on the steps of her Airstream, blowing smoke rings. A loneliness settled over Tilly—a loneliness she'd been unable to shake since she'd left Kaiser. She wondered if it would ever pass.

With the ladder up, she drew a bucket of hot soapy water, scrubbed the walls and wainscot and started to scrape the peeling paint. She was doing something useful, important. It had been more than a year since she'd felt productive. She would spend every spare minute at the cottage; she would make it a beautiful home. The work would take her mind off other things. She would work hard and be able to move on.

That Tilly was driving herself hard was immediately evident to those who loved her, especially her father. Three weeks into her mission, she came to breakfast like a sleepwalker.

"Morning, stranger," Paul said. He'd never known his baby to have dark circles under her eyes, and he noticed that it took multiple cups of coffee to get her talking. She'd worked every day. He served her an extra-large portion of oatmeal and passed the honey.

"It's not as hard as welding," she said, "but I'm feeling the hours." She stretched her arms overhead, pushing up on her elbows. Paul didn't tell her that he was worried about her, or that he was in awe of her.

"I have some time today," he said. "I can come over and show you how to caulk windows. Did you get a caulking gun?"

"Floyd at the hardware store helped me pick one out," she winked, "but you'll need one too." She gave her father a hug, and he gave her a ride to the cottage.

John had volunteered to help and was already on the front porch with his tools waiting when Tilly and Paul drove up. He tried to hide his disappointment. He'd thought he'd get to spend a Saturday alone with her, away from the factory job and his crew, doing something she wanted. Now he'd be working with Paul. He had to remind himself that he wanted to help Tilly.

He watched as father and daughter removed the trim from the inside and lifted a double-hung window from its track. Paul explained how the weights and ropes worked to keep everything moving smoothly, and John, more or less ignored, climbed to the roof to patch the leak above the bedroom. They worked through lunch; Paul offered to buy, but Tilly didn't want to take a break. Then she left at three o'clock for the roadhouse.

Jose and Ida were also concerned about Tilly. "Perhaps you should take tomorrow off," Jose said as he locked the door behind the last customer. He poured her a ginger ale. Tilly sat and watched as he restocked the bar, and this concerned Jose, because she usually helped. He thought she might doze and slide off the stool. Her energy had seemed to evaporate with the last customer. Jose wondered if she'd fall asleep in her clothes.

"I'll take you now," he said, helping her off her perch. "I can start early in the morning."

In the car he hesitated before saying he was worried about how hard she was working. "My dear niece," he said, "you're losing weight again."

She shook her head. "I need to do this, Uncle Jose," she said. "I'm just not as smart as Doris, and I want to show her that I can work hard."

Jose put the car in gear and delivered her home to her sleeping parents.

In early September, Doris resigned her job at the bakery and packed her few belongings for the move to Montara. John agreed to pick her up, and she bought him a whole devil's food cake for his trouble. She presented it to him after he loaded her bags in the back of the truck.

"I see," he said as he peered into the pink box, "that you had the wisdom to have it cut into manageable wedges."

"I can't stand to see a man frustrated," she winked.

He left the tailgate down and motioned for her to take a seat beside him. "I've worked up an appetite driving here. I could use a snack." He gave her the first slice, then took one for himself.

Doris watched him lick the frosting from his lips. He saw the look she gave him and felt the blood rise in his neck. He coughed and changed the subject.

"Tilly's done a hell of a lot of work on your cottage," he said. "I just wish you could have seen it before she started." He poured her a cup of coffee from his thermos and consumed a second piece of cake as they had a good laugh about the morning Doris set out to walk to the coast.

• • •

"Helen, I don't understand what's getting into you," Paul said. He leaned against the frame of their bedroom door. "What's going on?" His wife had been irritable before, but lately he noticed that Tilly was avoiding her. Helen seemed to be under a tremendous amount of stress, and he couldn't understand what was at the root of it. She sat at her dressing table nearly tearing her hair out with her brush.

"What don't you understand? They've hired John Callen to expand the dining room at the roadhouse. You know those plans that Jose's had—to add more view tables? Well, he's decided that now's the time to do it. So when John's done with the candle factory in October, he'll go straight over to the roadhouse and start working on the dining room. He was supposed to be going to school on the G.I. bill, but Jose, being the wonderful and generous Jose, has given him a great contract to make some more money before he becomes a student."

"What I don't understand is why you're so passionate about this," Paul said. He folded his lanky frame into a side chair and leaned back as if to show detachment, impartiality.

"You don't understand what I'm passionate about?" Helen caught his eye through the mirror, before turning to face him. "How about Tilly's future? Is that worth being passionate about? John is seeing Tilly. The longer this goes on, the more serious they'll get. Jose's just signed him up for another six months." She turned back toward the mirror and slammed the brush down on the dressing table.

"I like John. I think he's a fine young man," Paul said. "I don't know what will happen between him and Tilly, but if he's her choice, I'll support her in that. I know you're trying to get Tilly to go out with the new sheriff, but honestly Helen, I don't think she's at all interested."

Helen turned sharply. "Can you imagine having the Callens for in-laws? Is that what you want?" Paul leaned forward and shook his head, which Helen mistook for agreement until he spoke.

"What I want," he said, "is for Tilly to make her own decisions, and so far, I think she's done a damn good job. Look at what she did with the cottage. Did you see how hard she worked, for months, because she felt she needed to do more for the partnership?" Paul stood. "Did you ever offer to give her a hand? Since she's been back from Richmond, you haven't supported her in anything she's wanted to do."

"That's not true," Helen said. "I wanted her to get a house of her own. I encouraged her to get a house of her own."

"You wanted her to spend her savings on a house instead of going into business. Hell, you didn't support her in working for the war effort, but you had plans for her savings when she returned." Paul paced the room. "You're not just at odds with Tilly, you're at odds with all of us." Helen said nothing, but sat staring at her brush. Paul shook his head and left.

Helen Bettencourt put her head in her hands and sobbed.

• • •

Tilly was on the porch swing Ida and Jose had delivered as a housewarming present when the truck pulled up, and she charged across the front yard to hug Doris. She'd clocked over four hundred hours in the cottage; John and Paul had worked with her on weekends. It was a real home.

"It's even nicer than I imagined," Doris said, and gave her partner a hug. Tilly was happier than she'd been since coming home. With Doris as her roommate, it would be like living in the Land of C all over again. She lifted Doris at the waist and carried her one step over the threshold.

John looked on and smiled. Then he carried Doris' luggage inside.

Doris wasted no time assuming the lead for the Bluegate Partnership. She insisted that Tilly take a break. "You've really had three jobs," she said, "construction manager, handywoman and waitress. I think I can manage." John was waiting in the wings, eager to help her enjoy some of that free time. With the factory built, he was ready for a little rest and relaxation with his girl.

CHAPTER 17

THE CANDLE factory was deemed complete with the final inspection. Fire Chief Eastman accompanied the county building official on the tour. John stood by with a notebook in hand, ready to record any changes needed before approval. Doris and Tilly watched, but they weren't consulted. The officials directed their comments to John.

A compact structure, the factory was sixteen hundred square feet total, comprised of a workshop, storage and loading areas, and retail and office space. It was single story, stoutly built and very well ventilated, with ample natural light. Tilly recalled the first stakes the surveyor had driven six months earlier, delineating the driveway. She wanted to remember every conversation, every decision she'd been a part of in those exciting days. She hoped she'd enjoy working in the factory as much as she'd enjoyed working on it.

Chief Eastman gave the project high marks. He wrote:

"I'm more than satisfied that the owners and builder have done as much as possible to fireproof the building, and I must say that I am impressed. They've greatly minimized the

potential for fire with the design and equipment selection. I'd say the factory is safe, short of serious accident or arson."

Tilly and Doris were cleared to start working as candle makers. They stood respectfully until the chief drove off, then ran shrieking down to the beach and splashed and ran and laughed until they were soaked and exhausted.

John was hoping Tilly would be up for a nice relaxing dinner. He had something special in mind—to celebrate. But Tilly and Doris were like kids on Christmas day, eager to play with their new toys. In a way, he envied their enthusiasm. He knew few people so happy to get to work.

"What should we try first?" Doris said.

"Pumpkins." Tilly held the metal forms. "Aunt Ida has ordered them for the roadhouse."

"It's a two-color pour," Doris said, "but we have to try it sometime." She took a section with four pumpkin molds from the larger tray. "We'll start with just a few, until we figure it out."

She went through the steps she'd read and memorized, checking that the molds were clean, then applied an aerosol releasing agent. She cut wicks to a length that would clear the wax, with enough extra to trim after the candles hardened. The top of the pumpkin mold was the bottom of the pumpkin, which simplified color separation. The candle would have a green-brown stem and an orange body.

Doris consulted the manuals again and again as they proceeded, oblivious to time.

Tilly watched her mix dyes to get the stem color and worried that it would fade when the candle solidified. "Fortunately," she said, "the raw materials are cheap." Doris poured the liquid wax into the mold, gently, to keep air bubbles from forming. She wanted to hold the stem color strictly to that portion of the assembly.

When they were satisfied that the green stem was sufficiently cooled, Tilly took a turn, melting and dying orange wax for the pumpkin bodies. She stirred carefully with a wooden paddle, thinking of the care her aunt took in preparing silky custard. Though the sun was low, they kept working.

The molds were hung on a special Ferris-wheel-like rack that kept them level as they circulated through the water in the cooling tank. Timing was critical. They were working with machines Doris had researched thoroughly; nevertheless, it would take many days of trial and error before they were comfortable with them. Tilly thought back to the day the equipment arrived from Kansas City on an International flatbed—a good omen, Doris had told her, since she'd first come to the coast in an International pickup. To this Tilly simply responded, "I arrived by stork."

Doris recorded the time, temperature of the water, room temperature and weather, while Tilly looked on. A few minutes passed and Doris checked her watch again. "Okay," she said. "Let's try one and see if it's a keeper."

Tilly loosened the fasteners that held the two halves of the hollow metal pumpkin together, removed an orange wax globe, and set it on the workbench. They stared as it slumped before their eyes, like an unbaked cake. Their smiles turned into straight lines.

"Too soon," Tilly said.

"Yeah, its core is still soft." Doris made another note.

"It's got pumpkin creep up the stem." Tilly pointed to the green wax stem that had shrunk after the first pour. The orange for the pumpkin body had filled the void, so the color break was not where nature intended.

"They'll all be like that," Doris said. "I wonder if we can dip the stems into green or brown wax and fix the color mistake by adding another layer?" She was pulling a double boiler off the shelf as she spoke.

"We could make them more textured that way—really unique," Tilly said.

"Somehow I don't think we're going to have a problem distinguishing ourselves from the competition," Doris said.

They looked at their squat, discolored creation and laughed.

Tilly rolled up her sleeves and prepared to start over. She flexed her left arm and showed her bicep. "We can do this," she said. They *were* doing it. They were candle makers.

They would always remember the walk to the roadhouse just after dawn, to see if Ida was up early, baking pies. The cool, moist air revived them and they took turns carrying the box that contained their precious delivery.

"Compliments of the Bluegate Candle Factory," Doris said.

"We've been at this since three yesterday afternoon—fifteen hours." Tilly was leaning against the doorframe. "But we did it."

"And we wanted you to have our first run—a very limited run," Doris said.

"Very limited." Tilly broke into a contagious giggling fit.

"They're beautiful." Ida picked one up in each hand. "They have a special hand-crafted quality." Both young women had a good belly laugh.

"Punchdrunk," Tilly explained.

"I can't wait to show Jose," Ida said. Though she begged them to stay for coffee and apple pie, Tilly and Doris said that what they really needed was sleep.

They walked home arm in arm along the Great Beach, noticing the pastel colors of the dawn sky, the texture of the sand and how foam formed on waves. They were considering how they might reproduce all of these things in wax, when Doris mentioned Sylvia. "I wonder if she'd come and visit?" she said. "Reno's not that far away. I bet she'd love to see the factory. It would be just like the old days."

Tilly felt a knot in her stomach and immediately changed the subject. "And your mother," she said. "I really want to meet her."

Doris took the bait and called home as soon as she got back to the cottage. Her mother was enthusiastic.

"I've read that passenger rail service is getting back to normal," Joan said, "and I'd love to get a break from the snow and ice."

"You're going to love this place," Doris said. "You might see whales migrating. They go to Mexico to calf."

"You bet, honey, count me in," Joan said. "White Christmases are overrated."

Doris knew that mastering the craft would take years, but she had a plan for learning all the standard techniques. She wanted to build enough inventory to open the shop by Christmas and worked very long days. Tilly worked beside her. They melted and experimented with hundreds of pounds of wax.

It was two weeks before Tilly stopped by the roadhouse for a visit after work. Her aunt had placed a sheaf of wheat and dried flowers on the door. She'd put gourds on the tables with their first-run pumpkin candles, which Ida had proclaimed too beautiful to light.

"But they're candles, Aunt Ida. How can we stay in business if no one burns our candles?" Tilly said.

Her father was at the bar and Tilly pulled up a stool. "I thought I saw a familiar truck out front," she said and gave him a hug. His smile was subdued.

"How's business, Tilly?" he asked.

"Let's say it's keeping up with production," she said, "and we need to get a whole lot better at production. We're working on building up inventory."

Paul looked around the room and winked at Jose. "Looks like you have a happy customer here."

"The Marine View is our favorite account. Oh, and I have news: Doris' mother is coming to visit."

Jose poured Tilly a ginger ale on the rocks and put a cherry in it. He set it in front of her on a cocktail napkin.

"In that case, we must celebrate," he said. "This will be a very special Christmas, and we must have a very special Christmas dinner."

"Dad, I told Doris her mom could stay at the cottage and have my room over Christmas," Tilly said. "It's okay if I move back in with you and mom for a couple of weeks, isn't it?"

Paul shot a glance at Jose, who looked at the bar. He took a deep breath and turned to his daughter.

"Honey, I think there's something you should know. Your mother and I have been having some tough times. I've been sleeping in your old room since you moved out."

Tilly stared, stunned. Paul took her hand and told her it was normal to hit rough patches in a marriage. "All couples have their ups and downs," he said. "Don't you worry about us. You have a business to run."

She didn't go home when she left the roadhouse; she went back to work. It was the old malaise that she'd felt since Kaiser. She was learning to be a businesswoman;—it was more than she'd hoped for. But life felt so unsettled. Restlessly, she uncrated a box of Christmas decorations she'd collected for the shop. She would stay and decorate and surprise Doris. She heard the rain on the roof.

The Tilly Mark saw hanging a garland in the shop window was thinner than he remembered; less girl, more woman. She'd gone from very pretty to gorgeous. He watched her for some minutes. In the twilight of the December late afternoon, she appeared from the outside an actress on stage.

His mother had told him she'd bought holiday candles at the shop, and he had to see it for himself. This was the woman he had expected to marry, still wanted to, but she'd done this instead. He was at once proud and heartbroken. Deep down he knew she wouldn't spend Christmas with him, or follow him back to Los Angeles.

It started to rain. He couldn't imagine a reunion, after five years, sopping wet; he'd have to go in now.

How would he look to her? After Germany, he had returned to Los Angeles for college and would go on to dental school if his academic success continued. He'd gone with lots of girls, but he wanted Tilly. His mother said she had a boyfriend who was a carpenter. He was going to be a dentist.

The bells on the door jingled when he turned the knob. He could smell the pine. He removed his hat. "Merry Christmas, Tilly."

She was standing on a chair with a garland in both hands, looking down at him with what he took to be a look of surprise and not much else. "Hello, Mark," she said.

"You've cut your hair." He regretted saying it as soon as he heard the words. He recovered quickly with, "You look great."

His worst fear was that she'd ask if he'd come to buy candles. She didn't. She didn't say anything, just stayed on the chair.

"I'm home to visit my mother," he said. He heard her say that was nice; he didn't hear her say it was good to see him. He looked at his hat. "Congratulations on the business," he said. And then, when making small talk became too painful, he left the shop. The rain was falling hard.

• • •

Two hundred fifty miles east, Reno was digging out of a snowstorm; the day was still blustery.

Sylvia watched Ellen get out of bed and sort through the clothing on the floor. She shook her garter belt and stockings from inside the half-slip and stretched the elastic as she inserted one long, lean leg and then another, pulling the belt around her narrow hips. Behind her, the frost on the windows provided privacy. Her hair was dark and long, but not as luxurious as Tilly's. Ellen had been a disappointment, but Sylvia would stay with her through the holidays. How she hated to be alone at Christmas.

Sylvia had first seen Ellen in a club lit largely by candles, where she'd had a few martinis and was feeling sorry for herself. It had been thirty days since she'd posted her last letter to Tilly. There'd been no reply, and she was sure there'd never be one. She regretted the day she mailed it.

Sylvia told herself she had to try and reach out, that it was the right thing to do. She was sure Tilly was a lesbian and unaware that there were others like her. Sylvia had thought Tilly would be relieved and respond quickly. Instead, she received a chatty letter from Doris, describing how she and Tilly had gone into business together. She needed to write back.

Ellen kissed her on the mouth and closed the door quietly. Sylvia felt heavy and couldn't manage the energy to get out of bed. Perhaps she needed to take that road trip, in the spring, to see the candle factory.

Ida saw the "*Welcome Joan Jura*" banner Tilly had strung above the door to the shop and turned into the driveway.

"Is she here yet?" she asked.

"The train's late," Tilly said, "it's been snowing in the mountains."

Ida gave Tilly a hug. She said she liked the holiday decorations, especially the tree, which was decorated with Bluegate candles. "Look at all of these," she said, "even more beautiful than your pumpkins."

"Joan is Bluegate's first important visitor," Tilly said. She showed her aunt the seasonal displays and their best-selling item, bells cast in red and green.

"Thanks again for the room," Tilly said. "I don't like it that I'm displacing paying customers."

"We want Doris' mother to feel at home," Ida said, "and we want everyone to have the best possible Christmas—that's what's important to Jose and me." She leaned against the display table.

Tilly was happy to have a few minutes alone with her aunt. She pulled a chair from the office. They saw each other almost daily, but never really talked. She wondered if Ida would answer questions her mother refused to. She was most curious about Judge Callen.

"What do you think will happen with my parents?" she said.

"I won't take sides," Ida said, "though I want to support my sister in whatever she's going through."

"It's hardest on my dad, I think," Tilly said. She told her aunt that she'd walked in on one of their conversations; Paul was trying to tell Helen that she was distancing herself from the whole family. "She wouldn't respond," Tilly said. She held the bundle she was wrapping up, and Ida put her finger on the ribbon to hold it, while Tilly tightened the bow. Satisfied that the welcome gift was ready, Tilly hopped up on the counter and sat with her legs dangling.

"I've been meaning to ask you," Tilly said, "because my mother—well it's hard to explain—but did something happen between my mother and Judge Callen?"

"He used to come to the roadhouse regularly during prohibition," Ida said, "so I'm sure they've met. But your mother was your age then, and he was in his forties. They didn't really know each other."

"Do you think he's corrupt?" Tilly asked.

"There isn't anyone on the coast that wanted a different judge when the railroad went under," Ida said. "The real villains were the railroad barons. The Board of Directors of the Ocean Shore was selling snake oil. They convinced us to buy land out here—from them—then they couldn't keep the trains running so people could get to it. They expected us to make our payments, but it was near impossible to make a living. And it took years to settle the claims."

"She says that John's family has done bad things," Tilly said, "that his grandfather is one of the most notorious men in San Mateo County." Tilly couldn't tell if her mother knew

Judge Callen or if she just knew of him, but she'd never known Helen to feel so strongly about anyone.

Ida shrugged, "Robert Callen is a friend. When the railroad failed, those of us who invested found ourselves isolated. Both roads, to San Francisco and San Mateo, were dirt tracks, then."

"Even I can remember when they paved the road," Tilly said. "There was a bankruptcy proceeding and a land sale," Ida said, "which is likely how Stanley got his property, and the Judge crafted some creative deals. Your father was an employee of the Ocean Shore and to the extent that he got anything from the settlement, Judge Callen is responsible. But I guess you know that."

Tilly nodded. "I also know about the bootlegging."

"Yes, the bootlegging. And of course, Judge Callen loved good Irish whiskey."

"I've heard John telling tales," Tilly said. "The old Carry-Callen feuds went on for decades."

"I know less about that," Ida said. "The first Sheriff Carry never came over to this side of the hill," she laughed, "which is why we saw so much of the Judge." Ida smiled to herself and then looked up at her niece. "It all happened so long ago. Your whole lifetime ago."

The bells on the door jingled, and a young family of three, entered the shop. "Well, I'm keeping you from your work." Ida said. She pushed the chair toward the office.

"Let me do that," Tilly said.

Ida stood back and looked at her. "It will be all right. Everything will be okay."

When her customers left the store and she was alone again, Tilly thought about John and dinner the night before. After they'd left the restaurant, they parked at Rockaway Beach under the nearly full moon to listen to the waves break. She told him that it surprised her that after a lifetime on the coast, she still found the sound of the ocean compelling. And then he let her know how compelling he found her. She played along because she knew that other women would, but her mind, and clearly her heart, were elsewhere. She pretended she was with her leading man on the big screen and tried to make the right sounds and expressions while waiting for the moment to pass.

CHAPTER 18

December 24, 1946

TILLY LIKED JOAN from the first introduction. She was delighted when Joan wanted to prepare Christmas dinner at the cottage with her help. Joan told Ida that she couldn't bring anything, not even dessert.

"At least once a year you should sit down to a meal you didn't cook yourself," she said.

Paul helped rearrange the furniture so everyone could eat together at one table, and Jose mixed some creative libations that added much to the festivities. Everyone laughed late into the night.

Tilly was fascinated by Joan and wanted to know all about her job making ketchup and pickles before the war. Mostly she was amazed that a woman widowed young could do such a great job without remarrying. That wasn't supposed to be possible. If you were widowed, you tried to find another husband.

Tilly looked at Helen. Her mother worked too, but only as an extra during the busiest times, and she wasn't the breadwinner. She worked with family. Helen never had to figure out how to get along with strangers. Her mother was constantly surrounded by people who knew everything there was to know about her and could complete her sentences. Tilly wondered how long she would be able to stay in her hometown.

Four days after Christmas, Joan went for her morning walk on the beach, a routine she'd immediately settled into, leaving Doris and Tilly to their morning coffee. As she brushed her hair at her dressing table, Doris sighed. "It's hard to let my mom go," she said. "The time's gone by too quickly, and I don't know when I'll see her again. She's all the family I have."

"If the business does well enough we'll need to hire," Tilly said. "I bet she'd come west if we said we needed her."

Doris turned and smiled. Tilly hoped they could provide for Joan; she wanted Doris to be happy. She had an aunt and uncles who supported her; Doris only had her mother. She remembered how angry Doris would get, during the war, when letters to the editor suggested that working women mothered juvenile delinquents.

"We can't let her go without a sendoff," Tilly said, "and we can't just sit around on New Years Eve."

"Mom loves to boogie," Doris said.

"Then we should take her to Nick's at Rockaway Beach," Tilly said. They planned an outing they thought Joan would enjoy, and Tilly left for her parent's house.

Paul didn't sign up immediately. He'd been looking forward to a nice, quiet evening. He stood in the kitchen, munching a leftover Christmas-ham sandwich while Tilly did her best to recruit him.

"Come on, Dad," she said, "Mom's working and you'll just sit at the bar all night."

He opened a bottle of root beer. The foam spilled over the lip and ran down the side.

"We need another man in our group," she said. "John's going to have to dance with three women."

"Honey, there'll be lots of guys to dance with." He put the mustard in the refrigerator.

"I don't want Doris' mom to be sitting alone," Tilly said. "It's her last night here."

Paul wiped his mouth and looked at his lovely daughter framed in the doorway, knitted cap in hand and hair uncombed. How lucky he was to be included in her New Year's Eve plans, he thought, even if only to keep Joan company. "I'll go for awhile," he said, "but I can't stay late, so John will have to drive all of you home. Can four of you fit in his truck?"

Their New Year's dinner reservation was for eight o'clock, and they arrived right on time. Joan walked around the building, effusive about how close to the water they were. "Look at this view," she said. "The waves are so close they might break over the building!"

Hank Scaroni noticed Doris the moment she walked through the door, and he noticed that she didn't have a date. He'd gone to the bar early to secure a seat with a clear view of the entry. He elbowed his friend on the next barstool.

"Well I'll be. You called it right, Hank my boy," Fred said. "Looks like you may have a fine end to the year after all."

For months, Hank had tried to find a way to spend a little time with Doris without actually asking her out, a move he considered too risky. He bought too many Christmas candles from Tilly, disappointed that Doris wasn't in the shop. Always awkward around women he found attractive, Hank was absolutely inept with Doris because he feared she'd still be angry he'd forgotten to pick her up in San Mateo on her first visit to the coast. Tilly had been furious.

"What would she have done if John hadn't come along?" she'd said.

Hank looked at John, now a part of their happy group. He'd been so stupid, and yet he never sensed hostility from Doris. Was it possible that she didn't know he was *that* Hank?

After the break, the musicians made their way to the stage, squeezing past the excessive decoration. Silver and gold balloons hung in nets above the dance floor for the midnight drop. The set opened with a Count Basie number, "Blue Skies." A cocktail waitress balanced a flute of champagne on a tray and placed it on the white linen in front of Doris.

"You have an admirer in the house," she said. "He said to leave a slot in your dance card."

“This is so exciting,” Tilly said.

Doris blushed from her neck to her eyebrows. Her mother said she couldn’t wait to meet the mysterious stranger.

They placed their drink orders and turned their attention to the stage.

“It’s a shame to be wasting great music on the dinner hour,” Joan said. “The band’s terrific.”

“Let’s dance, Mom,” Doris said as she slid out of her chair. “Why do we have to waste it?”

“Why yes, you may have this dance,” Joan said. She took Doris’ hand.

They were alone on the floor. Joan led, as she had when Doris was a little girl and crazy to learn. They wore new party dresses in nearly the same size, dresses they’d bought in San Francisco the day after Christmas. Doris was in green, Joan in red.

Heads turned as the mother-daughter team waltzed on the worn maple; the bandleader smiled and an older man at the next table uttered the word “delightful.”

Hank watched too, and as he did, ordered another round. “Just to get loosened up,” he told Fred. “I don’t do that much dancing.”

The salad course came, too quickly followed by the steaks, a detail Tilly was quick to point out. “This would never happen at the roadhouse,” she said as they moved their salad plates to the side.

“Dancing on the table would never happen at the roadhouse,” John said.

The bar was getting crowded. Hank loosened his tie.

"You're not going to be able to ask her to dance if you don't slow down," Fred said. "Maybe we should get some food in you."

Hank shook his head. He knew tonight wouldn't be the night. He was beginning to see two Dorises. It was that dancing that put him off; he just wasn't a dancer. "I'll literally start off on the wrong foot," he said.

Fred sighed and asked the bartender for a glass of water.

Dinner service was cleared by ten, and the band went into its third-set pace with "Boogie Woogie Bugle Boy." The floor filled with the couples who frequented postwar parties, serious dancers trying to make up for the lost years. John took Tilly's hand and they carved a space for themselves, moving like a wooden girl and boy in a room full of real children. Tilly accidentally kicked a woman wearing midnight blue satin.

"I'm a failure as a father," Paul said as he watched his daughter try to follow. "This is painful."

"We always danced at home." Doris winked at her mother. "Mom was a pro."

"I used to love it," Paul said. "But I haven't been out in years."

Doris and Joan looked at each other and smiled.

From the corner of her eye, Tilly caught a flash of color as the crowd parted and made room for a couple of real dancers. It was Joan's red cocktail dress. Joan was dancing, really cutting the rug, with her dad.

"Wow," Tilly said. "This is something special." She and John stepped back and just watched, and Tilly considered how her father often surprised her when he was away from his daily routine. She thought back to the morning he drove her to Richmond. He'd once had a life beyond the confines of Montara. She'd never asked him if he was happy.

"Hank, Hank buddy." Fred tried to rouse his friend from the barstool. He got him to a lounge chair and let him sink into the soft leather until his head rested on top of the back cushion. The party was heating up and Hank was out cold; Fred hoped he wouldn't snore. Once again, Hank had failed to pace himself.

Doris sat alone, watching her mother. Fred could see why Hank was so smitten. She was small but perfectly proportioned, cute. Not many guys would call strawberry blonds their type, but on her it was special. He crossed the room and held out his hand. "My name's Fred, I think we met one night at the roadhouse."

"Did you send me that flute of champagne?" Doris said.

"That was my friend Hank," Fred said. "He's, well, he's a bit under the weather, but if you don't mind, I can fill in for him."

Doris shrugged. "That's fine with me. Do you dance?"

He pulled her out of her chair and bounced her off his left hip. "I've always wanted a partner your size," he said.

John nudged Tilly when he caught a glimpse of Doris airborne. He shook his head. "Is there anything she can't do well?" he asked.

"I haven't found it yet," Tilly said.

• • •

Tilly listened as Doris explained that to be really successful in the new year, they'd need more than tourist and holiday sales; they'd need ongoing, repeat customers.

"But we've only been in business for one quarter," Tilly said. "Shouldn't we give it more time?"

"We need to market ourselves," Doris said. Then she told Tilly that they should try to land the San Francisco Dioceses as a customer. "There's nothing to those sacramental candles, they're just white columns—not even tapers."

"They need to be blessed," Tilly said.

"They can do that themselves," Doris said. "It's not like the Pope has to do it."

"What about the designs, you know, the symbols?"

"Applied after the candle is made," Doris said. "I went into the church yesterday afternoon when no one was around."

It wasn't hard for Tilly to imagine Doris climbing up on the altar to inspect the sacramental candles. She was at once proud and horrified.

"So you want me to go to San Francisco and talk to the Bishop?"

"You're Catholic," Doris said. "I think it's best if you go. And it's probably not the Bishop himself. It's probably someone a few rungs down the ladder."

"Maybe the Bishop has a secretary," Tilly said. "I could talk to the secretary."

"We don't want all the churches," Doris said, "just the ones in this county."

CHAPTER 19

January 15, 1947

SYLVIA BELIEVED that she was being practical as she packed her '39 Olds in the frigid morning wind. Work was always slow after the holidays, and those who still went out usually tipped less. Valentine's Day would be worthwhile, but for the most part, the next two months would be a drought. Reno would have to manage without her.

She looked across the clear, cold morning and hoped the high-pressure system would hold until she crossed the mountains. The course she charted took her past Donner Lake, through Sacramento and Oakland, and across the Bay Bridge to San Francisco. Tilly had talked about driving across the bay with her father on her first trip to Kaiser, and Sylvia thought a stop at Treasure Island might be in order. She would spend a day in the city before taking the Coast Highway south. Only Doris knew she was coming.

Sylvia had ended the affair with Ellen and tried to convince herself that things were improving. For the first time, she was leaving a woman before the woman left her for a man.

Perhaps it was a hopeful sign. She found she was now specifically attracted to tall, lean brunettes.

Sylvia needed to see Tilly again—to be sure. She needed to get over her. She'd spent little of her Kaiser savings and had worked constantly in Reno. She deserved and could afford a vacation.

It had been Doris' idea to make the visit a surprise. Sylvia could tell from their conversation that Tilly had said nothing about her letters. Why would Tilly talk to Doris about "sisterly love?" Doris seemed oblivious to any tension between them and chatted on about how great Tilly was doing and how handsome John was. Doris described the prank she wanted to play on Tilly, and Sylvia said she was game.

She locked the door to her flat and made a stop at the post office to have her mail held, then started her long drive with the morning sun to her back. She decided to spend a night in Sacramento, have a look at the state capitol and walk along the river. The river reminded her of Missouri.

The next day, she drove through acres of almonds and other crops in irrigated fields. She didn't detour to Richmond to see the shipyard again, though she considered it. She thought she'd save that stop for the return trip. She'd had a fantasy about buying Airstream No. 28 and using it for its intended purpose—travel. Maybe it was possible.

She reached San Francisco on schedule and had Italian, her favorite, in North Beach. She walked down Polk Street and found the bar she'd heard about—mostly a girls' place—and a young redhead approached her, but she wasn't feeling sociable. She had to admit that she liked Frisco.

She called Doris with her E.T.A.—estimated time of arrival. "I'll be there if I can drag myself from this fabulous city," Sylvia said.

"Wait until you get here," Doris said. "Remember how Tilly used to talk about her aunt and uncle's roadhouse? An astonishingly beautiful cove—this whole stretch of coast, really."

And it was. Sylvia already knew the California winter was to her liking and as she drove the Coast Highway, she tried to remember why she'd gone to Reno after she left Kaiser. As she logged the final miles through Pacifica and Devil's Slide, then on to Montara, she had to admit that at the end of the war she'd simply felt too old to make any real life changes. Working for tips in Reno was more of the same.

At thirty-seven, Sylvia had become the spinster aunt whose only nephew had been killed in combat. She drank too much. She had some money put away but had no real plans to use it, save for doctor's bills in her later years. Losing the best job she'd ever had was harder than she'd thought it would be. Hadn't they always known that returning soldiers would replace them? Still, it was difficult. Doris had made a business plan. Sylvia had no plans. She didn't know what she had to look forward to, except somehow finding a woman to fall in love with. It was too late for her to pretend she might be able to live with a man.

She had to concede that it was good that Tilly had John. Perhaps Tilly would be able to have the family that Sylvia, in her stubbornness, had rejected. Sylvia hoped she'd see Tilly with her boyfriend and be happy for them, then be able to move on.

Doris' directions to the cottage were easy to follow, and Sylvia arrived early. Afraid that she might run into Tilly, she spent her time alone at the beach, growing envious that her friends inhabited a cottage just five hundred feet from the bluffs. The sound of the surf would surely be audible from their home.

She pulled into the driveway at two-thirty and Doris ran out to greet her. The women embraced and laughed and told each other how good they looked. Then Doris hid Sylvia's bags under her bed, and Sylvia tasted the spaghetti sauce simmering on the stove.

"You're right," Sylvia said. "It's not as good as mine." Doris poured red wine as Sylvia minced some extra garlic. "The secret," she said, "is to build the flavors in layers. The garlic you add in the beginning will mellow from all the simmering. You want to brighten it up at the end with some fresh stuff." At that moment, Sylvia thought it might be a metaphor for life. "I really miss Kaiser," she said.

As Doris watched Sylvia, a fellow midwesterner, she considered how lucky she was. She and Tilly were in business for themselves, and they were beginning to turn a profit. They lived in a wonderful place. Their home was tiny, but comfortable. If she never had more, it would be okay. As she listened to Sylvia's stories from the Nevada desert, she thought about the other fine women she'd met in Richmond and wondered what they were doing. "I know I'm lucky to be here and in business," Doris said.

"You've worked very hard," Sylvia said. "You've made your luck."

They set three places at the white, wooden table. In half an hour, John would pick Tilly up at the factory, while Sylvia hid in Doris' room. After Tilly had a chance to taste a few bites of the spaghetti, Doris would ask her if the sauce was as good as Sylvia's and that would be Sylvia's cue.

Tilly had a line of pink cupids on the workbench. She was trimming wax from the seams of their backs as John watched. He said they reminded him of Roman legions, and Tilly said she had no idea what he was talking about. Something about the little pink cherubs with arrows lined up on the bench struck John as funny. Tilly carefully boxed them, and John suggested they head to the cottage for dinner.

"Doris said she was cooking something special," he said.

"Maybe she got a new account," Tilly said. "She said she was meeting someone important this afternoon."

John opened the truck door for her.

With Sylvia parked around the corner, nothing seemed out of the ordinary when John and Tilly pulled into the driveway. Doris was shaking water from the spaghetti steaming in the colander as they walked through the door.

"Smells great," Tilly said.

They took their seats around the table, and if anyone noticed how little Chianti was left in the bottle, it wasn't mentioned. Doris opened a second bottle and poured all around.

Then she ladled the thick meat sauce over their pasta and passed the grated cheese.

"So how did your meeting go?" Tilly asked.

With a wave of her hand, Doris indicated that her mouth was too full, and John said the sauce was really delicious. Tilly agreed, and Doris asked, "But is it as good as Sylvia's?" And then Sylvia appeared in the doorway and said, "Well, is it?"

Tilly had just twirled a big forkful of spaghetti and had bitten off most of it. She started to cough. John rubbed her back; Doris poured water. Sylvia stood frozen with a half smile on her face. Then her gaze went to the Chianti, and she quickly refilled her glass.

When Tilly caught her breath, "What are you doing here?" were her first words.

There was a fat moment of silence before a perplexed Doris regained her composure and said, "Why, Sylvia's teaching me to make spaghetti sauce."

• • •

Tilly pulled off her shoes and collapsed on top of the down comforter. Somehow she'd made it through the evening. She'd called her Aunt Ida and had asked if there was a vacant room, and thankfully there'd been a cancellation. So she insisted that Sylvia take her bed, and John delivered her to the roadhouse. Now that she was alone and the door was bolted behind her, she let go and cried. Everything was wrong.

She knew Doris would never have staged the "surprise" if she'd had any idea what was coursing through her emotionally; she would never have withheld word of Sylvia's pending visit. But Doris had no way of knowing. When they'd had their farewell dinner in Sylvia's Airstream, they'd called each other "sister."

As Tilly looked back on the evening, she could hardly believe that "What are you doing here?" were her first words to Sylvia. How could she have been so cold? Sylvia tried to make light of it, said something about wishing she'd had her hair done, that she'd been breaking cameras all week, but the awkwardness of the moment was not trumped by levity. Tilly recalled Doris' look of alarm—she just couldn't imagine what was wrong.

Thank heaven for John. He was able to make small talk about Sylvia's trip and eventually, well into the second bottle of red wine, the group settled into a comfortable banter. Sylvia said she was going to Kaiser to try and buy her old Airstream, or one like it. She talked about the "road trip of a lifetime," as she called her dream to see America. Tilly looked away.

Tilly realized as she looked back on the evening that she never touched Sylvia, never hugged her, and after she started to relax, she knew how desperately she'd wanted to. Instead of showing affection toward Sylvia, she'd leaned into John. She reacted to Sylvia by sliding her hand under the table cloth, and running it along John's thigh. He was confused by the come on—it was completely out of character—but nevertheless, he seized the moment. On the way to the roadhouse he pulled the truck off the road at Bluegate Cove, and Tilly told herself that she was going to learn to enjoy sex.

The next morning Sylvia was gone. Doris found a note thanking her for the hospitality. *"You really do make a great red sauce,"* she said.

• • •

"Happy Valentine's Day, my lovely." John put the roses aside and handed Tilly a little velvet box, a perfect two-inch hinged cube. She stared head down, unable to look at him.

"Aren't you going to open it?" he said, already knowing it wouldn't matter that it was the most elegant ring he could find—that he'd gone all the way to San Francisco for it—and that he'd spent more than he should have.

"I already know it's beautiful," she said. She was crying.

Doris was in bed reading when she heard Tilly come in, brush her teeth and go to her room. It was early. She wondered if something had happened with John.

It wasn't the first Valentine's Day Doris had spent alone, though she hoped there wouldn't be too many more. Her mother was her only family and having one of her own was important. She worked so hard to take care of herself. She rolled over on her side and thought she could hear Tilly crying. She remembered Tilly's kindness on the day she learned of Stanley's death; she'd try and console her. She put ice in a glass of water and knocked softly on the door. "Is there anything I can do?" she said.

"Come in," Tilly said. She was still dressed, on top of the blankets, shoes near the bed where they fell. Doris handed her the glass, then sat in the rocking chair opposite. "John proposed," Tilly said.

Doris felt the muscles in her abdomen contract and hoped that Tilly didn't notice her wince. She was sure she hadn't. Tilly was wiping her eyes.

"Are those tears of joy?" Doris asked, immediately regretting that she'd said anything.

"No," Tilly said. "I've never felt worse. I feel responsible for his happiness, his future. But I couldn't say yes."

Doris felt a flutter of hope then.

"I know it sounds crazy," Tilly said, "but I'm not sure I want to marry anyone." She didn't say that she wasn't attracted to men—she couldn't say that. "I love my father and uncles, but not my aunt and mother's lives." She sat in the bed with her shoulders against the backboard and stared out the window at the moonless night. "I know you will marry and leave this cottage one day and I will be left alone," Tilly said. "And maybe then I will regret turning down such a kind and capable man."

Doris thought, kind, capable, handsome and sexy. In all her interactions with Tilly and John, she thought that Tilly treated him like a brother. Maybe Tilly saw it too. Maybe there was still a chance.

She'd had two dates since New Years Eve, but really didn't feel like she had much in common with Fred. And supposedly his best friend was infatuated with her, but she'd never had a conversation with him. She thought it strange. Maybe that's how it was in a very small town. She wondered if she was making a mistake, building a business in such an isolated place. John, she thought, would make living in Montara a dream.

• • •

When Doris suggested they take sample candles to shops and restaurants "over the hill," Tilly volunteered. She'd been looking for an excuse to visit the main county library, in Redwood City; she needed to conduct her research in secret. In Redwood City, she could remain anonymous. Everyone would know her in Half Moon Bay.

She was at once anticipating and dreading the trip. She needed more information about her "condition." Surely there was a remedy, some sort of fix for what ailed her. Surely women didn't go through life longing for other women. She was preoccupied with these thoughts as she walked to the nursery to borrow her father's truck.

"Be safe," he said as he handed her the keys. Tilly failed to understand why he worried so much about her driving.

She turned south to Half Moon Bay, where she picked up the tortuous but now familiar road through the redwoods and over the Coast Mountains. A logging truck nearly sideswiped her on a tight curve near Pilarcitos Creek, and she was jarred from her thoughts. She was continuously replaying John's proposal in her head. He'd taken her to the lighthouse after dinner and pointed across the cove to the roadhouse drive, where they met on the day he delivered Doris to the coast. He said he'd been infatuated with her from the first moment he set eyes on her and then, as he got to know her, fell completely in love. He said that nothing would give him greater happiness than having her as his bride. He called her his lovely, as he always did, and handed her the velvet box. And at that moment, when any normal woman would have cried for joy, she cried for Sylvia.

She wasn't sure how or why she formed the words, but she heard herself tell John that she wasn't ready yet—that she and Doris had just begun and that she needed more time. And then she heard him say, "Take whatever time you need." She was sobbing then and telling him how much she appreciated everything he'd done for her. Appreciated? Did I really say that? Tilly worked to remember every detail. She couldn't recall telling him that she loved him, but he had decided that she did and had decided to wait for her.

Doris had been a good and supportive friend and tried to be a comfort, and Tilly wanted to tell her about Sylvia. But what if Doris didn't understand? Tilly didn't understand herself. What if Doris didn't want to be in business with her? Tilly would lose everything.

No, there had to be a cure for this condition. She would find the cure, and get on with her life.

The brick library building had two story arches and beautiful windows. Tilly found a private corner in the stacks, away from the reference librarian and near the psychology section, to conduct her search. She pulled several texts on abnormal psychology and checked in the indices for "*women.*" Often, women's conditions were described as "*hysteria.*" In the third volume, she came across a word she'd seen twice, but didn't understand; she turned to page two hundred and found the definition for lesbianism, "*female homosexuality—sexual orientation of women to other women.*" Her psychological disorder had a name.

Tilly researched the cures for her condition: they ranged from hormonal therapy to psychiatric analysis to electric shock treatment while looking at pictures of nude women. All were terrifying. Yet the prospect of going through an isolated life as an invert was more than she could endure. She got into the truck and aggressively pushed her sample merchandise. She would need to make enough money to pay for treatment.

CHAPTER
20

May 12, 1947

PAUL WOKE the second time the fire alarm sounded. He dressed as he ran down the stairs, pulling suspenders over his shoulders and grabbing his jacket from the hook next to the kitchen door. He heard Helen ask what was going on, but he didn't have time to answer.

"Probably only a false alarm," she said as he climbed into the cab. "Coffee'll be ready when you get back."

He had traveled less than two blocks when he smelled smoke. "No, Helen, this isn't a false alarm." He turned onto Main Street and saw dense gray clouds blowing across the beach. "My God!" He hit the brakes on the loose gravel drive and turned into the skid, stopping near the fire station's roll-up door.

The engine was manned, siren wailing. Paul pulled some gear off the rack, threw it in the truck bed and followed the rig to the fire. Chief Eastman had already established a command post.

"These are our objectives," Eastman shouted into the bullhorn. "The wax is flowing like lava. Get a team down there to trench and direct it toward the water. Paraffin burns like kerosene. Do not apply water to the paraffin fire. I repeat, no water on the west wing."

Four men, including Paul, ran to the engine and started stretching hose toward the north side as Eastman continued his instructions.

"We'll need sand to smother the wax when it burns down. George, go wake Bob Havice, he's the closest, see if you can get a tractor with a bucket down here. Finally, we'll water the lighthouse to protect it." As he lowered the bullhorn, flames shot sixty feet into the air. Paul looked up for only a second.

Tilly watched, alone. She'd had trouble sleeping, and when the alarm sounded twice, she knew something had happened. Doris had heard it too—had poked her head out of her bedroom door, but Tilly couldn't convince her to come along.

"Not me," Doris had said. "I have to be up in a few hours to box candles for an early shipment."

Tilly had sprinted the last quarter mile toward the blaze, nearly spraining an ankle, not certain what was burning. She held her breath as the fire came into view, then gasped and understood. When she got close enough, she saw her father working with the others, connecting the pumps. She'd never seen him move so fast. No one noticed her .

Chief Eastman kept the megaphone at his lips. "Watch those pumps, tide's coming in and we don't want to lose them."

Deputy Carry arrived and lit flares on the paved road to alert motorists. Tilly was only a few feet from where he tossed the fifth flare, but he didn't seem to notice her. One of the men called to his partner in a voice loud enough for Carry to hear, "You think we need more fire?"

The seawater spit as pumps pushed air through the hoses. Two volunteers guided each stream, one checking and moving the fully pressurized canvas, another directing the spray from the brass nozzle. Tilly wondered if anyone involved in fighting the fire thought any part of the building would be saved. She knew they'd spend all night trying.

A volunteer working on the east side of the factory ran up the beach to the command post. "Chief Eastman, come over here."

Eastman followed him, entered the structure and exited quickly. He ran to Deputy Carry. Tilly saw Carry jog toward the lighthouse.

Meanwhile, the flames, fanned by a steady breeze from the southwest, became multicolored—spectacular against the night sky. Tilly realized the fire had reached the stockroom and was feeding from the largest shipment of wax they'd ever received. They had purchased white paraffin to fill an order for sacramental candles.

Everyone, everything around Tilly was in motion, from the volunteers to the incoming tide to the bluff edge collapsing beneath her feet. She sat on her heels trying to steady herself.

The back-up pumper truck from El Granada arrived next, and more men stretched more canvas across the sand and pressurized more salt water, all against a consuming backdrop of smoke. The sound of steam escaping the burning building and the caustic smell of seawater on flame and hot metal reminded Tilly of the welding stations in the Kaiser Shipyard another lifetime ago. She was crying; she listened intently to the chief's commands and heard him use the word "containment." Despite the tremendous effort, their candle factory was disappearing.

The chief motioned to Paul and sent him running toward his truck. Maybe Dad's been sent to get Doris and me, she thought. She pulled herself from where she'd become rooted in the shadows and looked for a way down to the beach. She trodded carefully aware of the crumbling trail.

Chief Eastman and Deputy Carry conferred on the sidelines where half a dozen residents had gathered. Carry tilted his hat back and stroked his chin. "You're the expert on fire, but it does seem like this one might have been set. It's as if the building started burning from all four sides at once, and then there's that damn smell of gasoline."

The chief nodded. "You see any footprints?"

"There's footprints all over the place now," Carry said, "but it looks like covered tracks around the gas tank at the lighthouse generator."

"If it was gasoline, someone had to bring it in," the chief said. "They don't store fuel on site; I've inspected the factory. The other curious thing is that the hot spot is where the burners melt the paraffin, but this fire was burning just as vigorously in the office suite. Hank Scaroni pulled the alarm. I need to talk to him about what he saw."

Carry jotted "Scaroni" in his notebook.

Chief Eastman's attention was on the firefighters, particularly the volunteers closest to the building. The megaphone was barely audible over the din. "Let's pull back. Collapse imminent. Pull back now!"

The sheathing had completely burned away, exposing the post and beam skeleton. As the corrugated roof heated and expanded, nails popped from the rafters. The sound of metal on metal was eerie, especially against the crash of the surf. Tilly thought it sounded like the call of a metallic gray whale. The building's structural members, engulfed by flames, were near failure. Again, the chief called the men back; they pulled hoses from the water and stood at a safe distance to watch the final collapse. The east wall went first, and within minutes the form of the structure was indiscernible.

"Has anyone seen Tilly and Doris?" The chief turned to address the onlookers; Paul hadn't returned. Tilly stood in the shadow of the bluffs she'd descended. She'd come into earshot in time to hear Mike Carry utter the word "arson."

Paul sped over gravel streets and took a sharp left turn at the cottage. The moonlight was blocked by cypress trees and the dome light in the cab cast a faint yellow glow. He jumped over the two porch steps and struck the wooden screen door with his fist. "Tilly, Doris, wake up! Tilly, it's Dad!"

Doris was still for a moment, not comprehending, not wanting to stir from beneath the warmth of her comforter.

"Tilly, wake up, it's Dad!"

Light spilled into the hallway from the back bedroom as Doris emerged, tying a powder blue robe at the waist. She looked past Paul to the truck, with driver's door open and engine running. "Mr. Bettencourt, what's happened?"

"Wake Tilly." He rushed to Tilly's room and flipped on the switch. Her bed had been slept in and her pajamas were on the floor. "Where is she?"

"What time is it?" Doris asked. Before Paul could answer she said, "Did you hear the siren just before two o'clock? Tilly woke and wanted to see the fire."

"Doris," Paul said, "the factory's burning. Get dressed." Doris stood and stared.

Paul's voice softened. "I'm sorry, but it's bad."

The blaze consumed the factory by six o'clock; the tide had come in all the way. There was no wind or threat to the lighthouse—the closest structure—from smoldering embers. Chief Eastman released spent firefighters as morning broke over the hills, and many headed to the hotel dining room for breakfast. "I'll cooperate with the department as best I can," he told Deputy Carry, "but it'll be up to you to secure the crime scene."

The deputy nodded. This would be big. He was silently rehearsing his call to Sheriff Wick.

A rooster crowed in the distance as Tilly said good night to her father. He gave her a bear hug and held on longer than usual. He'd been on the fire crew all his adult life. Losing a building was never easy, but this time, it was personal. For his sake, to the best of her ability, Tilly held her breath and forced a smile. Paul pushed a strand of hair away from her face, nodded and turned to leave. Tilly swallowed hard and tried to remain calm, but after he pulled out of the driveway, she let herself sob. With her fist at her teeth, she backed up to the porch steps and sat down on the worn wood. The neighborhood was still again, as it had been before the fire, but with a lingering smell of smoke. In the early morning quiet, the breaking surf was audible, hypnotic, occasionally punctuated by the foghorn at Pillar Point. Her savings and livelihood were gone. She would not be able to pay for treatment. Maybe she should just marry John. This was just too hard.

Inside, Doris stared at the wall in a numb state where sleep and reasonable action were equally impossible. "One thing at a time," she said to herself. She put water in the coffee pot and sliced bread for toast.

Tilly remained fixed on the porch steps. She felt a chill that started behind her neck and traveled down her spine. She shuddered a little and hunched forward, pulling her sweater tightly around her torso. Her head dropped onto her knees. She was suddenly too tired to go to bed, too tired to move. She heard Doris' movements in the kitchen, the sounds of making coffee, pulling it together, managing. Shivering advanced to shaking. The warm tears on her face eventually chilled her further. She could smell the coffee beginning to brew. She wondered what Doris was doing and lifted her head to squint though the screen. Doris was backlit in the kitchen, toasting bread. She was actually toasting bread.

"Tilly, you want coffee?" Doris was speaking, and she needed to answer.

"No, thank you," she said.

Doris opened the door and looked out. The expression on her face gave Tilly cause to sit upright. With eyes wide, Doris sat next to her.

"It will be all right," Doris said. "No one was hurt, that's the important thing." She put her arm around Tilly's quivering shoulders. "My God, come in. You're freezing."

"They said it was arson," Tilly sobbed.

"There will be an investigation," Doris said. "No one knows what happened last night. We have insurance; we'll rebuild."

"Doris, how can you be so matter of fact? Someone's done this awful thing."

Doris ran into the kitchen and threw the oven door open. The toast was burning.

"Tilly, we don't know that and besides, what choice is there? Come in, come in, you're shivering. I'll get you a blanket."

She dealt with the toast first, trying to make a joke about having already burned enough for one night. She draped the afghan around Tilly's shoulders.

"This is my home, Doris. Do you understand? I've lived here, with these people, all my life. And now one of them has burned our business."

"I'm sure there's an explanation..." Doris went on, but Tilly wasn't listening. Things burned down on the coast because people were careless with what they had, or impatient with what they no longer wanted. They didn't burn each other's property, yet she'd heard what the sheriff had said. She was suddenly seized with a terrifying thought. Perhaps someone knew about her. Perhaps someone wanted her to go away because she was abnormal. Did someone see her in the library? Doris buttered the toast and put a plate on the table.

Tilly drank two sips of the coffee and had a bite of toast before her stomach began to cramp. She stood up and tried to clear her cup and saucer while holding the blanket around her shoulders.

Doris stopped talking and helped her down the hall to her room. Tilly kicked off her shoes and, wrapped in the afghan, fell into bed fully clothed. Some of the sand in her socks stuck to the bottoms of her feet and made its way into her bed; the rest left prints on the carpet. Under the weight of all the blankets, Tilly eventually warmed and stilled and fell into a deep sleep.

Doris was left alone at the kitchen table. She put her head on her arms and cried. For thirty minutes, she let herself go; then she squared her shoulders and started a list of all the things she needed to do. She ate the last piece of toast.

CHAPTER 21

May 13, 1947

JOHN CALLEN heard about the fire at breakfast, astonished to see the hotel dining room filled by the volunteer crew. "Did something happen last night?" he asked the waitress as he sat down at the counter.

"The candle factory burned," she said. "Sure was a big one. Coffee?"

He ran out of the building and spotted Hank in the parking lot. "Where's Tilly?" he said.

"They've gone home," Hank said, "Paul drove them."

Callen looked toward the smoking rubble. "How in hell could a thing like this happen?

The fire chief had posted a volunteer at the top of the driveway, with orders to keep everyone out. They'd return after the heat dissipated to sift through the rubble for clues. As Deputy Carry was leaving, he noticed something metal near where the door had been. He used his handkerchief to pick up a crow bar. "Is this part of your gear, chief?"

Eastman shook his head. "All our tools are marked," he said.

Carry carefully stowed it in the patrol car and drove to the office. He couldn't wait to call the boss; he finally had something to report. The phone rang six times before the sheriff answered.

"Do you have any idea what time it is?"

Carry took a deep breath, "Six-thirty, sir."

"That's right, six-thirty a.m. This better be good," Wick said. "I'm in the hallway dripping, holding up a towel."

"We had ourselves a suspicious fire over here last night, boss. Seems it started sometime between one-ten and one forty-five. I'm going to need backup."

"What was so suspicious about it?"

"Burning pattern with multiple hot spots and a strong smell of gasoline," Carry said.

"Anyone hurt?" Wick said. "Anyone home at the time?"

"It was the Bluegate Candle Factory."

"The candle factory?" the sheriff said. "The one those dames started?"

"That's right, boss. They were doing pretty well, too."

"Sit tight and make sure no one goes digging in the ashes," Wick said.

Carry rubbed his hands together and looked around his office. Sheriff Wick didn't have much cause to visit, but this would be different. The press would be on it, too. He cleared a mug of cold coffee next to the phone and stopped before tossing a half-eaten piece of cherry pie in the trash can. He finished the pie. He hurriedly straightened piles of paper on his desk and slid a few files into a drawer. He took the trash out. Satisfied that the substation looked respectable, he drove back to the crime scene.

Sheriff Wick turned off the paved road, and Deputy Carry ran to move the barriers at the top of the driveway. Wick unfolded his six-foot-four-inch frame from beneath the steering wheel and nodded as he looked across the beach. "Looks like you boys had a busy night here," he said.

"The gals took a big shipment of paraffin for making church candles," Carry said. "It was a hot one."

The sheriff walked toward the water line, along the channel volunteers had dug to contain the molten wax. "Well, I'll be," he said. "Looks like a lava flow." He pushed his hat back slightly and scratched his forehead. "Detective Gustin's about half an hour behind me. He'll assist; he's got some experience in fire. From the look of this place, he may need to get a room and camp out over here for a few days."

"One of the firemen smelled gasoline as he broke into the east wall," Carry said, "You couldn't mistake it. There's a fuel tank over at the lighthouse—could have been the source."

"Any footprints?"

"Someone took pains to cover his tracks," Carry said, "and it was an incoming tide."

"Tricky thing about arson," Wick said, "is that you have to rule out all possible accidental causes. You have your work cut out for you with a candle factory." He pulled his left ear lobe. "Assuming we find an accelerant was used and the gals confirm that it wasn't on site at close of business, it looks like we have a crime on our hands."

It was past noon when the sun cut through the fog and Tilly emerged from her bed over-warm and thirsty. Her clothes and blankets were tangled; she felt sticky. She noticed that she smelled like smoke.

She stripped and drew a bath, then slid against the back of the slipper tub until she was completely enveloped by hot water. She took a deep breath and held her head below the surface for a few seconds, washing away the scent of fire. For a few moments she just soaked, enveloped by warmth. She wanted to call Sylvia—just to tell her about the fire, but she couldn't do that. No, Doris would let her know. Tilly sudsed and shampooed and rinsed.

She was combing the tangles from her hair when she heard someone at the door. Through the blinds she saw the drab brown uniform and didn't answer. She wasn't ready to talk to Mike Carry and kept still, wondering if he'd come in; the door was unlocked. He didn't; she heard his footsteps on the porch and the patrol car drive away. She dressed quickly and left the house.

At Seventh and Main, Tilly crossed the paved road and, after a moment's hesitation, forced her gaze down the beach. She knew she had to see the remains, take it all in, get used to it. They'd done a good thing—a thing few women had attempted—and they'd been successful. Now it was gone.

There were two sheriff's department patrol cars in the driveway, and the fire chief's red truck was parked on the side of the road. For several minutes she stared, committing the details to memory. What was left would need to be razed; the upright sections might collapse at any time. She watched the men pointing and talking and lifting pieces of charred rubble and recalled the day they christened the factory "Bluegate" in honor of Doris' uncle. The standing timbers now looked eerily like a door to the ocean.

As she got closer, she could detect the diluted smell of a fire extinguished, like a giant ashtray full of cigarette stubs moistened by salt water. She kept a wide berth, not ready to be interviewed. As she circled the site, she absorbed what had happened and what it would mean in coming months. They would need to start over.

The smell of smoldering wood and scorched wax was sickening on an empty stomach. She backed away with eyes still riveted to the ruined building and sat in the dunes with her heels dug into the sand. A car she didn't recognize pulled over to the shoulder—tourists, she thought. Yesterday she might have sold them candles.

The sun was well past its zenith and was bathing her in warmth from the west. It felt good on her face and dried her hair. She became calm and began to feel hungry. Less than half a mile away was Aunt Ida and Uncle Jose's roadhouse and Aunt Ida's home cooking. She took off her shoes and walked in the surf. They would take it one day at a time. It was a serious setback, but not the end. Her mood began to brighten as she walked along the beach. Then she saw John.

He dropped his hammer and ran to her, and she felt the familiar sense of dread return. She told him that Doris had left her a note saying he'd been by, but she didn't thank him. It had been a comfort, but it also made her feel guilty. Standing near him on the beach made her feel guilty. He was so kind, remained so loyal. The treatment would have to work. But with the factory in ashes, she wouldn't have the money to pay for treatment for a long time. Everything she had was invested in the building.

"I saw Doris," John said, "catching the bus to Half Moon Bay, to the insurance company and the bank. She wanted to know if the price to rebuild would be about the same. I told her we could work it out."

"I saw her notes on the table this morning," Tilly said. "I don't think she slept at all." She was glad that Doris was taking care of things. She was sure she'd make a mess of it. She was so distracted.

"And my lovely, how are you?" John asked.

She winced. How she wished he wouldn't call her that. She wasn't lovely; she was abnormal. "I must be doing better," she said. "I'm hungry." She backed away from him. "I need to get to the roadhouse and get something in my stomach."

Helen, Ida and Jose held Tilly in a three-way embrace the minute she came through the kitchen door. "We talked to Doris," Helen said.

"I watched it burn," Tilly said, her voice breaking, "and I listened to what the chief and the deputy said. They said it was arson."

"I've lived here all my life," Ida said, "and I can't imagine anyone on the coast burning down your factory."

You don't know about me, Tilly thought.

"They'll do an investigation," Helen said. "They'll figure it out." Tilly nodded and sobbed in her mother's arms.

Helen served Mike Carry his afternoon pie and coffee at two-thirty. The dining room was closed, and he looked out of place in the bar, in uniform, perched on a stool. He was more animated than usual, Helen thought, odd for a man who'd been up most of the night. He needed more to do. Someone might think he burned the place down; he was enjoying himself too much. "How long do you think the investigation will take?" she asked.

Carry used a bit of his ice cream to whiten his coffee. "Well, it's hard to tell," he said. "We need to find someone with the means and opportunity to commit the crime, but also a motive. It's not that difficult to burn down a candle factory out on the coast in the middle of the night, but why? Does someone benefit, or is it the work of a pyromaniac?" The ice cream was melting around the fruit like a sauce. He sopped up as much as possible with the crust. "If we do have a pyro on the coast," he said, "it's likely he'll strike again before long."

Helen refilled his cup.

"Can you think of anyone with a motive, Mrs. B?"

Helen stood away from the bar. She scratched the base of her neck. "Can you keep it in confidence, between us?" she asked.

"If it's evidence, I can't withhold it," Carry said.

"It's not really evidence. It's just that John and Tilly have been arguing about the business. John wants to get married and, you know, settle down. Have a family."

Sheriff Carry's eyebrows rose. He swallowed the last of his coffee and left cash for food and service on the bar. He tipped his hat to Helen as he made his way to the door. John was outside on a ladder, and Carry waved as he pulled the patrol car onto the Coast Highway. On a hunch, he headed south to El Granada Hardware.

• • •

Tilly sat across the desk from Mike Carry, surprised by how little space he had to work in. She wondered if his office had once been a closet. He ended the phone call he'd taken with a "ten-four" before acknowledging her.

"How is everything?" he asked.

She suddenly remembered him lighting flares at the scene of the fire. He was the flattest tire in town. "I guess it depends on how long it takes us to rebuild," she said. "We're working with the insurance company, but they need the report from your investigation." She smiled inwardly. She thought she was beginning to sound like Doris.

Carry nodded. "I'm going to ask you some questions. Just answer to the best of your ability. If something comes to you later or you need to add something to the information you give today, please get in touch with me."

Tilly crossed and uncrossed her ankles but couldn't get comfortable.

Carry had a paper in his left hand. He'd written out the questions. He leaned back in his chair and began. "Did you inspect and close the factory on the night of the fire?"

"Yes."

"About what time?"

"Six o'clock."

"How many people were in the building when you closed it?"

She recounted her closing routine, how she and Doris divided the labor, the type of equipment they used, and what materials were stored on site. He asked about insurance and beneficiaries and rebuilding plans. The questions kept coming in random order. Tilly couldn't decide if that was how his mind worked or if he was trying to catch her off-guard. She looked at her watch several times hoping he'd notice her impatience. Finally, Carry reached the end of his line of inquiry.

"How would you describe your relationship to John Callen?" he asked. He watched her closely.

She froze. What could he be getting at? Did he suspect she was abnormal? "Why, John's my boyfriend," she said.

Carry noted her hesitation and wrote "*Mother's comment regarding the business being a point of contention seems accurate.*" "Has John been supportive of your business venture?" he asked.

"Completely," she said. "He's helped Doris and me in many ways."

"Can you think of anyone else who would benefit from burning the building?"

"John won't benefit from the fire," she said.

"I'll be in touch if I need anything else," he said.

Tilly stood for a moment before opening the door to the back of the post office, anxious to escape, but feeling queasy over the line of questioning. She hesitated. She wanted to mention the unidentified silent partner but thought better of it. She didn't feel comfortable talking about Doris' uncle. Doris would tell him what she thought was important.

She stopped to check the Bluegate post office box. There were a few letters; one was an order for candles. She would need to write back and tell them about the fire. Canceling orders was the hardest thing to do. Then she turned over an envelope and saw the familiar handwriting. It was addressed to Doris and postmarked Reno, Nevada, and although she knew what she was doing was wrong, she found a private spot on her route home and opened it.

Dear Doris,

Thanks for writing—it was great to get a letter from you. I was so excited to hear that the business is going good and that you're really doing it—running your own company that is. Can I tell you I'm not surprised that you're president? Congrats too, on taking on such a fine partner.

I'm glad Tilly's doing so well. I'm sure she's been too busy to write—with the boyfriend and all. He seems like quite a catch—but then Tilly is too…"

She stopped reading. She tore the letter into the smallest pieces possible and, crying, threw them into the waves.

• • •

John Callen played with the choke a few times before the engine turned over. "Damn salt air." He had an hour to shower and pick Tilly up. He wondered if Havice would let him cut some flowers for her if he drove by the nursery. She'd been distant lately, but he still preferred her to more possessive women he'd known.

He noticed Carry's patrol car parked in front of the hotel.

"Glad we're eating at Nick's," Callen said under his breath. He grabbed his denim jacket and locked the toolboxes on both sides of the truck.

Carry was talking with the attractive blond clerk at the front desk, leaning on the counter to bring his gaze more in line with hers. She was checking the room reservation records. His brown uniform was a little tight around the middle and his white undershirt was visible beneath his open shirt collar.

"Have a minute, John?" Carry turned when the door opened, not lifting the left elbow from the reservation desk. He made eye contact with Callen.

Callen thought the pose made him look like a rooster. "I'm on my way to dinner," he said. "What's this about?"

Carry stood and squared his shoulders. The blond looked up appreciatively. "We have some business to discuss." He motioned toward the lounge, which was closed.

Callen followed, checking his watch as he walked. Surely, he thought, Sheriff Wick would assign someone competent to the investigation. The fire was the biggest thing that had happened on the coast in years. They sat at a table near the rear of the empty room.

"I want to talk to you about your activities on the night of May 12, 1947," Carry said.

"The night of the fire," Callen said. He leaned back in the chair. His grandfather always told him to get comfortable—act bored. John unrolled and re-rolled a shirtsleeve.

Carry removed a notepad from his breast pocket. The receptionist brought two cups of coffee and put them on the small cocktail table. Carry winked at her. "Thanks. You're a doll." He poured cream and passed the pitcher to John who took it from him and placed it on the table. Carry smiled. "I suppose I should have asked if you wanted coffee."

"How long is this going to take, Deputy?" Callen said, "Because I really am running late."

"Where were you on the night of the candle factory fire?"

"I worked all day; I came back to my room and showered. I ate meatloaf in that dining room right over there," Callen motioned to the foyer and the restaurant beyond, "then I went back up to my room, read for a while and fell asleep."

"About what time did you eat?" Carry was writing the specifics in pencil.

"Five-thirty, six maybe. Does it matter?" Callen looked at his watch. If the interview took too long, he wouldn't have time to get the flowers.

"Did you have dinner with anyone that night?" Carry asked.

"I eat alone most nights unless I'm meeting my girl, which Deputy, I have plans to do tonight. If you don't mind, I need to get cleaned up." He started to rise.

"This will only take a minute more," Carry said. "About what time would you say you went up to your room?"

"Probably by seven," Callen said. "I get to work early and work late. That particular day I moved a lot of earth. I slept right through the fire alarm."

"So there's no one who can confirm your whereabouts on the night of the fire?"

"I was in bed that night, like ninety-nine percent of the folks in town. Are you interviewing them too?" He stood. "If you're asking if I slept alone, the answer is yes. Now, if you'll excuse me." He pushed the chair in, under the table.

"How much will you make rebuilding that factory, John?" Carry showed no sign of standing. He was looking up at Callen.

"Are you insinuating that I'd burn my girl's business so I could rebuild it?" His eyes were wide. Callen's voice was sharp, though he was trying hard not to show emotion.

"You must know that many in town believe the business is a point of contention between you and Tilly." Carry sat back and stretched out his legs.

Callen hesitated for only a moment before shaking his head and striding out of the room. Carry drank the last of his coffee and poured the cream from the pitcher into his empty cup. He took a clean white handkerchief from his pocket and dried the inside of the creamer, careful to preserve Callen's fingerprints.

• • •

"Can you think of anyone that would benefit from burning the building?" Carry finally asked.

"Well, I'm not sure," Doris said.

Mike Carry leaned forward in his seat.

"I don't know how much you know about our business," Doris said, "but the factory was built on land left to me by my late uncle. In settling the estate, I discovered he'd had a silent partner in something called the Bluegate Partnership. His role—managing partner—passed to me. I did what I could to find the silent partner, but no luck. I concluded the partner had died or moved away. A lawyer recommended that I carry on in my role and manage the asset, so I moved forward with the plans for the factory. It's why we call our business Bluegate."

"So you think the silent partner might have burned down the building?" Carry slid the pencil behind his ear.

"I don't know. I was thinking that someone—maybe someone a little disturbed—who knew the history, might burn it down. Maybe the silent partner came back through town, saw the Bluegate Candle Factory and went a little crazy. It's the only thing I could come up with," Doris said.

"Well that's why you have us," Carry said. "So you don't have to worry your pretty little head over criminal investigations." He winked at her.

Doris ground her back molars to maintain her composure.

"Is there anyone else you can think of that might benefit from the fire?" Carry said.

"I don't think anyone benefits from the fire," Doris said. Except you, she thought. You need to feel important.

"Miss Jura, you are acquainted with John Callen?"

"Yes."

"What is your relationship with Mr. Callen?"

"John's a good friend and the boyfriend of my business partner. And he built our factory."

"Are you aware that John sees your business as an impediment to his future with Tilly?"

"No," Doris said. "John has always been very supportive."

"When was the last time John Callen did any work on or made any repairs at the candle factory that would have required him to bring his tools?"

"It's probably been four months," she said. "He's been working full time at the Marine View."

"That's all I need right now, Miss Jura. I may have further questions later."

"I have all the information I collected on the Bluegate Partnership if you'd like to review it," Doris said. "I've brought the files with me."

"I'll let you know," Carry said.

Doris walked away from the substation slowly, startled by a barking dog patrolling his fence line. Her mind was elsewhere. She called her mother as soon as she reached the cottage; Joan's voice was a comfort. She slumped into the small sofa by the phone. "We've had a fire," Doris said. "Mom, the factory's gone."

After a long moment, Joan responded.

"We don't really know what happened," Doris said. "There's an investigation underway. They've declared the site a crime scene."

"Crime scene?" Joan said. "You mean it was arson?"

"It was suspicious," Doris said.

"Dear God. Doris, honey, who do you think would have reason to burn the candle factory?"

"I don't know, Mom. I keep going back to the whole silent partner chapter and wondering if there's some connection. If you can think of anything, anything at all about an associate Uncle Stanley may have had, someone who might know something about what he was up to, please call me right away."

• • •

"Let's get down to business," Sheriff Wick said. "Detective, we'll start by reviewing your notes and the fire chief's report." Detective Gustin opened a folder against the corner of the sheriff's desk and began to read.

"The factory was secured as a crime scene after the fire was extinguished," Gustin said. "Several volunteers detected a strong smell of gasoline in the office suite, not in the main manufacturing area, and this was suspicious. Due to the perceived presence of gasoline, firefighters working the hose on the east side of the building, including the father of one of the owners, switched to a fog nozzle to protect evidence not already burned.

"It appears that there was more than one point of origin for the fire, but most of the accelerant was used in the office suite. We found a charred three-gallon metal can on site, within the perimeter of the building. The owners of the factory could not identify the can, and we could lift no fingerprints from it. The owners had never brought gasoline into the building and had no need for it.

"We were able to get some samples of gasoline from the charred structural members directly on the foundation. When the cooled and hardened wax flow was removed from some of the wood, our investigators were able to detect the accelerant beneath it. The lab matched the gasoline from the fire with the fuel stored at the lighthouse. Given that analysis and the discovery of the metal can, I think we can say that the perpetrator took the fuel from the storage tank and then broke into the factory.

"We know the light keeper was outside working on the light apparatus until about nine o'clock, so sometime between nine and one-thirty, we believe the perpetrator entered the building with the gas and rigged some sort of starter. We can't say for sure what the device might have been—could have been something as simple as a lit cigarette with matches rubber banded around the unlit end to make it burn over several minutes, giving the arsonist time to flee the scene before the matches and fire ignited. We simply can't pinpoint exactly when the fire was set."

The sheriff tilted his chair back and looked out the window for a moment. He pulled on his left ear lobe. "Good work detective," he said. "So it appears we do have a crime. Deputy," he said, turning toward Carry, "what do you have for us?"

Carry looked at his notebook. "Hank Scaroni reported the fire by pulling the alarm at Point Montara Fire Station," he said. "He'd had a few too many at the Montara Hotel bar, and left around one o'clock. He managed to get down to the beach just north of the factory, where he fell asleep. He pulled the alarm at about one forty-five; he figures it took him ten minutes to run to the station. He saw nothing out of the ordinary and smelled no smoke when he first reached the beach. There were flames in two parts of the building when he awoke around one thirty-five.

"I've interviewed a number of witnesses including the lighthouse keeper. He was in bed by ten-thirty, and never heard or saw a thing.

"I picked up a crowbar from the scene and asked Chief Eastman if it was part of the firefighter's gear. It was not. Floyd at El Granada Hardware Store told me that John Callen had been in to buy a crowbar the morning after the fire, saying he 'lost' his. I was able to obtain fingerprints from Callen and the fingerprints on the crowbar are a match. Both Tilly and Doris have stated that John hasn't done work at the factory in four months—which is the length of time he's been working on the roadhouse dining room expansion project.

"I interviewed John Callen. He claims that on the night of the fire he had dinner in the hotel dining room at five-thirty or six, then retired to his room for the evening. A waitress at the hotel corroborates his story and believes she saw him finish his meal and leave the dining room around seven. No one I interviewed remembers seeing him later in the evening. He says he took a hot bath, read for a while and fell asleep. About midnight, he turned out the light and didn't wake until six the next morning. He found out about the fire when he went downstairs for coffee and immediately ran to the beach to find Tilly. Paul Bettencourt had driven Tilly and Doris home around five."

The sheriff interrupted. "Okay, you say that Callen hadn't worked at the factory for over four months, but his crowbar was found there—or at least one that had his prints on it—after the fire. Was that right after or during?"

"During, boss. I picked it up as the volunteers were leaving."

"So it was just left outside?" Sheriff Wick turned to Detective Gustin. "And you say a metal can was found that had traces of gasoline in it, but it was left in the fire?" Gustin nodded. The sheriff stood and walked around his desk. "Something's not right," he said.

"Could be carelessness," Gustin offered.

"Or two people involved," Carry said.

"I don't know," Wick said. "What possible motive could Callen have for setting the fire? Sure he'd make money rebuilding the structure, but there's lots of work for builders out there now. He could be building houses, probably more profitably than working for his girlfriend and her business partner. No, that's not a motive. Give me something else. Why would John Callen want to burn down the business?"

Carry cleared his throat. "Well, perhaps his girlfriend is more interested in the business than motherhood." Sheriff Wick cocked an eyebrow. "Callen's pretty sweet on Tilly Bettencourt, and she's not showing much sign of slowing down."

"But the building's insured, and he would know that," Wick said. "Let's look at this another way: does John Callen have any enemies? Would someone take his crowbar and leave it at the scene to try to implicate him?"

Gustin and Carry looked at each other and shrugged.

Sheriff Wick put his hands on his desk and smiled. "Good start, gentlemen. Let's reconvene when you have more information, this Friday or earlier if possible."

CHAPTER 22

June 16, 1947

JOHN CALLEN received a lumber shipment from the Tunitas Creek Mill and, before approving the delivery for payment, checked each piece for straight cut and tight grain. He muscled a thousand pounds of wood a board at a time, rejecting half a dozen.

Jose watched him through the window, delighted with the quality of his work. He told Ida that he'd never met a more exacting builder or a kinder man, but he worried that John's problems with Deputy Carry might land him in jail. He went out to the parking lot to check for trash and continued to watch John from the corner of his eye. How nice it would be to have him in the family, he thought. Jose considered John a fine match for the niece he adored and hoped that when Tilly was ready, they'd become a couple.

A black, late-model Plymouth sedan pulled into the circular driveway, and John looked up. He rushed to meet the driver, brushing his jeans as he ran. He wiped his hands on his thighs. In moments, his grandfather, Judge Robert Callen, was out of the car, embracing him.

"What brings you to the coast, Judge?" John said.

"My grandson and my past in that order. I thought it was time for a visit. You know, I'm not sure I've ever been to this gin joint in the daytime."

John laughed. "You sure you want me to know that?"

"This is progress, isn't it?" Judge Callen said. "Jose's expanding to accommodate a legitimate clientele. Torres has always been a man of vision." He winked at John. "Have time for a meal?" he said.

"I'm at your service," John said, "though I may serve you better if I clean up a little."

"Agreed," the judge said, slapping John on the back. "Think you can clean up by six o'clock? I'm going to stimulate my appetite with some of the fine libations this institution is famous for. You know, I don't get over here nearly enough." He looked out at the horizon, squinting from the glare off the water.

"Jose's inside," John said. "I don't think he's expecting you."

"He doesn't know I'm here because I didn't know I was coming. Dawned on me today that I should drive out and see the lay of the land for myself. Besides, I've always loved this place. It's as beautiful as ever, though I'm not sure about all this respectability." He looked at his grandson. "Do they feed you here, or am I going to have to buy your dinner?"

"Jose is very generous. I try not to take advantage of him too often."

"Well I certainly hope you'll take advantage of him tonight," the judge said, "and introduce me to this mysterious Tilly."

"Tilly may show up here before I do," John said. "She's got more time on her hands now that the factory's burned." He looked over his shoulder, "I'm worried that Carry will try to connect my re-building contract to a motive."

"That sounds about as ridiculous as his other fabrications. Who knows what churns through the brain of a Carry?"

John nodded. "He's not rational, but he is the law around here."

"My record with respect to the Carry clan is flawless, and this case will be no different," the judge said. "Tonight we dine; go and get cleaned up and don't be too slow coming. You don't want to leave me alone too long with a beautiful young woman." The judge clasped his grandson's shoulder and went inside.

Jose was in the kitchen when he heard the familiar, naturally amplified voice. He immediately knew who it was.

"Judge Callen!" He grasped his old friend's hand and motioned to a stool, then slipped behind the bar for a bottle of his best Irish whiskey. He poured a double shot on the rocks and noted that the judge's hair was a bit thinner than it had been on his last visit. The impeccably trimmed beard was now entirely white, but Callen still walked like a young man. His dark blue eyes looked clear and bright.

"It's wonderful to see you," Jose said. "I'm so sorry about this unfortunate mess with your grandson and Sheriff Carry."

The judge raised his glass. "I trust that Ida is well?"

Jose nodded. "She was just talking about you this morning. She said she thought you might turn up." He leaned forward on the bar and spoke softly. "John didn't burn my niece's factory, for Christ's sake, he built it. He loves Tilly and Doris. I wouldn't be surprised if Carry set the fire himself. Trying to settle some old Carry-Callen score by dragging John down."

"Your niece?" the judge said. "Doris is your niece?"

"Tilly's my niece," Jose said. "You didn't know? Tilly Bettencourt. My sister-in-law Helen's daughter."

The judge stared at his glass while Jose served a couple that appeared to be touring. They took a table near the corner. While the couple engaged Jose in chatter about roadhouse history, the judge sat alone and took a long drink. He removed his tweed jacket. "Helen Bettencourt's daughter," he sighed. He remembered Helen fondly. He could appreciate a woman who understood negotiation and the power of female persuasion. He wondered if Tilly was much like her mother and, for a moment, envied his grandson. One elbow rested on the bar, chin on hand; his other hand held the glass. By the time Jose mixed and delivered cocktails to the tourists, the judge had drained his whiskey.

"I'll have another," he said. He was smiling.

After Havice Nursery closed at five, a few of the Montara Hotel regulars stopped by the roadhouse, as they did on

Mondays when the hotel lounge was closed. Among the trio that anchored the end of the bar opposite Judge Callen, was Hank Scaroni, who'd heard that Doris Jura might be there for dinner. He had a habit of showing up when Doris was around. He'd rushed home from work and changed his clothes before jogging the mile and a half to the Marine View. Despite the wardrobe detour, he arrived only minutes after his co-workers. "Hank's afraid he'll miss something," Jim elbowed Ned, who was sitting to his right. Hank didn't speak while he caught his breath.

"How good it is to see you, Judge Callen," Ida said when she came from the kitchen. She grasped both of his hands in hers, and at the mention of Callen's name, Hank and the other nurserymen stopped speaking and stared. They'd been toddlers when the judge was settling Ocean Shore Railroad bankruptcy claims, but everyone in town knew the stories. They moved to a table in the furthest corner, but fixed their collective gaze on the bar.

"He's the one." Hank nodded over his shoulder in Callen's direction. Ida and the judge were laughing at some old joke. Jose filled a bowl with salted peanuts. "He's the one that settled Doris' uncle's claim against the railroad. He was a real wheeler-dealer."

"Yeah, well things were a lot different back then." Jim was nursing his beer; payday wasn't until Friday. "He probably made more money than the guys that owned the tracks. I suppose he's over here to visit his grandson."

"Deputy Carry sure has it out for John Callen. It might be a good thing he has a judge in the family." Hank said.

"If I were a betting man, I'd put my money on Callen. Carry couldn't figure out a two-car funeral. My favorite Mike Carry story has to be yours, Hank—the one about the night of the fire…"

"Yeah. Here we are, a bunch of volunteers, trying to fight an inferno. So the new sheriff arrives and we think, swell, a professional. And the first thing he does is put out road flares. Flares!" The boys leaned back against the chairs, slapping their thighs and the table.

Hank was about to order a second beer when his attention was drawn to the door: Tilly Bettencourt had come alone. He hesitated. "Maybe later."

Jose nodded and crossed the room. He offered his niece his arm, and with great chivalry, escorted her to the bar. She was wearing a blue dress the color of her eyes, and her hair had been washed and set. "Tilly, come and meet an old friend."

Judge Callen turned, his gaze fixed on her face.

"It's nice to meet you, Judge Callen," she said. He stared. She raised her voice and spoke more slowly, "I know your grandson."

"Yes, yes, of course. I've heard a lot about you." Callen picked up his glass and finished the last of his drink.

• • •

"May I come in?" Judge Callen said. It had been more than twenty-six years since his last visit. Helen stepped aside and let him pass.

"This is a surprise," she said.

He noticed that she'd aged well and had filled out nicely. "It's a surprise for me too," he said.

"Perhaps you should have a seat," Helen said. "I'll make some coffee."

"I won't be staying long, Helen, but perhaps we should sit down."

Helen led him to the kitchen and pulled out a chair. She gazed at the coffee pot as if it were an escape route. Despite his protests, she measured the grounds and water. She didn't look directly at him.

"My grandson's in trouble, Helen. You do know about this."

"Yes." She turned her back to the judge and fussed with the percolator.

"My grandson is dating Tilly."

"Yes." She was leaning against the tiled counter on both hands.

"But you've not talked to Tilly?"

"No," she said. "Did you expect me to?"

"Deputy Michael Carry, currently sworn scion of the law and order Carry clan, is out to lock up my grandson. He thinks John burned down the factory in a jealous rage, because Tilly won't marry him. Now where did he get that idea?"

Helen's hands began to shake. She sat at the chrome table across from the Judge and rested her forehead on her palms. The coffee brewed. "The sheriff has no real case against John," she said when she regained her composure. "If he left town, Carry wouldn't pursue him." She got up from the table and took cups and saucers from the hutch.

"That would be convenient for you, wouldn't it? I could write him a check and send him off somewhere for a fresh start. You gravely underestimate my grandson, Helen. He is not going to run away from this accusation."

"You could talk to him…" She did not try to pour cream into a pitcher. She placed the bottle on the table.

"I will not. I suggest that you need to talk to your daughter and husband. Has it occurred to you that Tilly will probably follow John?"

"She won't. She'll stay here with Doris and rebuild the business. I know she will. If John leaves, she'll find someone else."

"You have to talk to her, Helen. If you don't, I will. I must certainly talk to my grandson."

Helen placed the coffee pot on a trivet and motioned to the Judge. He poured her cup first. Finally, she spoke. "I see no need to tell anyone anything. Tilly and Doris are playing sleuth, and the more dead ends they run into, the more Tilly will suspect John. I don't believe the relationship will survive, nor do I think a Carry will arrest and, heaven forbid, convict a Callen. This will all blow over. Why should my husband and daughter bear the pain of deception after all these years? What is the point?"

"When I learned tonight that Tilly was your daughter…"

"I beg you," Helen now looked directly at Robert Callen, "leave the past alone. There's no need to stir it up."

Judge Callen never touched his coffee. He rose to leave and said, "I hope you are correct, but I will not allow my grandson to pay."

• • •

Michael Carry labored for hours over his final report to Sheriff Wick. There was no question that gasoline was used to start the blaze and that it was taken from the fuel tank at the lighthouse. It was a simple matter to draw down a few gallons and carry them the short distance to the factory. Anyone who could carry twenty pounds and knew the tanks were there could have done the deed, on foot. The tide turned while the fire burned; no distinct footprints were discernable in the sand.

Deputy Carry leaned back in his chair and chewed on his pen. His report would be the basis for the sheriff's approval or denial of a warrant for John Callen's arrest. Hank Scaroni had reported the fire, but only after the factory was engulfed in flames. He had little to offer the investigation except to note that the fire ignited between one-ten and one thirty-five. Scaroni had no comment on how the fire started.

The crowbar found at the scene, at what had once been a door, was Carry's tie to John Callen. Callen was the only man in town with anything close to a motive for setting the fire. Tilly had refused his proposal. She had made a decision to pursue the business over marriage. That just might make John angry enough to burn the factory.

Callen had no alibi. He was a lone wolf. He said that he was asleep when the fire started and that he never heard the siren. It was breakfast at the hotel before he got word of what had happened, and then he ran to the scene. Carry found this the hardest part of his story to believe—that his girlfriend's factory could burn just down the beach from where he was staying, and he'd be capable of sleeping through it. But then, he rubbed his chin thoughtfully, the lighthouse keeper had also slept through it.

There was one aspect of the investigation that was troublesome. Doris Jura seemed convinced that the fire had something to do with her late uncle's coastside business affairs, going back to the days of the railroad. Doris could offer nothing in the way of evidence. She had shared a file that she'd compiled after inheriting the land, detailing the steps she'd taken to clear title. Carry wrote in his report that *"had some silent partner decided to reclaim his share of the property, there'd be no cause to burn the factory. In fact, it could be said that Doris Jura had significantly increased the value of the parcel."*

Deputy Sheriff Carry swallowed the last of his coffee, signed the bottom of the report and put on his jacket. He fueled the patrol car and made his way to the courthouse over the coastal mountains, through the fog, and on to Redwood City.

CHAPTER 23

June 24, 1947

"THE INSURANCE company won't do a thing until the investigation is complete," Doris said, "and I have no confidence in Deputy Carry." She swirled her coffee mug to mix the cream. "Even if we could find a place to work temporarily, there'd be no money to retool or re-supply."

Tilly leaned back against the porch post. "It hasn't been that long," she said. "I worry that Carry's in too much of a rush."

"I've returned the deposits on orders we won't be able to fill," Doris said. "That was the hardest thing to do."

Tilly nodded and sat quietly on the step for several minutes, finishing her coffee. "Carry thinks John burned the factory because I won't marry him," she said softly. "I've brought this on John." She put the mug down and held her head in her hands.

Doris moved from the porch swing to the step to sit next to Tilly. "No, Carry's brought this on John," Doris said. "If he wasn't so lazy, he'd at least look at the documents I brought to the interview."

"I have to stop seeing John," Tilly said. "I can't keep stringing him along, but if I tell him I want to break up now, I'm afraid he'll think I suspect him. I can't handle that." Tilly started to cry. "I never meant to hurt John."

Doris put her arm around Tilly's shoulders. "It's okay," she said, "when you follow your heart, things have a way of working out. Just tell him the truth."

Tilly looked at her and started to sob.

• • •

"I don't think there's enough here for an arrest warrant," Sheriff Wick said. He pushed back his leather, swivel chair and faced the deputy; Carry's arson report lay on the immaculate oak desk.

Carry shifted in his seat, hat in hand.

"I'm intrigued by the Bluegate Partnership and the fact that Stanley Jura's silent partner was never identified," Wick said. "How much did you follow up on that?"

"It seemed like a dead end," Carry said. "Doris tried to locate the partner to her inheritance—she did what was required. No one came forward."

"So we don't know if the partner's still alive," Wick said. "Do you have anything on Stanley Jura?"

Carry looked at his hat. "I know he was Bluegate's managing partner," he said. "Doris inherited the role from him. The only asset she had to manage was the land in Montara."

Wick pulled on his left ear lobe, then took a cigarette from the wooden box on his desk. He offered one to Carry, who refused. "Do you know when the partnership was formed?" Wick asked.

"Doris didn't have the partnership agreement," Carry said. "The only reference to Bluegate was on the deed, and in the will."

"So Doris has the deed to the property?" Wick asked.

"Yes, of course." Mike Carry was shifting his weight in the wooden chair, still passing his hat from hand to hand. He saw Sheriff Wick glare at him and set the hat on the side table.

"In what year did the property transfer?" Wick asked.

Carry unbuttoned his collar. "1925," he said. "In 1925 it was transferred from the Ocean Shore Holding Company, which was the real estate arm of the railroad, to the Bluegate Partnership."

Wick exhaled and sat back in his chair. He didn't speak for several seconds. "1925…the Ocean Shore Holding Company…Mike, do you have any idea who settled many of the Ocean Shore bankruptcy claims?"

Mike Carry turned his palms upward. "No."

Wick nodded. "I didn't think so. Most of the claims were settled by Judge Robert Callen."

Carry shrank in his chair. "I admit the evidence against John Callen is largely circumstantial," he said. "Do you think someone would try to frame John as a way of getting even with his grandfather?"

"On the bench," Wick said, "Judge Callen was a fair man. His interpretation of the law was, in many cases, liberal, or maybe more to the point, creative. He made friends with the bootleggers and rumrunners on the coast, but even Judge Callen would have made an enemy or two. He was carrying too much baggage. I think this investigation needs to be expanded to include a look at the Bluegate Partnership."

Carry nodded again. That had been Doris' assumption all along. It was hard for him to admit that her intuition was better than his.

"I don't want you interviewing Judge Callen," Wick said, "Too much family history. Detective Gustin has some time, and I want him to start over here at the courthouse, seeing what he can dig up on this mysterious partnership. No offense to Miss Jura, but I like to think a trained investigator will have more success finding that silent partner. For now, keep your eyes and ears open and let me know what else develops on the coast." His nod indicated that the meeting was over.

As Sheriff Wick watched Deputy Carry leave the office, he shook his head. He'd known the first Sheriff Carry. The first Sheriff Carry had been no match for Judge Robert Callen, and this Carry was even less equipped.

• • •

The phone rang as Tilly was marking the shortbread in even squares. She grabbed the receiver with her left hand, her right still pressing the knife into the warm dough. If she waited too long, the treats wouldn't cut cleanly, and she wanted them to look perfect for Judge Callen's visit.

"Long time, no hear from," the voice said.

Tilly knew immediately who it was. Something was caught in her throat. It was impossible to speak.

"I'm sorry I left without saying good-bye," the voice said. Tilly blurted out the question that had been haunting her for months and months, "Sylvia, why didn't you ever marry?"

Doris got home just as Tilly was hanging up the phone, but there was no time to talk. She grabbed a cloth and quickly dusted the furniture in the front parlor. She was washing her hands when she heard Judge Callen climb the sagging steps. He knocked. The screen door rattled against the jamb and Doris ran to greet him, tossing her apron on the kitchen table. Tilly quickly took the cookies from the tin.

"Come in, sir. Thank you so much for coming," Doris said.

"Nothing is more demoralizing to an aging man than being called sir by a lovely young lady."

Tilly entered the room in time to see the judge framed in the doorway. He bowed slightly and removed his hat, hesitating on the worn carpet, between the couch and two chairs. He took the seat closest to the door.

Tilly placed the tray of homemade shortbread and a pitcher of iced tea on the coffee table. The glasses dripped condensation.

"Now this is hospitality: shortbread and tea," Judge Callen said. "Did you know my ancestors were from Ireland?" He looked at Tilly.

"John's mentioned it," Tilly said. She looked at her hands. The conversation was moving from pleasantries to the subject of John too quickly.

Doris crossed her legs at the ankles. Tilly had heard her rehearse what she wanted to say. With her hands on her knees, Doris cleared her throat. "We have information and ideas that may help you with John's"—she hesitated—"situation. We can't make sense of this arson allegation, Judge Callen, and there are some things you need to know about the factory—about the land it's built on."

The judge shifted in his chair, leaning away from the two women. Tilly passed him a coaster for his tea. He nodded and set the glass on the coffee table.

"I inherited the land from my uncle, Stanley Jura," Doris said, "and, well, he didn't own it outright. And I think maybe my uncle was involved in something, well he might have been involved in something illegal." Doris stopped to breathe.

Judge Callen looked at her with one eyebrow raised. It appeared frozen in a more upright alignment than the other. "Why do you think that?" he asked. He took another sip of the iced tea.

"He had a silent partner," Doris said. "He owned fifty percent of something called the Bluegate Partnership. The partnership owned the land, but nothing else."

"There's nothing illegal about silent partnerships," the judge said. "There are legitimate reasons to remain anonymous." His voice was soft, understanding.

"I know that, but, well, this was strange. My uncle was dead. I tried everything to locate the other owner and no one came forward: not the partner, not an heir, a bank, no one. It's as if they didn't want to be found. And then this—the fire—I, we, keep thinking there must be a connection." She looked at Tilly for support.

"Judge Callen," Tilly said, "we can't imagine why anyone would burn our business—certainly not John. Maybe the silent partner is deranged. Maybe he was unable to understand that Doris was trying to locate him. Not everyone reads legal announcements—I never do—and maybe seeing the factory on the land made him go into a rage. It's the only thing we can figure."

"We need to find the silent partner," Doris said. She leaned forward across the coffee table.

The judge glanced away and refused the shortbread. He sat back in his chair. "When did your uncle pass, Doris?" he asked.

"When I was at Kaiser—1942."

He hesitated for a moment, studying the pattern in the carpet. "How old was Stanley?" he asked. The familiar way in which he referred to her uncle caused Doris to sit back.

"Fifty-eight," she said.

"I'm so sorry," he said. "The older I get, the younger that seems." He ran his fingers though his hair. "I knew your uncle, not well, but this was a smaller place twenty-five years ago—

a kind of frontier. Anyone who made it out here to the coast knew all the others."

Doris' eyes were now wide, "You knew my Uncle Stanley?"

"As I said, not well. We crossed paths at the Marine View Roadhouse." He smiled at Tilly. "Your Uncle Jose and Aunt Ida are an institution, Tilly. They would remember Stanley, I think. I doubt they would make the connection with the land, but I think they would remember a steady customer. He worked for the railroad. I believe he was a construction manager."

"He was an engineer," Doris said.

"Well, engineering that railroad was certainly a feat," he said. "Geology and gravity won out in the end."

Tilly refilled the judge's glass while Doris appeared to be trying to decide which of a dozen questions to ask next. The judge never gave her an opening.

"You see, it doesn't matter who the arsonist is," he said. Both women stared. "I don't need to know who burned the factory to convince a jury that John didn't. Reasonable doubt works in our favor here." They sat with mouths open while Judge Callen continued. "No one saw John leave the hotel that night, and he's not the only resident of Montara to have slept through the fire. The crowbar found on the property is not evidence—John's truck was unlocked and anyone could have taken it. Only in Carry's imagination does John have a motive for arson. My grandson will be cleared."

"But Judge Callen," Doris said, "an arsonist shouldn't be allowed to go free." He cut her off.

"Ah, my dear," he said. "That's another matter. That's the sheriff's job, to catch the villain. My job is to defend my innocent grandson." The judge rose and placed the glass on the table. "I must be going," he said. "I like to stop by the Marine View when I'm on this side of the hill and pay my respects to Ida and Jose."

Doris unhooked his hat from the coat tree and stood on the porch watching as he got behind the wheel of the black sedan. He drove off. Doris didn't move for several minutes. Then she leaned back against the doorframe and said, "He knows who the silent partner is."

Tilly was on the porch swing. "Why do you think that?" she asked.

"Don't you find it a little strange that he waited to say he knew my Uncle Stanley?" Doris asked. The porch swing creaked.

"Well, I doubt he knew him well," Tilly said. "And he probably never knew he owned the land until you mentioned it. Why would he?"

"The Ocean Shore Railroad went bankrupt," Doris said. "Everyone knows that the judge was involved in settling the bankruptcy claims. I just never made the connection." She moved away from the door and sat on the swing beside Tilly. "Tilly, when I did the title search on the property, I found out that the owner before my uncle was the Ocean Shore Holding Company. The railroad owned the land. The judge was involved." Her voice trailed off.

Tilly rubbed her temples and leaned back on the swing. "Does it matter?" she said. "You're the owner of the property now, and the judge seems confident that John will go free."

"It matters to me," Doris said. She rocked the swing, and stared at the line of cypress trees. Tilly got up and cleared the uneaten shortbread from the coffee table, and put the glasses in the sink.

The next day Doris was gone before Tilly had breakfast, and she didn't return to the cottage until past seven o'clock. Tilly found her in the kitchen when she came in to wash some berries she'd picked. Doris was staring at a cup of black coffee.

"Did we run out of cream?" Tilly asked.

Doris looked up.

Tilly turned on the overhead light. The sun was low in the sky and the room was in shadow. "You take cream in your coffee," she said.

Doris looked at the cup on the table in front of her, got milk from the icebox and poured a splash into her cup.

"Is everything okay?" Tilly asked. She pulled out a chair and sat across the table.

"I just can't figure it out," Doris said. "Judge Callen knows who the silent partner is. I know he knows. I don't know how to prove it. Tilly, he may be the silent partner."

"Have you eaten dinner?" Tilly asked.

"Dinner?"

"It's past seven o'clock," Tilly said. "Have you eaten today?"

"I've been in Redwood City, at the courthouse," Doris said. "I guess I lost track of time."

"Have you been at the courthouse all day?" Tilly asked.

"I got the records on the land settlement," Doris said. "Judge Callen presided over the entire liquidation of the Ocean

Shore Holding Company. Tilly, he remembered my uncle. He has to remember who the silent partner is. How many settlements involved a silent partner? From what I can tell, only one." Doris picked up her cup to swirl the cream in her coffee and set it back on its saucer. "I'm sure there's plenty he's not telling us."

"If Judge Callen's withholding information, it's in John's best interest." Tilly said. "He wouldn't do anything to hurt John."

"And that's what I'm thinking, except he's been keeping this secret for a long time." Doris said. "There's something he's hiding. All this stuff with John is beside the point. This isn't about John."

"Of course it's not about John." Tilly said. "John didn't burn our business. Only that crazy deputy sheriff thinks John's an arsonist."

Tilly watched as Doris emptied her cup into the sink and turned to face her, "I need to talk to Deputy Carry."

"Carry? No. Doris, he's determined to put John away. Why don't you talk to the judge? If he knows that you know about the claims settlement, maybe he'll come clean," Tilly said. She traced the flower print on the oilcloth with her index finger. She did not meet Doris' gaze.

"I don't think he will," Doris said. "He hasn't yet. Whatever it is, it must be bad. Or embarrassing." Her voice trailed off, "Tilly, my Uncle Stanley, he must have known something… "

"Something about what?" Tilly asked. She looked up from the table.

"Something about Judge Callen. Something Judge Callen didn't want anyone else to know," Doris said. "I think they were more than acquaintances at the roadhouse. Tilly, listen, everyone knows that Judge Callen was a wheeler-dealer."

"True."

"My uncle got the land in lieu of payment for consulting work done. He was treated more generously than many Ocean Shore employees. So if the judge ended up part owner of my uncle's property, he might consider it fee for service. That sort of thing."

Tilly shook her head. "But if Judge Callen expected a fee for service," she said, "he would have cashed in. He would have contacted you for half the value of the land. He wouldn't burn down a factory. It doesn't make sense, Doris."

"I know," Doris said. "None of this makes any sense." She poured herself another cup of coffee.

• • •

"Robert Callen and Stanley Jura were the two Bluegate partners," Detective Gustin said. "Judge Robert Callen is the silent partner Miss Jura's been looking for." He handed his written report to Sheriff Wick.

"Give me the highlights," the sheriff said.

"It all happened in '25," Gustin said. "Jura wanted to build a hotel and resort on the coast. He was working some deals in San Francisco for the cash, but lost most of what he had by '29."

Sheriff Wick leaned back in his chair and pulled out a low drawer to use as a footrest. "Did Callen try to revive the business? He had money and a lot more buying power during the depression."

"No." Gustin walked across the room for an ashtray. He was almost smiling. "Even though Callen owned half the land, he wasn't signatory to anything Jura set up for the hotel. He had no involvement in the resort project."

Sheriff Wick tapped his pencil on the legal pad in front of him. He paused for a moment, "Why would Callen shy away from the action?"

"You tell me," Gustin said. "Maybe there's other evidence out there, but I haven't found it. Maybe just a gentleman's agreement."

Wick shook his head. "Callen's too fine a lawyer. Hard to believe he'd enter into a partnership without an ironclad contract. We'll never see it though, we'll never get a subpoena." Wick offered Gustin a light and lit a cigarette for himself.

"Jura wasn't an employee of the railroad," Gustin said. "He wasn't on the payroll. I was trying to figure out how he could come to a five-acre settlement."

Sheriff Wick took his foot off the drawer and sat upright, one eyebrow cocked.

"It appears," the detective said, "Jura was on contract to author the engineering reports they used to value the Ocean Shore Railroad's transfer to the Southern Pacific Company. Ultimately, the S.P. dropped the deal. I checked to see if Callen had a stake in the Ocean Shore or Southern Pacific, but couldn't find a link to him or his wife."

"When was Jura on contract?" Wick asked.

Gustin consulted his notes "He came on in '17 and stayed 'till the end, 1920." He looked up from his log.

Sheriff Wick rose and looked out the window, across Whipple Avenue. He rubbed his fist. "Okay, you say Jura worked for the railroad as a consulting engineer and the railroad went bankrupt. He wasn't on payroll, so he wasn't first in line for a settlement. Callen handled the bankruptcy claims, and Jura got one of the nicest little coves on the coast with the Judge signed on as an equal but silent partner. Jura died and Callen never came forward to claim his share."

"Yeah, boss. That's about it. What do you think?"

The sheriff finished his cigarette while he tried to fit the pieces together. He had a theory. "Callen wasn't interested in controlling the property," he said, "but he was interested in controlling Jura."

Detective Gustin flicked an ash.

The sheriff continued, "It's just a hunch, but we know that Jura probably got more than he was entitled to with the settlement. He must have had some leverage over the judge to be treated so generously." He blew a smoke ring. "But the judge would have been smart enough to limit Jura's advantage."

"Leverage? Do you think Judge Callen was being blackmailed?"

"Callen is the kind of guy that could make a few enemies," Wick said. "He's got some skeletons in the closet, no doubt. I don't know anything about the Southern Pacific deal, but who knows, maybe Callen had his fingers in that too." Wick sat down at his desk. "Jura knew something about Callen that Callen needed to keep quiet. Jura got his payment for keeping his mouth shut. Callen had his leash on Jura to make sure he didn't get too greedy."

Gustin let out a low whistle. "It fits. It does fit. It would explain why Callen didn't come forward after Jura's death. With Jura's death, that chapter was over."

"Maybe," Wick said, "or maybe not. Maybe someone with a grudge is trying to frame his grandson."

Gustin nodded.

"We need more information," Wick said. "I want you to go over to the coast. Talk to some of the folks that have been around for a while. Deputy Carry can help you make some contacts."

Detective Gustin rose to leave.

"We'll get pushback from the judge when he figures out the investigation is heading in his direction, and he still has plenty of friends over at the courthouse," the sheriff said.

"I understand, I'm on it." Gustin said.

Sheriff Wick turned his chair back to the window and sat quietly for several minutes. He considered how Judge Callen had successfully evaded his predecessor, the late Sheriff Carry, for a generation. He made a few notes, then dialed a familiar number.

"District Attorney's office." The secretary transferred him to Eric Guisti.

"I'm wondering if you have a few minutes to go over a case with me," Wick said. "What I'm about to propose might be a little unorthodox."

• • •

Deputy Carry turned into the roadhouse driveway, causing John Callen, who'd been thinking about lunch, to lose his appetite. “The coastside connoisseur of cherry pie has arrived,” he muttered. Carry pulled in next to his truck.

“Callen,” he yelled before he was out of the patrol car.

John was continually amazed at Carry’s need to begin a conversation from a distance of one hundred feet. “Over here,” he said.

Jose watched the two men talking through the front window and recalled how Mike’s father had sparred regularly with the judge. He laughed. Prohibition had been good to the Marine View. His thoughts were interrupted when a visibly anxious John Callen asked if he could use the phone.

“The bar phone or the one in my office?” Jose asked.

John gestured over his shoulder. “He’s not going to let me out of his sight,” he said.

Jose retrieved the phone from beneath the cash register and thought John’s anxiety lessened as he dialed his grandfather. He grabbed a bar cloth out of uneasiness and habit; he could hear the baritone booming across the wire.

“What can I do for you, young man?” Judge Callen asked.

“Mike Carry is here to arrest me,” John said. “He’s taking me over the hill.”

“Don’t tell him anything,” the judge said. “I’ll meet you at the station.”

John returned the phone and handed Jose his truck keys. “Please ask Tilly to move the truck to the cottage,” he said. “I may need a ride back.”

Carry locked the handcuffs around John's wrists and led him to the patrol car. It occurred to Jose that this was Deputy Carry's first coastside arrest, and that he'd be like a pit bull trying to hang on to it.

Carry made a quick stop at the substation to make a phone call. "Sheriff, I have Callen in the car," he said. "I thought you should know he's called his grandfather, and the judge is on his way."

The sheriff turned to Gustin. "It's going as planned."

CHAPTER 24

August 19, 1920

"We don't know how much longer the Ocean Shore Company can survive," Jose said. He was rubbing the bar towel across aged mahogany. "It appears they have abandoned the idea of bridging the arroyos south of Tunitas Creek, and there was another slide at San Pedro Point last week." The judge looked into his drink and Jose continued, "Without the railroad we are all in desperate straits."

"This is heaven," the judge said. "It's only a matter of time before the Board of Supervisors figures it out and builds a decent road west." From his seat at the bar, he turned slightly to the left, to watch the sun set through windows that reached to the ceiling.

"Yes west, west is good for you. But the real challenge is a road to San Francisco," Jose said. "That is where the ranchers and growers have the best markets."

"One day you won't need San Francisco," the judge said. "You have everything you need right here: excellent soil, weather, timber, water and this astonishing scenery."

"Everything we need except a railroad, or even a road that's passable year-round," Jose said, "and of course, a courthouse." He tossed the ice from the empty glass into the sink. "Another double?"

"Make this one a single," the judge said, and laid money on the bar. "This will be an early evening for me."

"My brother-in-law, Paul Bettencourt, he works for the railroad," Jose said as he poured liberally. "He thinks he will be laid off in the near future. They are no longer hiring to replace workers that leave the company, so he is taking extra shifts when he can. My sister-in-law is working here a couple of nights a week to save up some money. They are trying to have a family, and my wife says the good Lord is keeping Helen from getting pregnant until Paul finds another job. It's old wives' tales if you want my opinion."

Helen Bettencourt opened the swinging door from the kitchen and said good night to her brother-in-law without stepping behind the bar. "Thank you for helping out, Helen. Ida should be feeling better tomorrow," Jose said.

The judge looked past him to the lovely young woman. She was unwinding her long dark hair from the knot pinned behind her head.

"My pleasure," she said as she glanced the judge's way. She left the roadhouse through the back door. Judge Callen took a long draw of his drink, and smoothed his hair.

Jose turned his attention to the customers in the dining room, including Stanley Jura, who sat watching at a small table in a dimly lit corner. He'd become a regular.

"Excuse me, Judge, while I see if Mr. Jura would like to order," Jose said. The judge looked over his shoulder at the light-complexioned man with a round head. He had thinning red-blond hair combed over the left side.

"I need to push on, Jose," the judge said. "Thank you for your usual, extraordinary hospitality." They shook hands, and the judge tipped his cap to Jura. Then he crossed the circular drive to his unlocked black Cadillac sedan, where his passenger sat waiting.

Stanley Jura checked his watch, then settled in to enjoy his dinner. He liked soup as a first course and usually followed a chilled cocktail with a hot broth. This evening was no exception. He lingered over the beef Burgundy, soaking up gravy with crusty sourdough bread. The salad came after the entrée, and a half carafe of red wine washed it all down. He didn't hesitate when Jose suggested a slice of the house apple pie a la mode. He loved Ida's pies. He paid the check without comment, tipped a fair amount and checked his watch again before stepping out for the half-mile walk past the lighthouse to the Montara Hotel. Stanley, like other men working temporarily on the coast, took a room by the month.

From the north, a late-model black Cadillac sedan sped around the curve at Point Montara, spraying gravel across the shoulder of the road. When the driver saw Stanley, he went into a skid and swerved to avoid hitting him. Stanley caught sight of the driver illuminated by the flashing Point Montara light, though he already knew who it was.

CHAPTER 25

July 23, 1947

THE DAY WAS HOT, one of the warmest of summer, and coastsiders who'd traveled over the hill to Redwood City to attend the hearing shed the jackets and sweaters they needed at the beach. They draped them over chairs, flags of informality in an otherwise staid courtroom. At nine o'clock, the air was already heavy despite giant ceiling fans whirring above.

Judge Charles Kilian entered and sat at his raised bench centered in the front of the room. Before him, at floor level, were two large, wooden tables with plain straight-backed chairs: one for the prosecution and one for the defense. The judge gaveled the proceedings to order.

"This is a preliminary examination, not a trial," he said. "The purpose of this examination is to determine whether a crime has been committed and, if so, whether there is reasonable ground to believe that the defendant participated in the commission of that crime. Mr. Guisti, you may open for the prosecution."

The press was present, not only the *San Mateo Times*, but also the *San Francisco Chronicle*. The handsome alleged arsonist was the boyfriend of the photogenic young woman—and local success story—whose business had been destroyed. He was also the grandson of the legendary Judge Robert Callen, who was serving as defense counsel. That the arresting deputy sheriff was the son of the late Sheriff George Carry, former nemesis of Judge Callen, added to the intrigue.

Deputy Sheriff Michael Carry sat next to Sheriff Wick and District Attorney Eric Guisti at the prosecution table, while John and his grandfather sat across the aisle. Tilly and Doris were in the courtroom, but stayed to the rear, not sure which side of the room to sit on. They'd slipped in late and had successfully avoided attention.

The prosecution called Fire Chief Rob Eastman to the stand. He strode to face the bailiff, shoulders squared, in an impeccably pressed uniform, and raised his right hand.

"Do you swear to tell the truth, the whole truth and nothing but the truth?"

"I do."

"Please be seated."

Tilly suddenly felt as if she'd been written into a script. She looked around; she knew the actors. It was all real, as surreal as it might seem.

Eastman stepped into the witness box as Eric Guisti approached.

"Chief Eastman," Guisti said, "please tell us what you found when you responded to the fire at the Bluegate Candle Company on May 12, 1947."

Tilly leaned toward Doris, "I can't relive this," she said. "Let's go by your old bakery." Doris nodded. They closed the door gently and exited onto Broadway, taking care to cross to the shady side of the street.

"We can buy a devil's food cake for John," Doris said. "This should be over today."

Judge Callen did not cross-examine the fire chief, and Eric Guisti called his next witness.

"Sheriff Wick, do you recall a conversation you had with Deputy Sheriff Michael Carry on May 24, 1947?" District Attorney Guisti asked.

"I do."

"Please tell us about that conversation."

Sheriff Wick leaned toward the microphone. "Deputy Carry came to my office to discuss a warrant for John Callen's arrest in the Bluegate arson. I reviewed his report and asked him to do more research."

"Is this a copy of the report?" Guisti placed it before his witness.

"It is," Wick said.

"Please summarize for the court the preliminary findings of Deputy Carry's investigation."

"Fire Chief Eastman and Deputy Carry declared the site a crime scene after the fire was extinguished," Wick said. "Subsequent chemical analysis of some of the charred timber revealed that an accelerant was used, likely gasoline. The owners had just received a shipment of wax, which was stored in the melting area at the time of the fire. The fire burned so hot that there was little evidence of any kind left, but there was an iron crowbar found at the location of the back door that could have been used to gain access to the locked building." Sheriff Wick shifted his weight in his seat. "Deputy Carry's investigation concluded that the crowbar belonged to the defendant. Further investigation revealed that the defendant had no alibi for the evening and was staying at the Montara Hotel just up the beach from the fire. Deputy Carry also found the defendant had a possible motive for setting the fire."

"Let the court enter this report as Exhibit A." Guisti handed the report to Judge Kilian. "Now Sheriff Wick, you mentioned that you asked Deputy Carry to investigate further. What did you ask him to research?"

"The report includes summaries of interviews the deputy conducted with a number of individuals connected with the candle factory, including the owners. Miss Jura expressed concern that the arson might have been linked to an old business deal her uncle and benefactor was involved with."

Judge Callen looked up at the mention of the partnership, and John noticed his grandfather's interest.

"Was it your opinion that the silent partner may have had some role in setting the fire?" Eric Guisti tapped his fingers against the top of the witness box a few times and then stepped aside so Callen could see the witness.

"No, that was Miss Jura's thought, and she shared it with the deputy." Wick's gaze followed the District Attorney. Guisti turned again to face him.

"So tell us, Sheriff Wick," the District Attorney said, "what interest did you have in further research into the Bluegate Partnership?"

John Callen could feel the vibration of his grandfather's foot tapping. Judge Callen stared straight ahead.

"The land the candle factory was built on was transferred from the Ocean Shore Holding Company to the Bluegate Partnership in 1925," Wick said. "Further research revealed that Judge Robert Callen presided over the bankruptcy hearings and helped Mr. Jura secure the land he wanted." There was a murmur in the courtroom. Judge Callen rose.

"Objection."

"I will show relevancy, your Honor." Guisti turned quickly toward Kilian.

"Overruled, please continue," Judge Kilian said. He was now watching Judge Callen.

"So, Sheriff Wick, this is fascinating history," the District Attorney said, "but what was your interest in a twenty-two year old land transaction?"

"I wanted to rule out the possibility that there might be someone harboring a grudge over Judge Callen's settlement, someone who might take the opportunity to frame his grandson," Wick said. "Revenge is a powerful motive."

"What action did you take next?" Guisti asked.

"I assigned Detective Gustin to the case, to look into the matter further."

"Thank you, Sheriff Wick. I have no further questions." Eric Guisti walked back to his table.

"Counselor?" Judge Kilian acknowledged Judge Callen's turn to cross-examine the witness.

Judge Callen approached the stand. "Sheriff Wick, you say you read the initial report and responded by asking for more information on a land transaction. What was your opinion of the other facts raised in the case?"

"I felt the report was not conclusive," Wick said. "I didn't want to pursue an arrest warrant for John Callen without more information."

"I have no further questions, your honor." Judge Callen said. He took his seat next to his grandson and rubbed his temple.

Judge Kilian used his handkerchief to wipe his forehead and loosened the collar of his robe. He checked his watch. The midday heat was becoming oppressive in the courtroom. "It being eleven-forty-five," he said, "I recess this court until two o'clock for lunch."

The room began to empty, with newsmen gathering around Eric Guisti for quotes for their late editions. A reporter approached Judge Callen, but he quickly turned away.

John looked intently at his grandfather and asked, "Is there anything you want to tell me?"

Robert Callen hesitated, and then nodded. "Yes, I'm afraid there are some things you need to know," he said. "Things I probably should have told you a long time ago." He squeezed John's shoulder and asked the bailiff for a private place where he could speak with his client. They were granted a room, small and very warm, with an armed deputy posted at the door. John took his seat across the gray, metal table and watched his grandfather gather his thoughts. The judge ran a hand through his hair and nodded as if he'd just decided exactly what to say.

"Tilly Bettencourt is your aunt," he said. "She's your father's half sister."

John didn't breathe. He leaned forward, wondering if he'd heard correctly.

"Tilly's your aunt," the judge said, "my daughter."

John sat up abruptly. "You had an affair with Helen Bettencourt?"

"A very, very brief affair." The judge leaned back in his chair and sighed. "It was a long time ago. Helen was a beautiful young woman. Tilly is too, but Helen knew she was beautiful. She was afraid her husband wouldn't receive the money he was due in the Ocean Shore settlement and, shall we say, 'befriended' this old judge at the roadhouse. I didn't know until the very end that she was having trouble conceiving, but did so shortly after our liaison. I heard the news much later and was happy for the Bettencourts. Paul got a good settlement and a baby in the bargain; we all got on with our lives. I hadn't thought about it in years."

John was impatient. "But that's not the end of the story?" he asked.

"No, it's not," the judge said.

March 10, 1925

Judge Callen left his office just before noon and walked three blocks down Broadway to the City Hotel, trying to recall the man he was to meet for lunch. The name his secretary had written in his appointment book was unfamiliar and the note, *"lunch to renew acquaintance and discuss the Ocean Shore bankruptcy"* did not enlighten. But Callen seldom forgot a face, so he trusted that once he entered the hotel, the identity of his dining companion would become obvious.

Earlier in the day, Stanley Jura had arrived in Redwood City via the Southern Pacific line from San Francisco. He checked into a suite on the third floor and, at eleven-thirty, took his newspaper to the dining room, secured the most remote booth, and instructed the maitre d' to expect Judge Callen. The maitre d' was tipped generously for agreeing to facilitate a meeting between old friends who, Stanley explained, had not met in a while. "We may have become unrecognizable to one another."

Twenty minutes later, Judge Callen opened the copper-sheathed lobby door for an attractive woman who smiled in appreciation, and passed through reception toward the dining room. He encountered a colleague who asked if he could drop by the office later in the afternoon. Callen agreed to a two o'clock appointment, thinking an excuse to leave early might come in handy. The maitre d' greeted him warmly, advised that his friend had arrived, and led him to the booth.

The man, seated and reading a San Francisco newspaper, looked only vaguely familiar. He was on the short side of average, with thinning strawberry blond hair combed over a receding hairline. His eyes were small and dark.

Stanley rose and offered his hand. “How gracious of you to come after so much time,” he said. His accent sounded Eastern European.

“Are you down from San Francisco for long?” the judge asked.

“I hope to leave tomorrow,” Jura said. “That is, if we are able to finish our business.”

Lunch patrons were beginning to fill the dining room; the hum of conversation was punctuated by the sound of ice water filling glasses. The waiter took the order to the kitchen and the booth became a private office.

“Isn’t it a shame that we can’t have a good whiskey with our steaks?” Jura asked. “There are things about this country that are not so free, don’t you think, Judge?” He unfolded his napkin.

“You mentioned that the length of your stay depended on the time needed to take care of business that you called ‘our’ business,” Callen said. “May I ask what that business might be?”

The waiter placed a basket of warm bread and a slab of butter on the table. Judge Callen offered it to Stanley before taking a slice.

Stanley’s water glass was refilled, and he asked for a cup of coffee. When they were alone again he said, “I’m aware of your reputation for fairness, Judge Callen, and I find myself in a circumstance where I may not get what I am due without some intervention.”

Callen observed Jura carefully. He recognized him but had no idea why. He couldn’t recall an interaction; at best they had crossed paths somewhere. “My secretary noted that you wanted to discuss the Ocean Shore bankruptcy with me. Is that the nature of our business and your current circumstance?"

"Judge Callen, forgive me, but we Europeans are not so direct with our associates, especially at meal time. Let us enjoy our meal first and then discuss the details of our business dealings. It is better for the digestion, no?"

A small bowl of consommé was placed before each man. The judge pushed his aside as Stanley picked up a silver soupspoon and ladled a first taste of broth, allowing it to cool for a few seconds.

"Have you been to the Marine View Roadhouse recently?" Callen asked.

Stanley put the spoon down. "Ah, you do remember me," he said. "That's good. It will make our discussions go more smoothly."

Out of a sense of unease, Callen regained interest in the soup course and pulled the bowl back. The judge was the master of negotiation, but he was typically the third party. This was beginning to feel like a personal matter.

"The Marine View was a special place to me during the days I was involved with the railroad project," Jura said. "Jose Torres understands hospitality, how to make every patron feel relaxed and at ease. I was often in the background, observing the actions of others."

"What did you do for the railroad? Were you an employee of the Ocean Shore Company?" Callen asked.

"My specialty is construction engineering. The directors of the Ocean Shore grossly underestimated the engineering challenges they undertook in the route they selected. They had little interest in the practicalities of running a rail line over eighty miles of the most geologically unstable reaches of the Northern California coast. It was pure hubris that drove them."

"No, I think it was simply profit that drove them," Callen said, "and forgive me, Mr. Jura, but I suspect that you are motivated by the same."

The waiter cleared the consommé bowls quickly; the conversation paused.

"As I was saying," Stanley said, "the directors of the Ocean Shore Company took some financial risks in trying to complete the route all the way to Santa Cruz. The section south of Tunitas Creek was especially challenging from an engineering standpoint. They brought me on in late 1917 and I stayed on until the end, first to engineer a way to make the route whole, later to fix portions of rail they were losing to landslides and finally to prepare the valuation report for presentation to the Southern Pacific Company. The directors thought they could sell the whole ill-fated enterprise to the SP as a spur to their functioning railroad."

"Not an entirely outrageous plan," the judge said. "Southern Pacific owned a lot of the rolling stock."

"I never expected to be compensated for my effort in cash," Jura said. "You see, I was not an employee of the railroad—I contracted my services to them. In 1918 and '19, when they were barely making payroll and looking at options to liquidate all or part of the business, I negotiated a deal for payment from the Ocean Shore Holding Company. What I wanted, Judge Callen, was land. I had my eye on a particular cove near Point Montara."

The steaks arrived; they sizzled on iron plates inlaid in wooden ones. Callen hoped to finish last so that Jura would have to talk first. He ate slowly.

Robert Callen had been careful to keep most of his indiscretions to the west side of the Coast Range, a part of the world not visited by his wife or frequented by her associates. In twenty years, he had never felt a third party might threaten his marriage. Politics and morals aside, he truly enjoyed his wife. The judge didn't know what Jura wanted, but he imagined the worst and tried to think ahead to how he might respond.

Stanley ate only half of the steak before placing his fork and knife on the plate. The waiter took the cue immediately. "The service is good here, no?" he said.

Callen continued to chew, giving Jura time to finish his story.

"As I was saying before I was presented with that delicious but too large cut of meat," Jura said, "there is a five-acre parcel that I believe I am the rightful owner of."

"And this is in dispute?" the judge said.

"More in limbo," Stanley said. "As you are intimately aware, Judge, this Ocean Shore business may take years to resolve."

"There are literally hundreds of claimants to the settlement," the judge said. "The land settlements are particularly challenging."

"This one is not, I assure you," Jura said. "The parcel is owned entirely by the Ocean Shore Holding Company."

"Which is also in receivership," the judge said. "Mr. Jura, I think you misunderstand the limits of my ability in this matter. While I can author settlements for parties once they get to my courtroom, there is a sequence of settlement that I cannot control. Unfortunately, the land issues are most likely to be resolved last."

Callen's plate was cleared and the crumbs brushed from the table. When the waiter left to get the judge a cup of coffee, Stanley Jura said, "Judge Callen, I have information regarding your actions on the coast in 1920 that may be of interest to your wife."

CHAPTER 26

July 23, 1947

TILLY AND DORIS returned to the empty courtroom with the pink cake box.

"Just in time for recess," Doris said.

"I doubt they missed us," Tilly said.

At two o'clock, Judge Kilian gaveled the proceedings back to order. The gallery was filled with spectators. Doris noticed, for the first time, that many were women. One caught her eye and smiled at her.

Judge Callen immediately approached the bench and asked for a conference in Kilian's chambers. "Something happened this morning," Doris said.

The prosecution, defense and judge left the courtroom, and Tilly suggested they go home.

"It's about a hundred degrees in here," she said.

"I'm curious," Doris said. "Let's stick around for a while."

Tilly slid down in her chair and tried to get comfortable. She was dozing twenty minutes later when the bailiff asked if Helen Bettencourt was present. Doris looked up from her book and watched as the bailiff went to look for Helen in the hallway. She started to get an uneasy feeling. After another thirty minutes passed, Judge Callen took his seat next to his grandson, and the district attorney started to pack up his files. Doris put down her book and nudged a napping Tilly, and Kilian re-entered the courtroom. "The case against John Callen is dismissed," he said. "There has been a confession and the arsonist has been apprehended."

Tilly clapped and cheered and then blushed deeply when she saw everyone looking at her.

John embraced his grandfather, and as Doris was handing him the cake, the district attorney pulled her aside and asked her to come to his office in half an hour. Judge Callen quickly ushered John out of the room, "to process the release papers," he said over his shoulder.

Doris felt queasy, though Tilly was smiling and shaking hands with reporters. Something wasn't right. Judge Callen wasn't the type to skip the victory lap. He'd been in too much of a hurry to get out of the courtroom. She remembered his prediction: *"I don't need to know who burned the factory to convince a jury that John didn't. Reasonable doubt works in our favor here… My grandson will be cleared."* Had he known who set the fire?

May 12, 1947

Helen was sure she was doing the right thing. She was preserving the family, keeping a secret whose revelation would tear them apart. She arranged the shredded packing paper like a giant wick and sprinkled gasoline on it.

The pyre ignited immediately. Paraffin burns like kerosene, and Tilly and Doris had just taken their largest shipment of wax for making sacramental candles. Helen had done such a good job setting the fire that she couldn't put it out.

It was past one in the morning. Helen ran from the blaze and didn't stop until she reached her kitchen door. She left her shoes, full of sand, at the porch steps and then heard the alarm sound at Point Montara Station.

Buildings can be rebuilt more easily than families, Helen told herself.

She knew her husband, a volunteer fireman, would respond to the alarm and quickly busied herself in the kitchen making coffee, so it would look as if the commotion had woken her.

July 23, 1947

"You kept this from me for twenty-seven years," Paul said.

Helen sat frozen. There was no answer. She looked around at the photos in Judge Kilian's chambers. Her eyes rested on a family portrait.

"Her eyes are so violet-blue," Paul said. "How could I have been so blind?"

"If John hadn't fallen in love with Tilly," Helen said, "none of this would have happened. There was no reason to say anything."

"No reason? My God, Helen, how about honesty? You burned the factory for your lie and tried to frame an honest man—your daughter's nephew, I might add." He didn't look at her.

"Don't talk to me about honesty," she said. "You and Jose and Aldo were out running whiskey with money we needed to pay bills, while Ida and I prayed that nothing bad would happen. The good little women were expected to stay home and take whatever came our way."

"I see," said Paul. "The judge came your way and you made the most of the opportunity—is that it? I couldn't impregnate you so you found someone who could, do I have that right?" He paced the room. "And you were worried about my ability to provide after the railroad failed, so I suppose you took care of that detail at the same time. Come to think of it, I did get a good payout. How many of the nights I worked overtime did you have to work overtime too? You did well, Helen."

"I only wanted to be a good wife and mother," she said. "The judge meant nothing to me."

"You only wanted to be a good wife and mother?" Paul repeated. "Well, I only wanted to be a good father and provider. But it looks like I'm a failure on both counts."

He left the room and bailiff escorted her to the transport vehicle. Helen was going to jail.

• • •

Tilly and Doris followed the numbered doors down a long corridor. When Doris found the right room, Eric Guisti ushered them in. He closed the door and asked if they had a lawyer. They looked at one another—*why would we need a lawyer?* But the district attorney was suggesting that they might want to consult with one before making any decisions regarding whether or not to prosecute.

"We consulted a lawyer my uncle recommended when we set up our business and contracted for services," Tilly tried. "We could call him."

"Mr. Guisti," Doris said impatiently, "no one has told us who set fire to our factory. Can you please tell us what happened?"

He cleared his throat and shifted his weight in his chair. He looked at Tilly when he spoke. "This afternoon Helen Bettencourt confessed to setting the fire."

Doris put her hand on Tilly's forearm.

"I assumed you'd been told by now," Guisti said.

"No," Tilly said, her voice a whisper. She stared straight ahead. "I haven't talked to my mother; she never returned from Judge Kilian's chambers. I assumed she wanted to escape the courthouse as soon as she could. She was very uncomfortable about testifying."

Doris squeezed her arm. "Mr. Guisti," Doris said. "Did Helen say why she did it? I know she disliked John, but he was our builder. Burning the factory would just keep him in our employ."

"She wanted John to leave town, but it wasn't so simple," Guisti said, "and I hate having to tell you what I'm about to say. You need to understand exactly what happened so you can decide how you want to proceed." He paused as if unsure where to start. "Tilly, less than a year before you were born, your mother had an affair with Judge Robert Callen that resulted in your birth." He looked at Tilly. Her expression told him that she'd heard the words, but not the meaning.

Doris gasped, "My God, Tilly, you're John's aunt!"

"Are you saying that Paul Bettencourt isn't my real father?" Tilly asked.

"Judge Robert Callen is your biological father and John is your nephew." He waited a moment before continuing, "But there's more. Stanley Jura knew about the affair and was blackmailing the Judge, threatening to reveal the Judge's indiscretions to his wife."

"I knew it!" Doris sat straight up in the chair. "I knew the Judge was hiding something. Let me guess. He was the silent partner with my uncle."

"Yes," Guisti said, "he was the Bluegate Partnership silent partner. But it wasn't a normal blackmail routine. Stanley only wanted what the railroad owed him for his work. He shortcut the settlement route and worked on the judge because he wanted to be sure he would get his land and there were far more powerful interests in line to divide the Ocean Shore spoils. Callen didn't come forward when you were trying to clear title, Miss Jura, because he didn't think the sheriff would crack the case."

"But what caused Mrs. Bettencourt to confess?" Doris said.

"Robert Callen went to see her the night he met Tilly," Guisti said. "He tried to talk Helen into coming clean but she wouldn't. You should also know that she asked the Judge to send John away to school with a generous endowment. Judge

Callen was able to use what she said to him that night to force a confession out of her."

Tilly guessed where the conversation was heading. She could never press charges, particularly knowing how desperate her mother must have been. But the business belonged to Doris too, and they would have to agree on a course of action.

"Mr. Guisti," Doris said, "I can't speak for Tilly, but I have no interest in pressing charges against Helen Bettencourt."

Tilly looked at her friend. "Thank you," she said. And then she turned to the district attorney. "It would be best for all of us if we could tie up loose ends as soon as possible."

CHAPTER 27

July 24, 1947

JOSE HESITATED before refreshing Paul's drink. "I am hoping that you are planning to take the vacant room upstairs for tonight," he said.

"Helen's packing," Paul said. "I don't think she wants my help with that. Might be better if I wasn't around." He pressed his palm against his forehead as he leaned against the bar. "Of course, all of this has been hardest on Tilly. I don't know why I'm feeling sorry for myself."

"Perhaps you are grieving for her loss too," Jose said. "But I think you will soon find that nothing's changed between you and your daughter."

"Tilly's not my daughter," Paul said.

"She is still every bit your girl," Jose said. "Nothing has changed except a deception's been revealed after many years. In time, we will all be better off. The lie was affecting all of us."

"Did you know?" Paul asked. "Because it's hard for me to believe that the affair could have happened, and that Stanley Jura knew and you didn't."

Jose shook his head. "My place is behind this bar," he said. "It's where I've spent most of my life for the past thirty years. I know what people tell me, but I see very little. I swear I knew nothing about Helen and the Judge. Stanley ate here, but he took his room at the Montara Hotel. Whatever he saw, he was somewhere else."

John was driving by the roadhouse when he saw Paul's truck. "We're going to have to talk sooner or later." The side door behind the bar was ajar, and Jose and Paul started when they saw him. "No, it's not a robbery," he said. "Mind if I join you?"

Jose looked at Paul, who nodded.

"Please," Jose said. "It is best that we help each other through this most unfortunate situation." He placed a napkin on the bar. "I know you seldom drink, John. Is there something I can offer you?"

John took a stool a few seats way from Paul.

"How about a shot of that fine Irish whiskey my grandfather was so enamored with?" he said.

Paul Bettencourt smiled at John, who nodded in his direction.

"So, let's see," Paul said, "if my former daughter is your aunt, does that make me a former great uncle-in-law?"

"This is like a bad movie," John said. He took a handful of peanuts. "If it weren't for all the gut-wrenching emotion, this situation would have some real advantages. I'm out of jail, thank God. I've gotten to think of you all as family, hell, you are family. And then there's the matter of the Bluegate property ownership. Isn't it an amazing coincidence that the eventual heir of the property is also half owner of the business? I mean, what are the odds of that happening."

"Eventual heir?" Paul asked.

John asked for another shot. "Oh, that's the best part: my grandfather's the silent partner Doris has spent the better part of two years trying to locate."

"Judge Callen is the silent partner?" Paul asked.

"Yeah," John said. "Gentlemen, I beg you in advance to forgive any unsavory remarks I may make this evening, morning, regarding the patriarch of my family or, Mr. Bettencourt, your wife. But I have just been cleared of arson charges, learned the love of my life is my aunt, and discovered that my grandfather is even more of a scoundrel than the reputation that precedes him."

Paul lifted his elbows off the bar and sat back in his seat; Jose leaned against the back bar.

"My grandfather was being blackmailed by Stanley Jura," John said. "Jura knew about the affair, and he spooked the judge, so the judge got him the land he wanted. But Robert Callen is not a man to be outmaneuvered. He was afraid that Stanley would look to him for more; he wanted to build a hotel, and the land was the cheapest part." He paused to finish the whiskey and Jose repoured. "Jura was probably the most honorable character in this drama: that's the irony of the situation. He only wanted what was due him. My grandfather couldn't be sure, so he added himself on as silent partner. He had no interest in the development but retained control of Jura through the partnership agreement."

Paul shook his head. "Why didn't he come clean after Stanley's death and let Doris get on with her life?"

"Because he didn't think anyone would be able to figure it out," John said. "He has the only other copy of the partnership agreement. He knew Doris didn't have Stanley's copy and didn't see any downside to keeping quiet. He forgot about some old signature cards that the sheriff's department was able to dig up. If Wick had kept Carry on the case, who knows what would have happened? Detective Gustin happens to be more than competent."

Jose poured another round.

• • •

Helen's first call had been to her brother, Aldo, and he'd responded immediately. He drove to the jail from Monterey in his big, black Cadillac and took Helen home to pack her things. The shrewd old fisherman had prospered as a rumrunner during prohibition, with capital enough to operate a fleet of fishing boats during the war when the demand for canned salmon was extraordinary. He'd invested in farmland in Salinas and was shipping food to San Jose. He was his sister's safety net.

Now, Helen folded clothes into Ida's oversized suitcase as Ida sat on the foot of the bed. "Funny," Helen said, "I never needed luggage before."

"Keep it as long as you like," Ida said. "I'm hoping you will come back often. I'm going to need more time off to visit you. How can I live without my baby sister?" She began to cry and Helen sat next to her. "Why didn't you tell me?" Ida asked.

"I can't begin to say how sorry I am," Helen said. "And I don't know how I'll ever face Tilly."

• • •

Tilly rose at first light and walked to her parents' house. Her uncle's car was parked outside, and she knew her mother would be leaving early. It was six-fifteen; she'd slept little. The house was dark, and she resisted the urge to enter, make coffee and wait in the kitchen. Fifteen minutes passed before a light came on in the upstairs hallway. She rapped on the front door. Nothing. Then she walked around back and saw her mother measuring coffee into the enamel percolator, as she'd done every morning for as long as Tilly could remember. This would be the last performance of her morning ritual in this kitchen. In that moment, Tilly understood that her mother's loss was greater than her own and started to cry.

She was angry with Helen for the lies to her father, the destruction of the factory and for the investigation she'd put them all through. But she knew what it was like to keep a secret from the people she loved because she thought their lives would be better that way. She couldn't imagine keeping it for twenty-seven years.

Her mother's future—housekeeping for her wealthy widowed brother in a town where no one knew her—seemed a lonely sentence.

When Helen turned to put the pot on the stove, Tilly saw her crying and burst through the door. "Mom, why didn't you tell me?"

Helen knocked the percolator over. She sobbed for several minutes. "I'm so very, very sorry." Tilly took her hand.

When Helen was able to speak she said, "All I ever wanted was to be a good wife and mother. I couldn't tell Paul you weren't his daughter. I went crazy and thought, if I can get John to leave town, everything will be okay. So now I'm the one who's leaving." They cleaned up the coffee, and then Helen looked at Tilly. "Thanks for not pressing charges. Aldo can cover anything the insurance doesn't, and I'll work to repay the debt."

"How long will you stay in Monterey?" Tilly asked.

"Your father wants a divorce," Helen said. "I've been pretty hard on him, on everyone, over the past year. And who wants to stay married to an arsonist?"

Tilly wasn't ready to say things might work out, but at that moment she felt closer to her mother than she had in years. "I hope you'll invite me down for a visit. You know I can drive now."

Helen hugged her.

An hour later, Tilly watched her uncle turn the Cadillac down Seventh Street and into the fog. She stood on tiptoe waving long after it was out of sight, not ready to say good-bye. She'd never felt so lonely. She knew what she had to do, and dreaded it.

Doris was mixing batter for waffles when she got back to the cottage. "Perfect timing," she said. She checked that the waffle iron was hot enough and carefully poured the first batch.

"I just saw my mother off," Tilly said. "She's determined to work and cover whatever our insurance won't. It was more than generous of you to be so understanding."

"You would have done the same." Doris took a sip of her coffee and poured a cup for Tilly.

Tilly looked around; the tiny house had become a warm and welcoming home that she didn't want to leave. The steam escaping the cooking batter smelled sweet, and she inhaled slowly before she spoke. "What I need to tell you," Tilly said, "well, I haven't told anyone."

Doris put down her cup. She looked at Tilly, who sat with her elbows on the table and her head in her hands.

"I can't live a lie like my mother," Tilly said, "and spend the rest of my life hoping that no one learns the truth."

"What?"

Tilly sat back and put up her hand. "Please hear me out."

Doris turned off the waffle iron and sat facing her.

"You may not want to live with me or even be in business with me when you know—and I'll understand. Truly, I will. After what you've done for my mother, I owe you that."

"What are you saying?"

"There's no way I could have married John."

"I know, he's your nephew."

"No, it's not that—of course I wouldn't marry my nephew—Doris, I'm in love with Sylvia—I have been for years now. I want to be with Sylvia, not John." Tilly hadn't known what to expect, but she felt a tremendous release when she said she wanted to be with Sylvia—said it out loud.

"I'm going to move back into the house with my dad, Paul—no, my dad," Tilly said. "You can have the cottage. I think it's best."

Doris didn't move and looked past Tilly at the wall. Tilly couldn't wait to escape.

"If you decide you no longer want me as a business partner," Tilly said, "I'll move on." She said she'd be back later with the truck to pack up her things. She closed the door softly.

Doris put the waffles on a plate and stared at them. She sat alone at the table for a long time. Losing Tilly's friendship was worse than losing the factory. She wasn't part of a team anymore, part of the little community centered around the roadhouse. She was on her own. What had happened? Two days earlier they were planning a celebration for John at Nick's—they knew he'd be cleared. Paul and Helen were still together, and Paul was still Tilly's father. And her uncle hadn't been accused of blackmail.

Tilly and Sylvia? Nothing was as it should be. And yet, as Doris looked back on their years at Kaiser, it was obvious that Sylvia and Tilly had something special. She'd often felt like a third wheel when they were together. She'd told herself that Sylvia and Tilly were closer because they worked the same shift. She had to laugh. It was much more than that. Beautiful Tilly was queer.

She was roused by the delivery truck and went to the porch to bring the bottles in. It was twice as much milk as she needed. She'd have to change the order. She thought about living alone, about losing her best friend and business partner. Maybe she should just go home to Pittsburgh. She sat on the porch swing and cried.

Out of the corner of her eye, Doris saw a shadow cross the porch stairs. It startled her.

"What's that they say about crying over spilled milk?" John said. He tripped over the top step. She'd never seen him drunk. "Oh, your milk's not spilled. It's still in the bottle. That was a joke," he slurred. "Is my aunt at home?"

Doris used her sleeve to wipe her tears. "Tilly's gone to stay with Paul."

"Yeah, well I'm not in any shape to have a conversation. What's there to say? Gee, you're my favorite aunt?" he belched. "Do you mind if I just pass out here?" He sprawled out at her feet.

We're sinking fast, she thought, too much change for twenty-four hours. She stepped over him and carried the milk in. The waffles were cold; she had no appetite and threw them in the trash. Perfectly good food wasted—there's nothing wrong with it. She bent to put the lid on the can and stood up—*There's nothing wrong with it.* John was framed by the screen door and flat on his back. He looked beaten. He had no choice; the romance was over. But it wasn't the same for her. She had a choice. Why was she was throwing it all away? Tilly had given her an out, said she'd understand if she didn't want to be in business with a lesbian. Tilly had been brave enough to tell her the truth.

Doris watched John snore for a few moments. There had been so many happy times. She covered him with a blanket and went in to use the phone.

"Mom," Doris said, "I need your advice."

Joan pulled up a chair and let her daughter do all the talking. After a while, Doris asked what she would do. Joan didn't respond right away, wise enough to know that her girl would need to find her own answers.

"Do you remember telling me how angry it made you to read letters to the editor about working mothers raising a generation of juvenile delinquents?" Joan asked. "Do you remember saying that you and I should be judged for who we are?"

"Yes," Doris said.

"What about the black woman who helped Tilly when she went blind?" Joan asked.

"I remember," Doris said. "I remember Tilly's comment about the Nazis pitting race against race."

"We're all good people just trying to get by," Joan said. "Only you know what will make you happy."

Tilly still had every sheet of fine apricot-colored writing paper and matching envelopes that Helen had purchased as a going-away present. She'd carried them to Kaiser and back, but they had always seemed too special to use. Her mother had ordered a seal with her initials embossed, and there was some deep burgundy wax. Who could have guessed that wax would become so important to her?

She began to write. She lacked the courage to phone and needed time to compose her thoughts.

Dear Sylvia,

I'm sorry. I've treated you horribly. I pinned my fears on you, but in truth, I was afraid of myself. When you called and I asked why you never married—I should have told you then. I was too scared.

Some things have happened here. The factory's gone—burned to the ground. My mother set the fire in a crazy attempt to keep a secret she's been carrying around since before I was born. I don't want her life. I used to think that meant that I didn't want to do the ironing. What it means is that I need to be who I really am.

Please forgive me if you can. I have come to believe that you are my one, true soul mate.

Tilly

As she sealed the letter, she caught a glance of Doris through the window, walking up the driveway carrying—milk? She ran down the stairs.

"Our order came," Doris said. "It's more than I can drink myself."

Tilly nodded. She wiped her hands on the side of her jeans. Her palms were suddenly sweaty. "Would you like to come in?" she asked. "I made some coffee. It's still hot."

Doris followed her into the house.

Tilly filled two mugs and got the cream for Doris. She watched her swirl the cup. "It's one of the first things I noticed about you," Tilly said. "Do you remember when you showed me how to find the cafeteria at Kaiser, the day we met? I noticed that you didn't use a spoon to stir in the cream."

Doris nodded. "I was so happy to have you as a roommate. I'd seen Sylvia, and thought, I'm glad I don't have to live with that old battleaxe."

Tilly laughed. "It seems so long ago." She stared into her mug for a minute and asked, "Will you rebuild the factory?"

"Maybe," Doris said. She hesitated and then asked, "Will you stay on as partner?"

Tilly caught herself before she hugged Doris. She wanted to, but she didn't want Doris to take it the wrong way. "You still want me as a partner?" she asked.

"I don't think we should live together," Doris said. "But I'll never have a better business partner."

"I want to hug you, Doris," Tilly said. "Do you think that would be okay?"

August 15, 1947

They had to shout over the din of trains pulling up to the platform.

"I feel guilty leaving you to rebuild the factory," Tilly said.

"It's my turn," Doris said. "I hope I can do as good a job as you did keeping John under control."

"Tell your mom to rearrange my room however she wants," Tilly said. "I want her to feel at home. I think she's going to get along with my Aunt Ida swell. The roadhouse is a great place to work."

Tilly and Doris hugged; the conductor tapped Tilly on the shoulder and called "All aboard!"

"I love you," Tilly said. "You're the sister I never had."

"You're the family I've been looking for," Doris said. She brushed away a tear. "I saw Sylvia off when she left Kaiser," she said. "She's been talking about seeing some national parks in an Airstream since then. I'm glad you can go with her."

"Take good care of my nephew," Tilly said. She winked at Doris. "It's a fool that doesn't take advantage of every opportunity."

The train traveled north through Berkeley and on to Richmond. Tilly wanted to get off—for just a little while—but the stop was too brief. She craned her neck to see as many landmarks as possible; she wanted to remember every detail. And then the tracks turned east and she found herself farther from home than she'd ever been.

Smiling, she settled into her seat for the ride to Sacramento and on to the Sierra Nevada Mountains. Sylvia would be waiting for her at the station in Reno.

LIBERTY SHIPS BUILT DURING WORLD WAR II

Listed by Shipyard

Shipyard	*Vessels Completed*
Alabama Drydock & Shipbuilding Co. Mobile, AL	20
Bethlehem-Fairfield Shipyard Inc. Baltimore, MD	385
California Shipbuilding Corp. Terminal Island, CA	336
Delta Shipbuilding Co. New Orleans, LA	188
J.A. Jones Construction Co. Brunswick, GA	85
J.A. Jones Construction Co. Panama City, FL	102
Kaiser-Vancouver Vancouver, WA	10
Marinship Corp. Sausalito, CA	15

New England Shipbuilding Corp./ South Portland Shipbuilding Corp. South Portland, ME	244
(For legal reasons, there were two corporations, both a part of New England Shipbuilding.)	
North Carolina Shipbuilding Co. Wilmington, NC	126
Oregon Shipbuilding Corp. Portland, OR	322
Kaiser Permanente Metals Richmond, CA	489
Southeastern Shipbuilding Corp. Savannah, GA	88
St. Johns River Shipbuilding Jacksonville, FL	82
Todd-Houston Shipbuilding Corp. Houston Shipbuilding Corp. Bend Island, Houston, TX	208
(For legal reasons there were two corporations, both a part of Todd-Bath Iron Shipbuilding.)	
Rheem Manufacturing Co. Walsh-Kaiser Shipbuilding Corp. Providence, RI	11
(Walsh-Kaiser took over managment of the shipyard from Rheem.)	
Total	**2711**

SOURCE:

The Liberty Ships, by L.A. Sawyer and W.H. Mitchell. Cornell Maritime Press, Cambridge, MD, 1970.

ABOUT THE AUTHOR

THERESE HAS WORKED as a land surveyor's assistant, park and playground designer, bartender and fishmonger. She completed the UCLA Writers' Program in June 2009. You can follow her adventures victory gardening, docenting with the Rosies, and touring in her vintage travel trailer at www.womeninthe1940s.com. *Wax* is her first novel.